DAVID WHELAN

The Last Vatican Knight

David Whelan

ISBN: 1482320193
ISBN-13: 978-1482320190

For Ali and Josh

ACKNOWLEDGMENTS

As always a big thank you to my wife Ali, and son Joshua for allowing me write and complete this book. It is for them and our future that I put myself through the sometimes tortuous process of writing.
My dad, Tim, once again took the time to read and suggest changes, and the copy you have in your hands are due to his support and critique.

By the same author:
Chimera
Dragon's Theatre

For children:
The Story of.... (volume 1)

DAVID WHELAN

PROLOGUE

REVELATIONS 12:7

"And there was war in heaven: Michael and his angels fought against the dragon; and the dragon fought and his angels,
And prevailed not; neither was their place found any more in heaven.
And the great dragon was cast out, that old serpent, called the Devil, and Satan, which deceiveth the whole world: he was cast out into the earth, and his angels were cast out with him."

In the days before man, a rebellion took place in the kingdom of heaven. Displeased that God had made man and called them His greatest creation, there was discontent within the ranks of angels who refused to bow down to the lesser authority of mankind.

Led by Lucifer, one third of the total number of angels in heaven caused an uprising and attempted to overthrow the Supreme Being.

Through the corridors of Heaven, in the streets of paradise, and across the celestial plains, those angels loyal the Lord were forced into conflict and fights with those angels loyal to Lucifer.

God's Army was led by the Archangel Michael and finally

1

after the battlefield was strewn with the remains of the fallen, the Fallen Angel, the Morning Star, Lucifer was cast from Heaven and with his followers who dared to question the Lord God, were sent to pits of damnation for all eternity.

CHAPTER ONE

The crack of thunder echoed across the darkened sky seconds after the flash had died away. The rumble in the heavens reverberated through his chest, through his arms and down to the tips of his fingers that held tightly to the rocks. The rain pounded his face and body as Father Stuart McKellen took another careful step and inched himself higher into the rubble of the 13th Century church.

All around him the remnants of the building lay strewn around him. After years of neglect and abandonment the forces of nature finally won the battle and tore through the once magnificent church with fury.

Years had passed since that fateful night when 15 loyal worshipers had died while trying to save valuables from the church from a fire that had started by a lightning strike. Not much unlike this storm now, McKellen thought, as he carefully found a handhold and found his footing on the moss covered stone that formed part of a destroyed wall.

All those years ago, his mind wandered, all of those people, hundreds of years ago looking up at the elegant stained windows that were positioned right where he stood now. Incredible that so much has happened since, and that a new evil had descended once more onto this remote church.

With his clothes clinging as tightly to his skin as his hands to the soaked stones, McKellen continued across another jagged stone. Despite being soaking wet and cold from the strong wind whipping his face, McKellen breathed heavily and sweat broke out on his brow. He wiped the stinging dampness from his eyes and momentarily through the blur his eyes locked onto a shadow moving quickly over the ruins. The shape, clearly visible against the lightning illuminated sky, moved skilfully over the rocks.

Never before had McKellen seen such a beast, and after this encounter he never wanted to see one again.

He had been driving back from the Boorman's farm, 13 miles away through the driving rain after comforting the family for the loss of their daughter, Kimberly.

So young, he thought, so young to die. But the illness took hold quickly and the damage to her immune system was too great for doctors to do anything. An ambulance had been called to the farm and as McKellen pulled up at the farmhouse, the repetitive blue flashing of the lights greeted him. Kimberly's father Daniel was standing on the porch in the driving rain smoking a cigarette.

With eyes that filled with tears, but a heart and soul that was determined to stay strong for his wife, Daniel needed to take a few minutes to be alone with his thoughts when McKellen arrived. As he approached Daniel he knew there was to be no good news this night.

"She died 15 minutes ago." was all that Daniel said as he stepped to one side and allowed the priest into his once joyful and happy home.

Inside he had found the paramedics in the living room trying their hardest to comfort Anna as she fought to control herself as the news of her daughter's death still rung in her ears.

For the rest of the evening McKellen stayed with the family and spoke to them about the short but energetic life of Kimberly. He used words of consolation, gentle touches on the arm to give some sort of appearance of comfort. It was a difficult situation and he knew the best thing he could do was to allow the family to grieve in their own way.

It was a private moment, one they no doubt didn't want to share with a priest they only saw on Sundays, so when he felt the time was right he excused himself and left them to their pain and loss.

He felt guilty for doing that, but there was little more he could do. He had made drinks, contacted family members and talked to the parents, but in the end he knew they wanted to be alone.

As he drove back to his parish through the driving rain and buffeting wind his mind raced over the previous hours and his heart went out to the parents of little Kimberly. He didn't have any family of his own; no brothers or sisters or nephews and nieces. He was alone in the world and he started to think about who would mourn him if he was to die.

As the wipers swayed to their regular beat an object in his headlights ahead caught his attention. He slowed down and the main beams of the car illuminated two dark figures. One in black was crouched over the other lying on the road. McKellen sat there stunned at the sight and as he watched he realised that the object in the road was a dead sheep, its white fleece glimmering with rain and the lights from his car.

What had happened? Was this man helping? Had he struck the sheep with his own car? But where was his car?

McKellen climbed out of his car and pulled his coat close to him as the wind took his breath away. He walked slowly towards the figure in the road and called out. "Are you okay? Are you injured?"

There was no response.

Only a few feet away McKellen once more asked if the figure needed help.

The face that looked up at him wasn't that of a man, or even that of a person. With elongated lower teeth protruding upwards onto either side of the stretched snout, the red eyes glowed at McKellen and a growl of hatred rumbled from deep inside it.

McKellen froze where he was and took in the sight as the fur covering the creature's body dripped with rain and around its mouth drenched with blood. Slowly McKellen backed away, but the animal bowed its head low to the floor, sniffing and smelling the ground as it walked on all four legs, prowling towards him, hunting him.

At a shade under six foot tall, McKellen wasn't a small man, but this thing in front of him now equalled his height at its shoulder, and would easily double his height should it rear up onto the hind legs.

Long nails extended from all four feet and the scraping of the tips on the tarmac sent rivers of fear through the priest as he carefully backed up to his car and climbed back in. Luckily the engine was still running, and luckier still the animal was out of striking distance.

Without shutting the door McKellen found first gear and pulled away as fast as the 1.4 litre engine would allow. The tyres squealed and the steering was light, but he was moving, and moving fast. In the rear view mirror he saw the animal begin to chase but the car was too fast for it and the image disappeared into the distance behind him.

His breathing was hard, but the driving harder as the car followed the ribbon of wet tarmac as it cruised the contours of the land. He needed to find somewhere safe, somewhere he could make a phone call and tell someone about what he'd seen.

Damn it! He thought. Why did he leave his mobile phone at home?

Every few seconds he checked his rear view mirror for the animal, but it wasn't there. He must've travelled a couple of miles now and must be safe; he deduced as he eased off the accelerator and allowed the car to become more responsive and manoeuvrable in the treacherous conditions.

What was that thing? Was it a wolf? A panther?

There were rumours that a large big cat roamed the wilds of Scotland, but that area was miles away. Could it have travelled that far, he thought as his heart rate slowed and his breathing became more regular.

As he continued to drive with the radio quietly playing to itself a tree trunk suddenly fell without warning into the road and McKellen acted quickly to avoid it. Swerving off to the left the car skidded but miraculously the wheels found traction and grip on loose gravel and the stones bounced off the body work as the car careered off the main road and down a disused driveway. The lights bounced around in the darkness and instinct took over as McKellen pressed hard on the brakes. The wheels strained to gain any grip through the mud and the car skidded across the wet surface and angled off towards a tree.

The priest could see it coming and he braced himself for the impact.

But it didn't come.

The car had finally stopped a metre from the tree. God must be watching over him, McKellen thought as he let out a breath he didn't know he was holding. He sat for a moment and watched the wiper blades clear his view of the area he was now, inconveniently, parked in.

Where was he? Why did he recognise this place?

As he surveyed his surroundings a moving shadow caught his attention and McKellen saw to his horror the animal on all fours prowling towards him from the tree shadows.

Did it look more menacing? Had he angered it by running away before?

He had no time to answer these questions as he scrambled out of the car and headed anywhere he could to hide from the animal. The path he followed took him through a mass of trees and he weaved in and out of them, getting his coat caught on one of them in the process. With fear mounting McKellen pulled his arms out of the coat and continued towards the partially destroyed building ahead of him.

That was 15 minutes ago and now as he crouched on the rubble he watched the animal sniff around the ground hunting for his scent. He had so far managed to evade the animal but he knew he couldn't hide forever. He also knew that he couldn't fight whatever it was, he knew that he would have to try and escape, make his way back to the road and maybe flag down a passing car. That was the only logical thing he could do.

Being up high gave him the advantage of surveying the area and he picked his route to the ground that was as far from the animal as possible.

The wind seemed to be easing off and carefully he moved his hands to grip the stone wall, but with all his weight and balance now on his feet the loose stones beneath his shoes gave way and the fall was instantaneous.

Through the air he fell and with a dull muted landing he lay in the waterlogged ground and let the rain wash over his face.

He heard the footsteps before he could see the source; the breathing heavy in his ear and the warm breath covered his face as he lay paralysed by fear and pain. The dark matted hair on the face of the animal looked him in the eyes and bore its teeth at him.

A shout came from behind the animal, but it didn't move. The voice shouted again and slowly the animal stepped away from the injured McKellen.

Despite the pain in his neck and shoulders he looked up to try and find his saviour and there before him was a man dressed in black with a billowing cape hanging off his back.

He didn't make any move to help McKellen, in fact he was watching the animal as it sat next to him like a dog next to its master.

"Help me!" McKellen managed to say through the pain in his chest. The man didn't move or show any response to his plea. "Help me!" he repeated.

"Where is your master now?" The voice was deep, reverberating and powerful. "Where is the God you worship? Why

8

don't you ask him for help?"

McKellen was confused at the questions.

"You're a man of the clergy," the man continued, "pray now, and ask your God for help." The deep voice penetrated McKellen's mind and heart. A cold breath swarmed over him as he lay there, as if his soul was being touched.

"The rule of God is coming to an end. Prepare to watch your world be torn apart." the man said.

McKellen was about to shout back but the ice cold touch of the man's gaze gripped him where he lay and with fear he had never felt before he watched as the animal reared up on its hind legs and pounced onto his chest and tore at his flesh.

The last thing he saw before he passed to the celestial plains was the growling animal rip open his chest and feast.

CHAPTER TWO

For centuries the head of the Catholic Church has held his throne within the confines of the greatest cathedral in the world. The Vatican, built on the spot where St. Peter, the first disciple of Jesus Christ, was crucified by the Roman Empire.

As a place of pilgrimage for devout Christians, St. Peters Basilica slowly grew from a small place of worship to the smallest recognised independent state in the world covering an area of around 110 acres and housing approximately 800 persons.

With St. Peters Basilica taking centre stage, perfectly manicured gardens to the rear offered the visiting bishops, cardinals, state leaders and the Bishop of Rome himself a chance to contemplate their work and beliefs.

Cardinal Louis Franco Conquezla quietly walked through the gardens, needing some relief from the throngs of crowds awaiting the weekly Papal blessing. He seemed to absorb every moment of silence that surrounded him, gone were the cheers from the crowd, gone were the blast of car horns that Italian drivers were so keen on using, and gone were the thousand other noises that battered his mind every second of every day.

His role within the Vatican was of great importance, and needed a lot of attention to complete it successfully; however he made an effort every day to escape the basement office he and his team worked from and take at least 15 minutes to have for him.

It was a habit he enjoyed and one that he wanted his colleagues to enjoy too, but as keen and young minds often did, they worked solidly, sometimes not leaving the office from the moment they entered at sunrise, to the moment the sun descended below the horizon once more.

Rather uncharacteristically Conquezla walked barefoot across the lawn and the dewy morning still hung in the air. In the shadow of the walls marking the perimeter of the Vatican City, Conquezla continued to step carefully across the grass as his mind focused on the list of tasks he had set himself for the day. Behind him Fr. Stefan Jung called across the grass once more.

"Your Eminence?" he repeated, afraid to break the silence. "Cardinal Conquezla?"

Finally the Cardinal turned to him, his flowing robes billowing out behind him. "Are we ready?"

Fr. Jung calmed himself, "We are, Your Eminence."

Conquezla nodded and strode across the grass, and using Fr. Jung for balance replaced his shoes and together the two priests headed back to their office.

The Bishop of Rome, more commonly known as Pope Pius XV sat at the head of a long table. Under the gaze of precious art works depicting scenes from the bible and illuminated by high floor to ceiling windows overlooking the Vatican gardens, Pope Pius was reading a briefing that had been prepared regarding an upcoming state visit to Australia and the Far East.

Around the table were various people holding different titles within the church. They all wore black cassocks and only the skullcap and coloured belt determined their rank and title; red for Cardinals; purple for Archbishops and bishops. The Pope was in his customary white cassock.

The Vatican, as a recognised Sovereignty, had to act like one and many of the senior figures around the table were now more administrative in their roles rather than clergymen. With titles and roles similar to any global country the Papal Council met weekly to discuss matters of State.

Cardinal Pierre Moritz, tasked with arranging the state visits was speaking. "We have received an invitation from the Chinese government to attend the Hall of the People in Beijing for an audience with their leaders."

Pope Pius looked down the table at Moritz over his half mooned glasses. "I didn't realise that China was on the itinerary."

"It isn't Your Holiness," Cardinal Philip Houseman said from his side. Houseman was a close friend of the Pope and a trusted confidant, he was also the Pope's chief advisor on the worlds political and domestic matters. "But with China opening its borders over the past few years, it's a unique opportunity to visit and show the world that the Church is willing to embrace them."

"The visit is in eight months' time," Archbishop Ellett spoke up, "do we have time to arrange an extra country to visit?"

"We have a 2 day window in the schedule that could be used to visit China." Moritz said. "Given the efficiency of the Chinese Government they could be ready if His Holiness arrived tomorrow."

"And by efficiency you mean vicious control of its people." Cardinal Dominic Spencer said from the Popes right. "Your Holiness, China has a small but very devout Catholic community; priests are tormented by government officials and I know of one, a Fr. Cho Li was incarcerated for 7 years in the wilderness of the desert only to be released for a day and then once more arrested."

Cardinal Spencer was an American, born in Boston Massachusetts, all he ever wanted to be was a priest and his years of service now brought him to the table of the Pope. "Catholics are persecuted in China; they are hunted and beaten, and on some occasions killed for what they believe."

"Then surely a visit by the head of the Church would help the people understand the church, and help the government to be more accepting." Houseman said. "Sir, this is a unique opportunity and it will show the world that we can accept all regimes and all people."

Spencer shook his head, "And what of the public relations?"

"What about it?"

"When his holiness visits countries like America or Germany or Brazil there is a huge number of people there to see him. Outdoor masses are filled to capacity with people wishing to be there, just to catch a single glimpse of His Holiness." Spencer was addressing the whole table, "How do you think it will look if His Holiness was there and no Catholics were there to welcome him because they were too scared or intimated by the Government officials? Who will be there to attend? How will it look to the rest of the world when the majority of people attending are the stony faced bureaucrats of the Chinese Government, who, to add insult to injury, aren't even Catholic?"

"His attendance will draw the crowds and maybe give the people strength to proclaim their faith." Houseman said, casually flicking through the briefing notes, as if only giving a passing interest in what Spencer was saying.

"Indeed it will, and nothing will happen to the people while he is there, but what about afterwards?" Spencer shot back, sensing Houseman's lack of interest, "What if I'm wrong and a member of the congregation is beaten or worse killed? His Holiness will have to speak out on it and as soon as he does, the Vatican is dragged into a political mess that the United Nations have been trying to deal with for years with no progress."

"You think it's a bad idea?" Pope Pius spoke quietly.

Spencer nodded, "I do sir. I don't think your being there will help those Catholics that are there. It will give them safety for the period of time for your visit, but as soon as we leave and the cameras are off, the officials will clamp down.

"This is a unique -" Houseman started, but Pius held his hand to stop him.

"A unique opportunity, yes I understand that, but I also don't want to inflict further suffering on its citizens, and those brave enough to proclaim their faith publicly against a government that has persecuted its citizens." he said looking around the table. "But something needs to be done, I agree, something needs to be said. I see we're going to Japan, let me make a speech there condemning the Chinese handling of their Catholics, that way we recognise there is a problem, but we don't bow to their hospitality or blinkered view of the problem."

Cardinal Louis Franco Conquezla sat at the far end of the table and listened to the debate. He admired the pope; admired his logical mind, principals and understanding of the world. Conquezla was glad that he backed the former Cardinal Joseph Becker to be the next Pope from the start of the secretive conclave that chose the new pope 18 months previously.

The situation in China had been a difficult dilemma for many years and it was a political minefield that the Vatican didn't want to get too bogged down in. Conquezla nodded as he agreed with the new Pope and his assessment of the situation. It was the right thing to do.

From a doorway embedded into the decorated wall Fr. Stefan Jung appeared holding a manila folder. He bowed deeply towards the head of the table where the white robbed Pope sat and silently stepped to the side of his superior, Cardinal Conquezla.

He took the folder and opened it and quickly read the notes, this was not good news. He removed his glasses and looked down the table to the Pope who caught his eye.

"Cardinal Conquezla," Pope Pius spoke up over the debate that ensued, "you have something of interest?" the table fell silent and all eyes were on him.

"Yes," Conquezla said clearing his throat, "Your Holiness it is with great and deepest regret that I report that Fr. Stuart McKellen was found murdered in the grounds of St John's church in the Scottish Highlands this morning."

A murmur spread across the room as the news sunk in.

Quick prayers were whispered and rosaries kissed.

Conquezla continued, "The body was found by a dog walker and police are investigating the matter. As yet no more information is available."

"What do you suggest?" Pope Pius asked quietly.

"I suggest we allocate Fr. Andrew McCloud from Edinburgh to act as liaison on this matter. He will report directly to me, and I to you." Conquezla said.

"Very well," Pius said, "Cardinal, please make the necessary arrangements."

"At once, if you'll excuse me."

Pius nodded his approval and Conquezla gathered his papers and quickly exited the room followed by Fr. Jung.

Outside in the marbled corridor Jung took some of the papers off Conquezla. "Teeth and claw marks?" he asked Jung, referring to the initial medical reports in the papers that described the savage attack.

"Yes, DNA samples have been collected from the body but as yet the British Forensic Services have been unable to identify them." Jung replied walking beside the Cardinal, "Our contact in the British Government is sending over the post-mortem photographs now, I've asked for the teeth and claw markings to be sent first."

"Good, excellent." Conquezla said. "I need Fr. McCloud on the phone as soon as possible."

Jung pulled a mobile phone out and handed it to the Cardinal. "He's on line one, Your Eminence!"

CHAPTER THREE

Wall Street was buzzing with excitement as the countdown to the opening of the Sunrise Corporation's New York base began. No expense had been spared by the owner, Felix Masterson, to show off his company to the world.

For almost two years a 50 storey building had being constructed in the heart of New York's financial district. Completely hidden from view behind monolithic covers, nobody knew what the building was going to look like, or if it would sit in with the steel and glass constructions that laced Wall Street already. Masterson felt he was a king of dramatics, with his finger on the pulse of the media he knew what good a showman needed; panache!

In the weeks leading up to this moment the CEO of the Sunrise Corps travelled the country talking about the exciting new offices being opened in New York. Most of the people who saw the reports didn't care that another multi-billion dollar multi-national company was opening offices, but the media loved it, more importantly they loved Felix Masterson.

The schedule of events today was easy enough. Masterson would fly from his penthouse apartment on the company helicopter and land on the roof of the Sunrise HQ. As soon as they landed the drapes covering the building would fall away revealing for the first time the magnificent glass faced building.

Environmentally friendly with state of the art water and electrical supplies, it cost nearly $1billion to design and build. With the press and world media getting its first look at it, Masterson would have time to travel from the roof to the stage at the front to speak to the awaiting masses.

His press secretary had made some notes for him to say, but Masterson had brushed them away, instead trusting the event to blind luck and his quick mind. If he was truly honest with himself he didn't know how he felt on such a great occasion, and to prepare comments and a speech would only make the event feel fake. He wanted to wait and see what would happen and the genuine reaction of the press, and then he would give a true account of what he felt, that way it would be more honest.

The sun was setting across the East coast and the terracotta glow reached up from the horizon and danced off the tinted glass of the HQ. The observers were dazzled by this, and it was at this moment that Masterson walked out onto the stage and accepted the applause of the crowd waiting to see him. After a couple of minutes the applause died away, as did the blinding light shining down on the crowd.

Jesus had never made such an entrance, Masterson thought as he waved again and stepped up to the microphone. Behind him giant plasma TV screens beamed his image for all to see. Reaching the upper end of his 40's Masterson looked good for his age.

A slight receding hairline with a few grey hairs added a distinguished feel to him as his perfect teeth flashed across the screens. His whole working career had been waiting for this moment, and he was going to show everyone who ever doubted him, that he Felix Masterson, was finally the king among people.

"We stand here on the forefront of great technological advancements. The Sunrise Corporation works tirelessly to improve people's lives, your lives. With research in medicine and clinical trials we're a leading force in the fight against cancer, diabetes, multiple sclerosis, and many other diseases that have for so long crippled and ruined families across America and the world.

"With this new East Coast Headquarters complete, we can now focus our attentions on the important things in the world, success. Our engineers are working hard on making the production of electricity cheaper to help the less fortunate around us. They are working day and night to make everyone's lives a little bit easier. Let us take the burden from their lives." A ripple of applause broke out across the crowd, and Masterson paused to let the cameras focus on him as he gracefully accepted the attention.

"We need to reduce the damage we have for so long inflicted on the world, and it is for that reason that the carbon footprint of this building is almost zero. With state of the art solar panels that collect energy throughout the year no matter what the weather, and with electricity produced from energy sourced from the Hudson River, we are completely independent.

"In six months we should see the completion of Delta City, a unique purpose built city in Nevada that houses Sunrise International's headquarters. Using state of the art technology, developed by our in-house scientists Delta City will be the epitome of design and technology.

"This here today is a stepping stone towards a utopia where nobody should fear anything. Ladies and gentlemen, distinguished guests it gives me great pleasure to invite you to the future. I give you, Omega Tower."

The crowd erupted in applause and the guards at the front of the crowd stepped aside and allowed the VIP's, honoured guests and more importantly the press, the first chance to see Omega Tower. Masterson smiled broadly as he watched the people swarm inside.

Descending the steps he paused for a moment as he realised that his hard work of fighting through University, working in a pharmaceuticals lab and finally owning and running his own company was all worth it. The sacrifices he had made, personally and professionally were all worth it now as he watched the masses enter his world, the world he had created and was now master of.

The drinks flowed freely as the guests gazed with awe at the magnificent interior of Omega Tower. Mezzanine floors seemed to suspend over the foyer, held up by nothing more than a subtly positioned struts and supports.

The mechanics and engineering of the building used the ethos that to make something as strong as possible, it should be as light as possible. Hidden joists, beams and pillars were cleverly woven into the architecture of the building that had 3 mezzanine floors over-looking the marble floored entrance plaza below.

Despite the thronging crowd of nearly 500 guests the noise level was dissipated by the acoustic artistry woven into the plans. The grand space didn't echo and nobody had to shout to be over heard.

Felix Masterson chatted casually with members of the press and his press secretary ushered him across to sit in front of another camera to answer the same questions he had answered 15 times previously that morning. It was hard work, but the surgically enhanced smile beamed out towards the camera and the reporter was immediately seduced by his charm and charisma.

On the 3rd floor mezzanine balcony Laura Kennedy watched as the crowd bustled and everyone tried to get a glimpse of the mastermind that was Masterson.

Team leader for medical research in South America, Laura was a graduate of Harvard Medical School and had worked across the world from St Bart's hospital, London, to the Cancer Unit at Hong Kong Hospital. Now she stood and watched her new employer work the media like a showbiz whore. She watched the mass of reporters below with her packed bags beside her as Alex Koplan, her deputy team leader and part time lover, joined her.

"You're going somewhere?" he asked as he took a sip of champagne he had taken the liberty of taking from a passing waiter while downstairs.

Laura looked at him. "South America, somewhere in

Venezuela I think."

Alex nodded, "That's a bit vague isn't it?"

Laura smiled. It was vague but that was all she had been told herself. "Other people will be sorting it out for me, I go, I arrive, someone meets me, I work, I come back."

"The great oiled machine that is Sunrise Corps."

"Please Alex," Laura said, smiling, "you're forever trying to get business trips around the world. I've never met more of a freebie scrounger than you, so don't get jealous of me for this."

"It's why I took the job." Alex said finishing his drink. "What are you doing down there?"

Laura checked her watch, a limousine would be waiting at the rear entrance of the building and she didn't want to be late. "Checking up on childhood cancer patients. We need the data from the Venezuelan branch to compare to US, European and Middle East samples."

"Doesn't sound like fun."

"I like it," Laura replied quickly, "children are easier to work with than adults and their optimism is astonishing."

Alex shrugged, she was right but he knew he would prefer a trip to Miami or Sydney instead. "Will I see you when you get back?"

"Of course you will." Laura said putting one of her bags on her shoulder.

"No, I mean will I see you?" Alex said emphasising the personal nature of his question.

Laura looked at him, "We talked about this before Alex, let's talk about it again when I see you in the office next week."

Alex reluctantly accepted the knock back and watched as she walked towards the elevator and the doors closed behind her. She was gone from his life for another week, but as he always thought, when one door closes another opens.

He watched the crowd below him and saw a young lady in a red dress standing quietly on her own. A girl shouldn't be on her own at a party like this, he thought as he tidied his tie and took the stairs to go and meet her.

CHAPTER FOUR

Fr. Peter Morgan cheered proudly as the child scored his penalty kick. The ball sailed through the air and was caught not by the goalie who flailed around but by the nylon net. The child's team mates ran to him and with enthusiasm Morgan never thought he would see in this child again, they cheered and congratulated him.

The dusty makeshift pitch stood on the outskirts of Makenza town and suffered from the lack of shade and punishing un-relenting sunshine, and he was glad that he didn't have to wear the customary black uniform of his position within the church.

The south side of Makenza town was a slum, deprived and poor. These children in their ragged clothes and worn shoes were the result of a lifetime of hardship suffered by their parents, who wore similar clothes when they were young. But as the smiling faces of the children stretched across the pitch, the hardships and disappointment disappeared, if only for a moment.

As part of an initiative by the Church to help those in need, Fr. Morgan was one of the first to volunteer for the project in South America. Fluent in Spanish and Portuguese Morgan was comfortable in this area and loved the hope and desire to succeed he had planted in the minds of the youngsters here.

His role wasn't to promote Christianity and convert

people; Venezuela was a devout Catholic country so the early pioneers had taken care of that part for him, he thought on more than one occasion. He was there to help people, work with them, and to give them a helping hand and to better understand them. He saw his main role as a way of giving them hope when there was no hope, and let them dream when there were no dreams to fulfil.

He wanted the children, who suffered the most, to grow up with education and good health. He didn't care if they believed in God or not, they were children who wanted help and he wanted to be there to catch them when they fell.

Morgan had been in Venezuela for nearly 4 years and he'd worked a lot in and around Caracas. Wherever he went it broke his heart to see children living in squalor, but there was always a strong belief in them that they would get out of the slums and make something of their lives.

Some wanted to be doctors, one young girl he met had told him she wanted to be president, and for these boys now all of them wanted to be footballers. But no matter how much encouragement he gave them, no matter how much inspiration and no matter how much talent and ambition they had, Morgan knew that these young players would never play professional football.

They shouldn't suffer, nobody should, but children shouldn't have to suffer the fate of millions of others. As he stared at them now smiling and cheering Morgan knew that the cancer they all suffered from would soon come and take their young lives, and there was nothing he could do to stop it.

The evening was drawing in and the doctors and nurses from the hospital who had come to watch the impromptu football match led the young patients back to the 2 storey hospital that the waste ground they played on backed on to.

Morgan was packing the balls away when Carlos Jimenez, his liaison with the Venezuelan government came striding over with an auburn haired woman a couple of steps behind him.

"Padre Morgan?" Carlos said in his rich South American

accent as he skilfully flicked a ball up into the air towards Morgan. The priest turned and caught the ball.

"Carlos! Good to see you again." Morgan replied in perfect Spanish. "What brings you out here?"

The two men shook hands and Carlos turned and introduced Laura Kennedy. "She is from Sunrise Corporation in New York."

"Miss Kennedy, it's a pleasure." Morgan shook her hand and led them to a bench where equipment was piled.

"Likewise Fr. Morgan. I've heard a great deal about your work here and I thought while I was in Caracas I would come and see your work first hand." Laura said.

Morgan and Carlos picked up boxes of football equipment and the three of them headed back to the hospital.

"Miss Kennedy is head of operations for clinical studies in childhood cancer." Carlos explained. "Centres in Caracas are funded by Sunrise donations as are specialist units in Europe and North America."

Morgan nodded. He had heard of Sunrise Corporation, heard of its reputation, and had heard that it had funded Oncology centres in the Venezuelan capital. The company had pumped a lot of money into the health economy of the country for a number of years, but after 8 years of waiting, this hospital was still to see any of the funds that were supposedly being fed down through the system from the government and from the Sunrise Monetary Fund.

Yes, he had heard of the Corporation, but he was not impressed by their selectiveness of funding, especially with the eloquent discourse helping the masses displayed by the CEO Felix Masterson.

"How long are you here for Miss Kennedy?" Morgan asked politely as he held a door open for her and led her and Carlos along a dimly lit corridor in the bowels of the hospital.

Laura was careful where to step as puddles of water converged on the floor. "A couple of days. I have to be in Caracas at the end of the week for a board meeting."

Morgan opened another door for her. "Another redistribution of the wealth?"

"Something like that yes." she replied accepting the offer for the door.

Despite his Catholic upbringing, vows to uphold the church laws and the promise to himself to be the best priest he can be Morgan was seething underneath his calm demure, and he hated the corporate boards who dictated who would get money and who would be 'assessed later'. He hated that no money had come to this hospital. He had worked hard to get the local companies, mainly mining operations to donate some of their profits to the upkeep of the hospital, but there was a limit to their funds and patience.

Morgan and Carlos deposited the kit underneath a staircase and the three of them made their way up to the white corridors of the main hospital. Morgan led the way to his office and the air conditioning hit them all as relief after the humidity of the evening air.

The office was plain, white walled with a desk, chairs and a sofa against the wall. On the shelves were a number of books relating to trauma victims, coping mechanisms and Catholicism. On the wall behind Morgan's chair was a crucifix and a portrait of Pope Pius XV, below which was a short ivory and silver engraved baton, about 10 inches long.

These were the only outwardly signs that they were in the presence of a clergyman and as his guests sat down Morgan gave them a cold drink from the fridge beside the window.

"Miss Kennedy is here to gather data for her company's research, we've already met with Dr Gomez who will supply her with the data, but I thought it would be good for her to meet you Padre." Carlos said taking a refreshing sip of his drink.

Laura too took a sip and wiped her lip. "Carlos was eager to show me the palliative care you contribute here."

Morgan looked at her across the table. "I offer more of a support service to patients and parents. I wish I could do more for them."

"From what I've heard you've done a lot with limited resources." Laura said leaning back into the soft sofa.

"Resources are limited. I've worked hard to try and buy new sports equipment for the kids. The church can contribute only so much, but most of the things you see here are bought from my own pocket." Morgan replied calmly.

"Does the church or hospital not refund your expenses?"

Morgan smiled at the comment. "I'm not in this for money, the patients need help and I'm here to give it."

Carlos shifted in his seat in a feeble attempt to fit his bulky frame comfortably into the chair. "Miss Kennedy is also here to investigate other possible initiatives Sunrise could fund in this area."

"It's about time." Morgan said roughly. Laura was taken aback and stared at the priest.

"I don't quite follow Father." she said leaning forward.

Morgan didn't want to lose his temper, but sitting there watching the well preened woman who had her finger on the pulse of millions of dollars of funding, judge him and his efforts to be worthy of Sunrise funds made him sick. "I've been here for over 4 years and in that time I've seen the detrimental decline in health care in this area." he said. "I've watched organisations like Sunrise come in, flash their money around the Capital, make speeches and presentations about how they can help the poor people of the country, but then the money always seems to run out just before it leaves the city limits of Caracas and nothing gets to the people who need it most.

"We're the forgotten people out here Miss Kennedy and it makes me so angry that with so much money being pumped into the health system in the capital none of it reaches us out here."

Laura sat silently at the outburst from Morgan and quickly gathered her thoughts. "That's why I'm here."

"No -" Morgan interrupted, "you're here to collect data from the Doctors upstairs on the dying children who I work with every day. That's you're primary reason for being here, and everything else is academic and secondary. Like we always are, like we always shall be no matter how loud I shout, how high I jump or how many hoops I have to dive through."

"I never thought I would hear such an outburst from a priest." Laura said as calmly as she could, defying the anger that had started to boil up inside herself.

Morgan smiled at her. "What did you expect?"

"I thought you'd be full of kindness, compassion, understanding and be preaching about the good going to heaven and bad to hell."

"It may be surprising to hear that priests have opinions on things other than religion." Morgan said. "In fact one of the things I'm passionate about is getting as much funding as I can for the children of this hospital. My compassion lies with the people upstairs who are watching their children die, my understanding is with the families as they try to come to terms with the death of a child, and my preaching gives words of comfort to the parents who cry on my shoulder.

"I use the appropriate tone in the circumstances that call for it Miss Kennedy, if I'm gruff with you, or I shock you it's because I've sat here many times before and listened to people like yourself tell me what they're going to do for this hospital; how much money is going to be pumped in, but in the end all I get is a letter of rejection saying more worthy causes in Caracas are a priority.

"Too many times I've seen disappointment on the faces of the nurses and doctors as another potential beneficiary decides to send their money closer to the seat of power. The reason for this? It's sexier public relations to say you're helping in the capital city that people across the world have heard of rather than a backwater town like Makenza."

Morgan stopped himself from continuing any further and looked away from Laura. He didn't want to erupt as he had, but the emotions had got the better of him, and he silently cursed himself for not stopping sooner.

Carlos spoke up once more to break the silence. "I think it would be wise Padre if we take a break and discuss this later." He stood and Laura followed his lead. Morgan too stood and opened his door for his guests. "We're having a reception at the town hall tonight if you would to join us?" Carlos said.

Morgan and Carlos shook hands, "I'll try and make it." Morgan said and he turned to Laura who avoided his eyes. There was a wave of guilt building up inside him, a sensation he never felt often but was unmistakable now it was there. "Miss Kennedy, I want to help these kids and I've heard and seen things like Sunrise many times before. I just don't want to see them let down again."

"That's a noble sentiment Father." Laura said, shaking his hand, "It was a pleasure to meet you."

Despite the relative poor and shambolic living conditions for the majority of the residents in Makenza, the town leaders lived in relative luxury. Within a fenced off ornamental garden, lush green grass and exotic plants grew and flourished.

The house standing in the middle of this mirage was an elegant white stone villa with pillars guarding the entrance and overlooked by a veranda that allowed a panoramic view of the garden and mountains in the distance.

Working with such poor people Morgan felt it hypocritical to attend such functions during his first few months in Makenza, but he soon learned that the local business leaders attended such events to show off their money and wealth to each other, and it wasn't long before Morgan was using his influence as a man of God against them.

He had raised much money for the hospital by attending such events and skilfully playing one businessman off against another to get as much money as possible. To begin with the doctors, nurses and families at the hospital disapproved of Morgan attending such events, but once they saw the influence he had with the ability to make contacts they allowed him this one luxury.

Looking out across the garden from the veranda Morgan

sipped his iced water and watched as the evening glow of the sun bedded down for the night underneath the quilt of darkness. The stars began to glow and the moon shined down on the garden casting shadows across the manicured lawn.

To his side he sensed someone approach and the perfume on the air matched that of the scent that still hung in the air of his office. He turned and faced Laura Kennedy. Despite being a man of the cloth Morgan could appreciate the attractiveness of Laura. Her toned arms wrapped within a shawl, her hair pulled back to show off her eyes and face, and the plunging neckline of her evening dress that exposed the sides of her breasts.

Morgan wasn't always a priest and he had, in a previous life, indulged in the world of women on more than one occasion, sometimes with more than one woman at a time, but his professional standing at the moment forbade him from indulging in such activities and it took all of his inner strength not to look south of her face.

"Good evening Father." She said as she took a glass of champagne off the passing waiter's tray. "You look very, very -" she looked him up and down as he stood there in his black trousers and shirt, without his dog collar.

"Like a priest?" Morgan continued for her, smiling.

"Well yes." Laura said smiling too.

"It's okay. When I was back home I got funny looks for doing a weekly shopping trip." Morgan said. "I don't know how people think we stay alive."

Laura was embarrassed and looked away from him. "Sorry, I didn't mean it."

"Don't worry, I've gotten used to it. To be honest, it's the reason I don't wear the dog collar, it's too constricting at times. Both professionally and personally." Morgan explained. The ice between them was thawing somewhat, but as the waiter passed them by once more there was a silence. "Miss Kennedy, this afternoon I was out of line. I shouldn't have gone off at you like that. I apologise."

Laura was relieved that the afternoon's episode was mentioned. "I understand Father, it must be frustrating to fight for so long, be promised so much and be let down so often."

"It's like banging my head against a proverbial brick wall." Morgan added, "And please, call me Peter."

With the air cleared Morgan and Laura relaxed as the waiter came past once more and Laura took two glasses of champagne and passed one to Morgan. He declined it and shook his head.

"Sorry, don't priests drink?" Laura asked.

"No it's not that." Morgan said reassuringly, "Nearly 80% of this town's population live in poverty. I've worked with them for the whole time I've been in Venezuela and those people out there can only look up at this house and dream of the comforts that lie within and behind the high walls and manicured hedges. It would be hypocritical of me to enjoy the luxuries that they themselves cannot have. That means no wine, no champagne, no canapés, no food."

"No food? You don't eat while you're here? Then why do you come?" Laura asked astonished.

"To make contacts, and use the innate Catholicism that is bred into all of these businessmen to donate to the hospital."

"You con them?" Laura asked.

"Religion is not a con. People believe what they want to believe, I just remind them of what they were taught." Morgan casually explained as he nodded to a factory owner who came onto the veranda to light his cigar. "Religion and family are still strong factors in South America; I could walk from Mexico to the bottom tip of Chile with only a bible and dog collar and live off the generosity of the people. There is no other profession in no other part of the world that gets that treatment."

"So you preach to them? I can't stand being preached to and told that I'll be going to hell for not loving my family". Laura stated.

"I take it you're not a Catholic?" Morgan asked taking a sip of water.

"No."

"And you don't believe in God?"

"No. I'm a scientist and believe in the work of Galileo, Newton, Einstein and Hawkins."

Morgan accepted this and faced her. "These people do believe in God, for some it is the only thing in their life. The more material items you have the less need you have for a strong belief system. That's why the US, Europe and other wealthy countries are seeing a downfall in church attendance.

"The majority of people don't need the church anymore, but there's a small proportion that still do and while there are, the church will continue to make people fulfil better lives and treat each other well." Morgan paused for a second, "Surely trying to make people more tolerant of each other is worthwhile?"

CHAPTER FIVE

Focusing the lens on his custom made digital film camera, Dirk Woods sat silently in his wooden boat and waited for the great beast to emerge from the black waters. He had been waiting for hours to capture the moment but there was no sign of the animal.

Waiting hours under the Africa sun takes its toll on a man, but for a professional natural world cameraman like Dirk this was just another day at the office. Another half hour, he thought as he checked his watch without rocking the boat. It was getting late and he needed the remnants of the dipping sun to pack his equipment away and drive back to camp safely. Agonisingly slowly the seconds ticked away, and after another 4 minutes Dirk threw in the towel.

He switched off the camera, carefully un-hooked it from the stabilising tripod and placed it in the foam lined case underneath the seat.

In the corner of his vision he saw a movement and an object emerged from the water. Dirk froze still and watched as the nostrils and eyes of a 6 tonne hippopotamus rose from the water. Mesmerised by the sight of one of the most serene but vicious mammals in Africa emerge from its watery hide, Dirk slowly levelled the camera and clicked the record button.

The lens focused on the hippo and for 10 seconds neither

man nor beast moved. Dirk watched as the water droplets ran down the face of the hippo and for a moment their eyes locked. Dirk held his breath as the boat bobbed on the water and he watched the hippo through the lens. There was something wrong though. He had filmed hundreds of animals across the world, and in each encounter he had sensed a living being in the eyes.

He could never describe it, but when he watched wild animals in their natural environment there was what he could only describe as a soul behind the eyes. But it wasn't the case here. Dirk stopped the camera and emerged from behind the view finder.

It really wasn't right, he thought.

Despite the great head of the hippo staring at him there was no other movement, no other signs of life. The ears didn't flick, the eyes didn't blink and there were no ripples beneath its nostrils from its breathing.

Against his better judgement Dirk picked up a stone caught in his boot in the bottom of the boat and threw it out into the water. With a gentle splash the stone landed in front of the muscular face and water landed on its brow. But there was no movement, no reaction, no sign of life.

Going against all advice he had ever heard and against all the training he had received Dirk gently paddled the boat within 6 feet of the hippo. Wildlife photographers and cameramen across the globe vowed never to interfere with the order of nature no matter how much an animal is in distress, but there was something about this hippo that was strange. Carefully keeping his balance Dirk reached the paddle out across the water and dipped it in front of its nose.

Nothing.

Paddling closer still, he repeated the manoeuvre and tapped the paddle on the head of the hippo. If there was ever a time for the beast to move, it would be now, but it didn't. It continued to look ahead, not moving at all. The paddle rested on the head and as Dirk moved in the boat, the snout of the hippo dipped under the water and Dirk fell back into the boat and scrambled away from the edge in fear of an attack.

But it didn't come.

Carefully the cameraman peered over the side of the boat and saw the decapitated head of the hippopotamus float on its side in front of the boat.

"What the hell could've done that?" Dirk said to himself as he grabbed the camera and began to record the horrific image. With the nerves still shaking through his body he stood in the rocking boat filming the head and with his attention focused through the view finder Dirk Woods never noticed a silver head rise out of the water behind him.

With glowing red eyes the creature silently rose out of the water, its skeletal body with protruding rib cage lifted out of the water and from its shoulder blades a pair of webbed wings extended and stretched outwards to 12 feet in each direction.

So focused was Dirk on his filming that he never saw the dying sun glint off the razor sharp stalactite like fangs extend from the jaw and he never saw the outstretched arms of sinew and bone reach over to him and grab his shoulders.

Despite the fragile frame the creature was immensely strong and it wrapped Dirk within its wings and submerged him under the water as he beat and thrashed about in protest.

He couldn't win and the water soon calmed as the last bubbles in his lungs exploded on the surface. The water once more calmed and lapped gently around the head of the hippo and rocked the boat that still carried a recording video camera.

*

Morgan stood in the corridor watching through the grimy window as a doctor carefully examined a 9 year old boy. Suffering from leukaemia for over half of his life the time had come for him to breathe his last breath, and leave his earthly body behind.

The boy's parents were by his side and his mother whispered prayers into her hands as his father, a large powerfully built man, stood emotionally blank at her shoulder. He tried desperately to show no emotion, but Morgan knew it was difficult and he admired the man for showing strength in the face of such adversary.

From along the corridor Laura Kennedy joined Morgan. Despite their disagreements, Morgan accepted that she was good hearted and he knew it wasn't her fault that his work and these children were being over looked. After leaving her at the party two hours ago she had finally caught up with him.

"Peter, I've been thinking." Laura said as she too watched the family. "I think I'll be able to get a small budget together to allow this hospital to be included in the donation list from Sunrise. I've got to speak to a few people, but more money could be coming this way."

She was excited at this news, but Morgan didn't respond. He stared at the mother as the emotion took hold of her.

"Peter... did you hear what I said?"

Morgan kept his eyes on the child as the final breaths struggled past his lips. "That boy there is nine years old. When he was four he was diagnosed with leukaemia and ever since he has been on any number of drugs to try and control the disease. About a month ago he took a turn for the worse and now the time has come."

His voice was low and quiet, and Laura listened as she too watched the mother sob into the chest of her husband who wiped a tear from his cheek. Morgan continued, "The doctor is about to tell the parents that there is nothing they can do and that he will die today and when that happens I will have to go in there and try and comfort them.

"Nothing I say will be able to help them. They will need to mourn in their own way. I've gotten to know the boy, he's a bright child, enthusiastic about football, and loves his family; he hasn't hurt anyone and has no enemies. But the parents will ask me one thing. Why has God taken their son away? And I - I can't answer them. I'll try, but nothing I say will give them comfort. They'll get angry at me and despite being devout Catholics they'll reject the church, and her teachings."

Morgan turned to Laura who was wiping a tear from her own cheek. "Miss Kennedy, we don't need a small budget; we need a monumental budget that will pay for counsellors, and staff who are fully trained to deal with families such as these. I'm a realist and know cancer can't be beaten overnight and I know if we had the best medical facilities here, this boy would still be dying. It's the little things that matter, it's the care and support these people get now that matters. Their sons suffering is ending, but theirs will go on." Morgan stepped away from the window and opened the door to the room.

He turned back to Laura, "That Miss Kennedy is what we need." He entered the room as the mother wailed in pain at the loss of her son. Morgan turned to the window and closed the blinds so that Laura couldn't see anything.

*

"I'm telling you Scott you've got to see this footage!" Tom Willis said into his satellite phone. "I don't know what happened out there, but it was something I've never seen before."

He paced back and forth inside the spacious canvas tent that had been commandeered to be an editing suite. As the production manager for the wild life series it was a major shock to find the remains of Dirk Woods and he felt responsible for the loss.

His line managers back in California ordered him to pack his team up and fly back as soon as they could, and for the first time Tom didn't argue. Dirk's death was a severe blow to the whole team, but as documentary makers it was a risk they were prepared to take. Dirk wasn't the first to be killed while on location, but as Tom watched the footage, he was certainly the first to be killed by whatever the thing was on screen.

"No - I'm sending it you now. Yes - We're packing up camp and rolling out now. We should be back in town by tomorrow morning and then onto the airport by lunchtime. I think we should be able to catch the next flight to Amsterdam and then onto California." Tom said quickly as he sat down and clicked buttons on the screens. "Yeah, we should be back in two days. Look, Scott, the phone's dying but I'm sending it now. I'll phone again when we're closer to civilisation." He hung up and threw the phone onto the desk. He needed to get this footage back as soon as possible.

Chucky, one of the African support crew members came into the tent. Sweating hard, he was a strong well-built man and since seeing the footage from Dirks camera he had a gun strapped to his waist at all times.

"Mr. Willis sir," he said between breaths, "the main camp is down, we just need to collapse this one and pack the equipment."

Tom turned to him. "Do it, this has been sent. Myself and the team will head off now. Can you arrange to have this forwarded to us in the US?"

Chucky nodded. He was a local man, but enjoyed helping the Americans. It was well paid and while they were here he enjoyed good food and good drink. He had worked with Tom Willis before and never once found him to be patronising or condescending, as other foreign television producers were to the local villagers.

Chucky may not have been trained in the art of film production, but Tom Willis treated him like a member of the team and Chucky loved that. It was for that reason that he would keep his promise and would ensure that the equipment was returned safely to America.

After quick goodbyes to the African logistic team who had helped them through the trip, Tom leapt into the driver's seat of the 4x4 and turned to check on his team. Sally who was perhaps the closest to Dirk had tears streaming down her face and looked blankly out of the window; Robert, another cameraman studied the map from the front passenger seat and then he turned to - no, Dirk wasn't sitting there, Tom reminded himself. His vacant seat in the back was an ominous reminder of what had happened.

Tom turned back and started the engine that grunted into life and the jeep finally pulled away. They drove over the heavily pockmarked ground and away from the clearing and towards the dirt road some 10 miles away, but as they passed a lone bare dying tree a gunshot rang out.

Tom hit the brakes immediately and looked back at the camp. He saw that Chucky had his gun drawn and was looking at the sky as he came running over to the car.

"Mr. Willis, I saw something!" he said, scared and nervous as he pointed the gun to the heavens. "It was huge!"

Tom was eager to get away, as were his companions, but Chucky was a friend and he needed to be calmed. He got out of the car and looked around. "Chuck, I can't see anything. We have to go."

"No! I saw it. I saw it with my own eyes!"

For a moment the two men stood next to the 4x4 and listened. With the grumbling engine of the car there was nothing else to hear.

"Chuck..." Tom started to say but Chucky shouted and pointed his gun and shot at the sun.

"There!"

From the protection of the blinding sun a huge winged beast with sharp protruding teeth swooped down and with razor sharp talons it landed on the bonnet of the 4x4, puncturing the metal and piercing the engine, killing it.

Claws from its wings flapped down and grabbed Chucky who shot off another round before being crushed by the iron grip. Tom panicked and ran back towards the camp but he was confronted by another of the beasts as it forced him back to the car.

Inside Sally and Robert were screaming and shouting to get out but the noise aggravated the creatures more and with a co-ordinated attack the front creature smashed its head through the windscreen and attacked Robert as the rear creature pieced Tom's body with one of it fangs and ripped his body in half.

Sally screamed and never saw the attack from the side as a third creature ripped through the door to devour her flesh.

CHAPTER SIX

With a stinging hangover Lawrence eased his head off the pillow and carefully swung his legs off the side of the bed. Every muscle in his body protested at the movements but it was a necessity needed to relieve the pressure on his bladder.

Standing over the sterile metallic bowl he breathed a sigh of relief and tried to remember the events from the night before. Splashing water on his stubble covered 45 year old face Lawrence looked in the mirror. The face that stared back at him wasn't the face he remembered, but after 10 years of living on the streets it was the only friend he knew.

The room he was in was white, completely white with white linen, white tiles, white bedding. The only splash of colour here was the toilet bowl, the frame of the bed and the occasional rectangle opening that the guards used to talk to him through the door. He was a prisoner here but the problem was he didn't know where here was.

Two weeks previously he had been rummaging in a bin on the south side of Chicago when two men approached him and offered him a place to stay. He was led to the back of a truck where other homeless people were sat inside with a drink and sandwiches and convinced of what he saw he climbed aboard. All of them were driven like cattle for 6 hours across the city and country and they disembarked in an underground unit.

They were ordered to remove their clothes and wash, and then given new clean clothes. It had been years since Lawrence had felt the sensation of a freshly pressed shirt and as he sat down for a hearty meal with his new companions he felt getting on the back of that truck was the best decision he had ever made.

With as much cheap wine and beer as they could drink, they over indulged each night and now Lawrence was feeling the effects. Sitting on the bed he put his head in his hands and tried to rub the pain away, but the bright lights shining down on him made it worse.

He was an experienced drinker, and had spent many hours and days under the influence of intoxicating drink, but he had never had a hangover as bad as this before and decided the best thing to do was hide under the covers and wish the pain away.

On the security monitor Dr Ruth Powers watched Lawrence climb back onto his bed and under the covers. Like 10 subjects before him he was starting to show the symptoms that had become common with the drugs he had ingested.

Dr Powers watched impassively as Lawrence tossed and turned on the bed trying to get comfortable. She knew that he would be experiencing numb fingers and feet, tingling in his arms and soon the stomach cramps would strike. According to her notes, Lawrence was unlike the other homeless test subjects they had collected.

He was an educated man who had just fallen on hard times; previously married that had collapsed, Lawrence gambled his money away and soon found himself with no job and no home. To speak to him his intelligence shone through, and perhaps, Ruth thought, that in another life he may have been offered a job with Sunrise Corps. But it was too late for him now.

The drugs had been administered and soon he would succumb to the Carthage Virus.

Educated in Australia, Ruth Powers graduated top of her medical school class and was offered a junior position at Canberra General Hospital. Where there she took an interest in tropical diseases and her research took her to John Hopkins University in America. There she worked in a lab and experimented on small animals and her work soon came to the attention of Professor Tiberius Coolridge at Sunrise Corporation who offered her a job.

The pay was astronomical but the price of it was to suspend her ethical objections to human experimentation. Leaving her family and ethical blinkers behind, Ruth Powers joined Sunrise Corps four years previously and settled well into her role as Deputy Research Associate for Unexplored Viral Infections.

Ruth made a note on her clipboard and then asked for the next subject to be displayed on the screen and the writhing figure of Lawrence was replaced by a similar designed room with a middle aged woman standing at the door shouting.

It wasn't unusual for his meetings to last three or four hours, but with an empire as large as Sunrise Corps, Felix Masterson needed the time so he could keep abreast of all of his organisation's dealings.

This meeting was different though; in this one he wasn't discussing public relations, governmental contracts or property values, no, this time the meeting was solely about the research components of Sunrise. As a trained chemist, Masterson had a grasp of chemistry and it was on that foundation and that field that Sunrise was born.

But over the years his interests altered and biology became the new love, quickly followed by physics. Each of these disciplines had their own unique opportunities for development and Sunrise, under the careful guidance of Masterson, was there at the forefront of emerging technology and medical treatments.

During these marathon meetings Masterson usually found himself drinking copious amounts of coffee or fantasising about his secretary and her high cut skirt writhing about on top of him; a fantasy he had to remind himself he had already fulfilled.

But during this meeting his mind was totally focused and the first cup of coffee of the meeting sat in its original spot, untouched and bereft of warmth.

"So production of these new processors could create a net income of close to $500 million in the US alone." The head of IT development Wolfgang Krantz said, standing in front of a computer graphic showing the projected predicted growth pattern. "If we extend the release to Europe, the Middle East and Asia, we could be trebling this figure."

Masterson nodded and made a couple of notes. "That's an impressive estimate. How long until the kinks are smoothed out and resolved?"

"It's our top priority with all hands working on it. Within a month we'll be ready for complete trials and 2 months after that, should no problems arise, we can begin mass production." Krantz said.

"Very good," Masterson said. He was genuinely pleased by the progress of the IT team and was already thinking about the launch party he would have to show off the next generation of computer hardware. Perhaps at his hotel in Las Vegas, he thought. "Please continue with the work and keep me informed."

Krantz nodded and flicked his computer off. The meeting had started off with 20 participants, but as it progressed each presenter who was not needed for the following item was excused.

Finally it was the turn of the viral infections team and Professor Coolridge stood and loaded his data onto the computer. Wolfgang Krantz collected his papers and left the remaining four attendees to the final presentation. Once the double doors were closed Masterson flicked a switch that electronically locked them and the window blinds silently descended, shutting out the world outside.

Unbeknown to the other people in the room Masterson had also activated a white noise masking device implanted into the walls to stop all attempts at eavesdropping on the meeting from any of the many competitors who were desperate to learn the secrets of Sunrise Corps. The remaining meeting members were Dr John Walker, Deputy Viral Projects Leader; and Neil Pemberton, Masterson's 2nd in command.

With the lights dimmed Coolridge cleared his throat. "As you know," he began, "the viral infection team has been working on a number of experimental techniques to combat the possible threat of biological warfare." His voice didn't echo around the room, so good were the acoustics. None of the other men watching him flinched or moved; they didn't even make notes. "A genetically engineered virus, called Carthage Virus has been developed by our team in Arizona and we have been working to find a cure for it. So far the results have been promising in that no known cure currently on the market touches Carthage."

Coolridge gave a quick overview of the project guidelines; 24 subjects, selected from the general population, 12 randomly entered into the control group and 12 into the test group. The test group was split into three groups. Each one was given a different strand of the Carthage Virus and the results recorded. The virus was given orally, hidden in food, and the speed of the patient's demise was observed.

Coolridge explained that lab experiments had been conducted on other subjects in Arizona where different treatment options were analysed. None of the permutations of supposed antidotes were successful and there was a 100% mortality rate.

"How are our subjects doing?" Masterson asked.

Coolridge flicked the computer and a video image of Lawrence blazed behind him. "45 year old male, found on the streets of Chicago; he was in surprisingly good health." Lawrence lay on the bed in agony and moved about as he tried to get comfortable. "He was randomised into the test subject group and again into the Viral 3 arm.

"This footage was recorded 6 hours after being administered Charthage V3 and he was suffering from abdominal pains, numbness in his hands and feet, tingling in his arms and legs with severe pain to the head." Coolridge clicked the computer again and the image showed Lawrence once more on the bed, but he was curled up with his head hanging over bed. There was no sound on the footage but the viewers could tell he was being violently sick.

"This was 12 hours after administration and he is obviously being violently ill. From observations of other subjects our medics say that at this stage his stomach acid was intensifying and burning through the stomach wall, his lungs are failing and his heart has an irregular pattern."

The image changed again and had Lawrence lying in a pool of his own blood. "This is 15 hours after administration," Coolridge said coldly, "total organ collapse, the post-mortem revealed his organs were completely liquefied."

"My god!" Pemberton whispered.

Masterson showed no emotion. "How many test subjects remain?"

"Two." Coolridge answered.

For a moment none of the men said anything, the near silent whirr of the air conditioning was the only noise in the room. It was a horrific sight to see, a man dead on the screen in front of them. It wasn't a movie and it wasn't an actor; a real man had died at the hands of Sunrise scientists and all in the name of research. Masterson had personally asked for this type of research to be carried out and had scoured the earth to find a scientist willing to head up such projects.

It wasn't easy and the salary he paid the researchers demonstrated how high a price it cost to keep people silent. He knew that if the public and authorities ever found out about this work it would be the end of Sunrise. There had to be no evidence, no trace, no trail of what happened in his labs.

"The research has been a great success," Masterson said, "and you and your team should be very proud of the advances you have made. But with this new set of results, am I right in thinking that the work has gone as far as it can?"

Coolridge thought for a moment and removed his glasses, "The research has been taken as far as it can, yes. Mortality rates are 100% and the rate of demise has an average of 16 hours. The Carthage Virus is as potent as we can possibly make it, and I believe it will be ready for military use soon."

"How long do the remaining 2 test subjects have?" the CEO asked.

"Based on the mean averages of the others, I would predict 2 hours at the most." the Professor answered.

Masterson stroked his chin and thought for a moment. He had a decision to make, one he had made before, but was never easy no matter how many times he did it. However, it was a necessity and with a new project about to be launched he needed his best people free to focus on the Hades project, as his new sponsor had called it.

"Let them go without intervention and dispose of the bodies in the usual manner. For the control group, dispose of them as you feel fit."

Coolridge had heard the order before and knew it was difficult for the CEO to give it, and it was harder for the scientist to follow it, but he nodded and accepted the order.

"I want no survivors, Professor." Masterson continued, "No witnesses, no stories." Masterson stood and the other men followed his lead. "We have a new project starting soon Professor and I need all of your people to be ready."

"We'll be ready." Coolridge said.

Masterson thanked the attendees and pressed the button that unlocked the doors and raised the blinds. With his folder under his arm Masterson strode out of the meeting room and headed back to his office for his next appointment regarding the Hades Project.

CHAPTER SEVEN

Fr. Andrew McCloud stood at the back of the room as the reporters filed in and took whatever places they could in the seats available in front of the briefing desk. Television cameramen, journalists and reporters all readied their equipment, Dictaphones and pens ready for the police briefing on the vicious and suspicious death of Fr. Stuart McKellen.

McCloud had met Fr. McKellen on a number of occasions and found him to be a tolerant and pleasant man. He was quietly spoken dealt with hostility with a calm outlook and soothing approach. McCloud was as shocked as most at the news of the death, and in his grieving he was taken aback once more as he received a phone-call from the Vatican office of Cardinal Conquezla, his mentor, to investigate the death.

Honoured to be asked, McCloud travelled up from his parish in Carlisle in the North West of England to this briefing in Edinburgh.

Standing at the back he removed his dog collar as the overt sign of his role would encourage the swarm of reporters to surround him and question him about the dead priest's life, the role of the church and his own personal thoughts on the matter; topics McCloud was eager to avoid.

From a door at the front a highly decorated police Chief and two other officers entered and sat behind the desk littered with microphones from across the country. Cameramen focused their lenses on the men, and flash bulbs exploded in blinding lights. The policemen took it in their stride and sat down.

"Good afternoon," the lead officer spoke with a wisp of a Scottish accent, "My name is Chief Constable Philip Rooks to my right is Detective Chief Inspector Hugh Stevens and to my left Superintendent Gavin Fisher." Rooks paused for a second and took a sip of water before continuing.

"As recent news reports have indicated a priest was murdered two nights ago. I can confirm the victim was Fr. Stuart McKellen from St Joseph's Roman Catholic church. Fr. McKellen was travelling back to his parish after visiting and comforting a family in distress. During this journey his car swerved off the road and hit a tree in the grounds of the abandoned St John's church in the Highlands and his body was discovered some 200 metres from his car."

The reporters erupted in a frenzy of questions. TV reporters pointed microphones and journalists shouted over each other to be heard. Chief Constable Rooks waited and raised a hand; experienced in dealing with the press he knew how to handle them. "This is an on-going investigation and I am not going to speculate about what happened. I will pass this briefing to Chief Inspector Stevens."

Hugh Stevens thanked his superior and his thick Scottish accent rolled across the briefing room. "At this time we have no suspects to question; friends of Fr. McKellen described him as a quiet, pleasant man with a positive outlook. He had no enemies and friends indicate that there is no reason why anyone would want to harm him. A post-mortem has been conducted and the initial findings indicate that Fr. McKellen suffered severe lacerations to the abdomen and face, there were defensive wounds on his hands and arms and it is clear that a struggle occurred. The cause of death was severe loss of blood caused by the lacerations. He was pronounced dead at the scene."

A reporter shot his hand into the air and asked his question before anyone had a chance to stop him. "Is there a chance that this is a religiously motivated crime? And if so what has the church said about it? And if so what are the other religious leaders doing to calm those people who will take advantage of this incident for their own violent obsessions?"

Inspector Stevens looked at the reporter, "Let me be clear about this now. From the beginning I want to make it clear to each and every one of you who are sitting here listening to me, there is no evidence to suggest that this attack was the result of a religiously motivated crime. I have spoken to church leaders and they are as shocked as we are. Neither they, nor I, think this is a hate crime. Because we are not following that line of enquiry at this time I am not in a position to comment on the thoughts of other religious groups. I would imagine they are saddened by the loss of a valuable member of the community, whatever his religion."

That was it, McCloud thought, the three words that would be in every report the following day, religious hate crime. It didn't matter if it was true or not, the tabloid papers would say it would be the start of religious fanaticism sweeping the country, but would contradict themselves in the next paragraph.

Experts would be questioned and quoted saying that the police were wrong; extremists groups would surface and members would hold up banners outside mosques and temples and tensions in the religiously diverse communities would rise. The papers would, of course, report all of it and use it as evidence that they were right all along.

Despite not being a betting man McCloud bet himself that at least one tabloid paper would run a "Campaign to Stop the Violence."

For the next half an hour more questions were shouted out and the police officers calmly answered or deflected them. Some of the reporters asked questions in a different manner and context to try and thrown and confuse the senior officers, but with experience of giving evidence in court and interviewing suspects, the officers couldn't be tricked into saying something they shouldn't.

Chief Constable Rooks brought the briefing to an end and the men left the stage. McCloud quickly followed them out of the door and down the corridor. It took a couple of calls to them before they stopped and acknowledged him.

"Sorry sir this area is off limits to the press." Superintendent Fisher said forcefully holding a hand up as if stopping traffic.

McCloud stopped short and dug into his pocket for his ID. "No, I'm Fr. Andrew McCloud from Carlisle. I've been assigned as the Vatican liaison in this matter." He handed his ID card to Fisher.

The ID had McCloud's picture on it next to the seal of the Vatican; the crossed keys of St Peter below the white mitre of the Pope. Next to this was the unusual emblem of a dagger with a snake wrapped around the hilt piercing a red heart.

Fisher handed it back to McCloud. "We had notice from the Foreign Office that a representative would be here, we just thought that -"

McCloud interrupted "You just thought it would be a Cardinal in billowing red robes? I thought it would be wise to keep a low profile in there. A priest at the police briefing of a murdered priest brings too much attention to me."

Fisher agreed and introduced Chief Constable Rooks, who made his excuses and headed back to his office, and Chief Inspector Stevens. The three men headed up to the CID incident room where fresh coffee was being made. The officers working on the case were on phones writing notes or reading reports.

Inspector Stevens ushered the two men into his office and cleared one of the chairs of paper for his extra guest. McCloud and Fisher sat down and Stevens poured all three of them a coffee from his own percolating coffee pot.

"It's not every investigation that we have people from the

Vatican assist us; in fact this is probably the first time we've had anyone on the inside who isn't a police officer." Stevens said sitting in his own chair.

McCloud nodded as he poured milk and sugar into his cup. "I realise that. In fact just to clarify, my parish is in Carlisle, I'm representing the Vatican, not actually from there." He sipped the coffee and sat back. "There is a limit to what I can tell you, but contacts within the Metropolitan Police in London and the Home office alerted the Vatican about the murder and the brief outline of the circumstances."

Fisher sat forward, "Wait, you mean details of this investigation were passed to a foreign government, which is essentially what the Vatican is, without our consent?"

McCloud didn't react to the hostility, "Yes. It's an agreement all governments have with the Holy See."

Fisher was about to protest about this, but Stevens got there first. "It doesn't matter how you found out, just that you're here." he said. From the top of the papers on his desk he passed McCloud a folder of documents and booklets of photographs.

"That's everything we have so far. I shouldn't have to remind you that everything in there is confidential and that the photographs are of the crime scene and post-mortem. They are graphic."

McCloud flicked open the first crime scene photograph booklet and saw the bloodied mass of the former Fr. Stuart McKellen lying on his back with his chest cavity ripped open. Stevens watched and expected the priest to close the photographs in shock or turn away as most people do, but instead he was impassive and continued to look through the photos.

"When you said in the briefing that he died of loss of blood you meant loss of vital organs?" McCloud asked.

Fisher nodded, "Yes, we didn't see the point in telling the press that his lungs, liver, heart, kidneys, stomach and intestines were removed."

"Those look like claw marks on his face." McCloud said

holding the pictures closer to his face.

"That's what our pathologist said too." Fisher agreed, "Although the marks are like nothing he's seen before."

McCloud was quiet for a moment and closed the booklet. "Claw marks on the body, a savaged body, this looks like a wild animal attack. Why are you classing it as murder?"

Stevens and Fisher exchanged looks, as if checking what information to pass to the priest. "Three things," Stevens said. "One, there are footwear marks in the mud around the body. None of the marks match those of our officers, the paramedics or the poor chap who found him. Two, unidentified DNA was found on the body. Skin cells were also under his fingernails where he tried to fend someone off. These are still being analysed but as yet, nothing has come back; and three, marks on his neck show bruising consistent with a hand gripping his throat."

"He was strangled?" McCloud asked flicking open the booklet again to find the picture.

"Restrained we think." Stevens corrected, "The fact that it's bruised indicates that he was alive when throttled. Whoever did this restrained him whilst whatever animal it was feasted on his bowels."

Standing at the spot where McKellen's car skidded off the road, Fr. McCloud and Inspector Stevens looked up and down the remote road. The tyre marks on the tarmac were still there as were the tracks in the mud leading down through the bushes and directly to the scarred tree that brought McKellen to a sudden halt.

"What caused him to swerve off the road?" McCloud asked looking about him. The road was covered with leaves and in the rain, the road would be like an ice rink, he thought.

"We're not sure," Stevens replied stepping into the middle of the road that had been cordoned off. "McKellen was on his way back from comforting a family," he explained pointing up the road, "some 30 minutes away. We think that on his way back he came across something."

"Like what?" McCloud asked trying to piece together that fateful night in his mind.

"Officers found the remains of a sheep in the road," the Inspector explained, "we didn't think anything of it until trace evidence from McKellen revealed sheep hair and blood. We examined the carcass of the sheep and found similar marking to its body that were on McKellen."

McCloud fitted the pieces together and gave his assessment before the police officer could. "He stopped to see what was going on, got scared, drove down here at full pelt, lost control and went off into the bushes and was caught by whatever spooked him?"

Stevens was impressed, "You should be a detective." he nodded, "That's what we think happened yes." Stevens walked down the road along the path the car took. "He came down here, lost control possibly because of the slippery conditions and careered off the road and into the bushes."

Stevens continued down into the bushes and McCloud followed him watching his step so as not to fall in the mud. They emerged with the sun shining in front of a ruined derelict church.

Stevens continued his assessment. "The car came to a stop at that tree there and McKellen got out and headed towards the church. We found him at the base of that wall." He added pointing to a moss covered wall some two storeys high.

From his coat McCloud pulled out copies of the scene photographs and orientated himself so as to get a feel for the scene. As he looked at the images Stevens continued his commentary.

"We found fragments of stone and moss in the palms of his hands which match samples from the wall up there. For some reason he was climbing up high but he fell. The pathologist noted that he fractured his right shoulder blade as a result of this fall. He was side on to the wall when he fell and we've got cast impressions of foot marks, paw marks or something approaching him from his feet and from behind him there are other footwear marks.

"When we found him we discovered drag marks in the mud where it looked like he had been moved with his feet facing the wall and arms outstretched to the side, why, I don't know."

The sun was shining down and shadows were falling on the crime scene. McCloud looked from the photographs to the shadows and back again. There was something there, a sign. He looked up into the trees overlooking them and saw what was making the shadow.

"I know why he was moved." McCloud announced. Stevens was surprised and looked quizzically at the priest. McCloud saw the look and quickly explained. "Look, here in the photos he is facing with his head away from the wall with arms out stretched like the traditional crucifixion form. Now look at the shadows."

He pointed at the grass and Stevens saw for the first time the crucifix shadow cast on the grass in the near exact spot where McKellen was found. The priest continued. "Crucifixion wasn't a new thing, yes Christ was perhaps the most famous victim of it, but the Roman Empire used it as a form of punishment for all criminals. Jesus was after all crucified with two thieves."

"I'm not following Father." Stevens said.

"Look what's causing the shadow." McCloud replied.

Stevens looked up into the trees and saw two thick branches crossing each other, but it was an inverted, upside down crucifix. McCloud continued his own commentary, "Whoever did this wanted McKellen to be lined up with this shadow; they wanted us to see the symbolism, the message."

"What message? All I see is an inverted cross."

"In Christian theology Jesus was the most famous, for want of a better word, person to be crucified. The second was his Rock, the first he chose, St Peter. But Peter when caught by the Romans and sentenced to crucifixion asked not to be strung up like his master, but to be crucified upside down."

He paused and let the information sink in, but Stevens still looked blank. "That cross up there represents St Peter. This isn't just a religious hate crime; this is a person who knows the symbolism of such things. But why St Peter? He was the first and most loyal disciple, but surely if this was a hate crime, they'd be more inclined to focus of Jesus, not one of his followers." He continued to talk, muttering to himself, mulling things over in his head, walking back and forth, in front of the crime scene and the shadow of the inverted crucifix. "Why St Peter?" he said to himself out loud.

"Could it be a place?" Stevens asked. "A clue to another church where another attack will happen?"

McCloud stopped walking and looked at the police officer. "What do you mean?"

"Some notorious sadistic murderers get complacent and decide to try and play games with the investigating police officers." Stevens said, "They try to act clever and leave clues as to their next step, subtle clues, but clues nonetheless. Is there a church near here called St Peter's?"

McCloud shook his head. "Not near here. The closest bearing that name is about 50 miles away."

"What about elsewhere?"

"Of course there're many church's bearing that name, the most famous being in Rome, the Vatican." McCloud said. "But how can what's happened here be linked to the Vatican?"

McCloud began pacing again, thinking, trying to work out any sort of motive for the murder of Fr. McKellen. Was it religious hatred? Was it revenge? There were too many questions running through his mind.

Since he had received the phone call from Cardinal Conquezla's office, and speaking to the Cardinal himself, his mind had been active, always thinking, always trying to work out the next step so as to assist the Cardinal in Rome. The Cardinal, he thought, had been his mentor throughout his training for the Vatican Knights, and McCloud remembered the first meeting he had had with him; his first training session and the hours and days of studying the mythical creatures of Hell.

Suddenly, McCloud stopped his pacing and asked for the

file photographs of the post-mortem examination of McKellen. Stevens stood next to the priest as the wind picked up and he pulled his coat close to himself.

McCloud seemed to ignore the cold wind as he flicked through the bound photos and stopped at the clear close-up photographs of the lacerations and wounds.

There was something familiar about them, he thought, as if he had seen them elsewhere. Walking again, more slowly, he allowed his mind to wander and to try and remember.

For five minutes he slowly retraced his steps in the wet grass, Stevens quietly watching the priest as the wind picked up and a gentle drizzle started to fall on them. "These look like animal marks, the lacerations?" he asked Stevens.

"That's what we thought." Stevens replied. "But what type of animal, we have no idea. The nearest zoo is miles away and there's been no reports of a wild cat, well, never. It could be a private collector who's pet has escaped. I've got officers checking that out."

"Hmmm – maybe." McCloud said. "But there's still something about them." He looked at the photos and rotated them to view them from every angle. He wished he could've seen the body for himself.

Suddenly McCloud shut the photos and tossed them to Stevens. "Well?" Stevens asked.

But McCloud wasn't listening and he quickly headed back up the path to the cars, pulling his phone out of his pocket. He weaved across the path, holding the phone in the air to try and get a signal. "Fucking technology!" he said under his breath.

"Father," Stevens said, falling in step beside him, "what have you thought of?"

McCloud finally found a signal and quickly dialled the phone. "Excuse me, Inspector," he said with a pinch of panic creeping into his voice, "I need to speak to Rome."

CHAPTER EIGHT

Morgan sat in his office with his feet on the desk. It had been a hard couple of days with some of the children's conditions worsening. The doctors did what they could to help, but it was a battle they couldn't win.

It was at times like this that he needed someone to talk to himself, but nobody on the medical staff would understand the stresses he was under in trying to help and reassure so many families from a spiritual point of view. He leaned back in his chair and closed his eyes and for a moment, tried to shut the world out.

He respite was short lived as a knock came to his door. Without moving, and not caring what he looked like to whoever it was, he called for them to enter.

It was Laura.

Over the few days she had been at the hospital Morgan had slowly began to appreciate her. Initially he was against her presence, or more likely he was against the presence of a multinational corporation representative with no real interest in helping people and being around people he cared so much about.

But Laura was different and she showed general compassion with the families and children, and for this, Morgan was beginning to warm to her. She was dedicated to her beliefs in wanting to help those people who needed it, but was also loyal to her company that made the final decisions and had the hand on the purse strings.

Over the past day she had been in near constant contact with the New York office and was trying to secure funding for the hospital through research grants or sponsorship. So far various departments within Sunrise had shown an interest, but she needed to talk to more important people before a final decision could be made.

Laura sat down in the chair opposite Morgan, so accustomed she was to his office she put her feet up on the chair.

"Rough day?" Morgan asked looking at her as she too leaned back in her own chair.

"I've heard that some research projects have had their funding cut short," Laura said not looking back at him. "Luckily my team hasn't been affected, but there's a rumour going around that more teams could be cut."

Morgan got to his feet and from the top drawer of his filing cabinet produced a bottle of malt whiskey and two thick bottomed glasses. He poured them both a drink and they chinked glasses.

"Sorry, no ice." He said. Laura smiled and took a sip that sent a shock through her body.

Morgan, more accustomed to the taste sucked air through his teeth as the spirit warmed his throat.

Sitting down again he caught Laura staring at him.

"You don't act like a typical priest." she said.

Morgan smiled at that, "They're usually stiff and sombre." he answered, "But those are the older priests, those stuck in their ways who don't want change."

"You're more like... I don't know, but there's something behind the eyes." Laura said, "A hidden past perhaps?"

"I joined the priesthood relatively late," Morgan said sitting forward and topping up his glass, "I had a life before this, went drinking, dated, I was even engaged once, so yes I do have more of a past life than most clergymen. Some other men of the cloth disagree with my past life, but I think that having been in love, been exposed to vices, demons and temptation puts me in a better situation to deal with it than someone who has lived every living moment to please God." He knocked the whiskey back in one and returned the bottle to its hiding place.

"It shouldn't matter how we got here, it should only matter that we are here, all of us are here to help. But some priests don't see that, they only see some of my past deeds and use them against me." His tone softened and his mind slipped and began to reminisce.

"What past deeds?" Laura asked bringing him out of his memories.

It was many years ago when Morgan had decided to join the priesthood. Following a massive personal trauma and spending an extended period in hospital, Morgan remembered his path to the priesthood. It was long, difficult, and full of self-sacrifice. Morgan snapped out of it and silently cursed that he had let himself be exposed momentarily like that. "Nothing, it's in the past." he checked his watch, "Shouldn't you be checking in with HQ?"

Laura swore and checked her own watch. She finished her drink, thanked Morgan and left the office dialling a number on her mobile phone.

Morgan put the glasses on the side and looked out of the window. The clouds were darkening, a storm was on its way and he opened a window to allow the electrified air to attack his senses.

*

"Alex - Alex, listen to me," Laura said into her phone as she paced the corridor, "I'm not talking about millions of dollars here, just maybe 100 grand to pay for staff costs."

Alex Koplan on the other end of the phone talked to her, but it wasn't good news. Laura scuffed her feet on the floor and opened a window to watch the heavy rain start to fall.

She interrupted him, "But it's the palliative care they need, nurses, care assistants, doctors. That's what they need here, not a multi-million dollar machine and a dozen administrative staff to push bloody papers around."

She turned away from the open window as static interfered with the phone. "Why? What? Alex I can't hear you - Why am I doing this? There's a priest here who has put his heart and soul into helping these kids and he's running on empty now. He needs help and I think we can help him."

As Laura talked a dark shadow fell across the window and blocked out the setting sun. The six inch claws clamped down on the window ledge, an elongated black skull dipped inside the window and the muscular body with long arms and razor sharp blades for fingers stepped inside. Dripping with rain the wings eased back behind its shoulder blades and the jaw opened to reveal two rows of mini razor teeth. A forked tongue whipped out licked the top lip.

Laura had her back turned to the beast and continued to talk as the beast, despite its size of over seven feet tall, silently approached her. Laura hung up the phone and turned but only to be met by the iron grip of the claw around her throat. She tried to scream but no air escaped her lungs, but also no air reached them. Her eyes were wide with terror as she kicked and thrashed about but the beast didn't release any pressure on her.

She didn't know what it was or where it had come from but in those suffocating moments of hanging from its vice like grip she could almost see a smile flick across it's skinless face as she struggled to breath. Scrabbling with her hands she scratched at the face but her finger slipped into the empty eye sockets and the bare skull moist with rain sent a shiver of fear through her body.

This was it, she thought, she was going to die.

The beast opened its mouth and leaned in, the tongue lashed around, excited by the meal about to come. The teeth sparkled in the dimming lights as they got closer and closer to biting her face.

"Hey!" came a call from her side.

Painfully she turned her head and saw Morgan standing in the middle of the corridor. The beast turned to him, but Morgan didn't flinch.

Laura tried to shout warnings, somehow she needed to tell him to escape, but she couldn't, and from the look on his face, Morgan wouldn't. The priest took a step forward and in the dim light Laura saw he was carry a short staff, the same 10 inch staff that was on his wall in his office.

The beast, still holding Laura against the wall with its arm outstretched, was focused on Morgan.

"Rasth-amal garlgath munalresh farlga munisha" the beast gurgled.

Laura had managed to grab a breath and was transfixed by the beast and how Morgan hadn't flinched or moved once.

"I know what you are; I know where you've come from, and if you're here for the reason I think you're here," Morgan paused as he stared at the creature in front of him, "your Master will be disappointed." He said, his voice, calm and low, almost soothing Laura thought.

Without another word, without another flicker of emotion, Morgan took a step forward and began to swing the staff around and upwards. With a subtle flick of his wrist as it travelled in its arc, a silver blade emerged from the end of the shaft, with integrated sections sliding out and automatically locking in place, a perfect steel blade was formed and with a razor sharp edge the blade whipped through the air and sailed upwards between Laura and the beast.

Morgan halted his advance and stood ready for any counter attack from the creature. For a moment nothing happened. The beast stared intensely at him and then focused on its own outstretched arm. Laura followed the creature's cold gaze and saw that the sword had severed the arm and Laura fell to the floor and quickly removed the limb from her throat.

The beast roared in anger and quickly turned on Morgan who, in the tight confines of the corridor, parried the razor claws, stepped to the side and sliced at the beast's leg.

Another roar of pain echoed down the corridor as Morgan, now behind the beast sliced away in smooth arcs at the beasts back and ligaments in its legs. The creature fell to the floor and with a strong heaving thrust Morgan pierced his sword through its ribs that penetrated the chest cavity and emerged through the breast plate. The beast cried out and fell forwards, releasing itself from the sword.

Silence fell on the corridor and Laura stared at the beast and then at Morgan who had hardly broke a sweat. He turned to her and with another flick of his wrist the sword collapsed back into the hilt.

He stepped over to her. "Are you okay?" he asked quickly checking her over.

"What... what was that?" she asked through pants for breath and the desire not to cry.

"Are you sure you're okay?" he asked again checking her arms and hands, seeing the small grazes and scratches on her skin.

"I'm fine. What was it?" she repeated.

Morgan looked at it. "It's a Hashalanth Scout." he said helping her up.

"A what?"

"Hashalanth Scout" Morgan repeated. "The problem is; they travel in pairs."

Morgan looked around them, through the windows at the rain pounding against the glass. Suddenly there was a scream from somewhere in the hospital, shouts and crashes came from somewhere down the corridor.

"Come on!" he said as he grabbed her hand and led her away down the corridor towards the sound of the screams.

Morgan led Laura down the corridor and through double doors. Nurses, doctors, patients and families were scurrying through the corridors and heading for any available exit. Ahead of them in a ward the sounds of crashes, smashing and shouts were heard. At the doors to the ward Morgan turned to Laura.

"Stay here," he said, "I can handle this." She grabbed his arm and stopped him leaving. Panic was setting in and her voice creaked with tension.

"I'm not leaving your side. I'm coming with you."

Morgan with a surprising strong grip removed her hand from his arm. "No, you stay here and help anyone who comes out."

"But that thing upstairs -" she started to say looking over her shoulder back at the way they had come. She didn't want to face that thing again.

"Is dead!" Morgan said completing her sentence. "It's not going anywhere, but this one in here is going to hurt and kill the children. This one is the priority. Stay here and you'll be safe."

He released her hand and with the hilt of his sword ready he entered the ward and the doors closed behind him. Laura slumped down onto the floor and sat against the wall, hanging her head down in her hands.

From inside the ward she heard Morgan shout at the Hashalanth and the hissing rasping response to him. Her hands started to shake as the past few moments flashed through her mind again and again.

She would never forget the feel of the ice cold claw clamped around her throat; would never forget the fight she put up for a last gulp of air; and she would never forget the sight of the calm Fr. Peter Morgan producing a sword wielding it gracefully and skilfully through the air and expertly disposing of the creature.

Despite her own fears she somehow drew strength from the calmness in which Morgan had acted; he wasn't like normal priests, that was for sure, but his actions were something different. He had an aura of strength and skill that she had never known before and from his own disregard of his own safety and determination to help others, it was an innate quality that made her feel safe in his presence, much more safe than being here in the corridor.

Wiping tears from her face she crawled on the floor and opened the ward door. She could see lines of beds down each of the side walls and at the nearest bed she saw a young girl cowering on the floor crying.

She needed help and Laura took a deep breath and scrambled across to her. The child saw Laura coming and held her arms up to the safe protection of a woman. Holding the child's head close to her chest Laura looked up over the bed and saw Morgan with his sword clasped in his hands swing and attacked the Hashalanth.

The iron claws deflected the attacks and Morgan too parried a blow from the wing that came sweeping down from behind the Beast. He took a step back and regained his composure and the Hashalanth took a step towards him and with a clenched fist it lunged for him as Morgan side stepped it and swiped at the protruding wing and sliced a good portion of it off.

The Hashalanth cried in pain it swung round quickly and caught Morgan unawares. The muscular arm catapulted Morgan off his feet and threw him against the wall. With a sickening crunch he hit the wall and fell to the floor crashing into a bedside cupboard and overturned bed. His eyes closed as the pain took hold and he fell unconscious.

The Hashalanth took no more notice of Morgan and began to once more advance on a family at the far end of the ward. The father tried his best to shield his family; wife and two children, from the Hashalanth but it stood over them almost anticipating the next meal it was about to feast upon.

The razor claw reached down and grabbed the father by his arm and pulled him up off his feet. He screamed in pain as his shoulder took the weight of his bulky frame and the skull like face of the Hashalanth came within inches of the long thin, forked tongue as it flicked out to taste the sweat on his skin.

From behind the bed Laura could see that Morgan wasn't moving and the innocent man was about to be killed. With the child still clinging to her chest she stood up and passed the girl to a nurse hiding behind an upturned trolley bed.

Together the nurse and the child cried into each other's arms. She didn't know what she was doing, but she couldn't sit there and let this man be killed in front of his family. On the floor beside her there was a bowl and Laura picked it up and threw it as best she could at the back of the Hashalanth. The bowl flew through the air and caught the beast between the shoulder blades.

The darkened eyes turned to her as she stood alone in the middle of the ward. The Hashalanth now faced her. With a disregard for the man in its claw it dropped him to the floor where his wife crawled over to where he was.

Now for the moment the man was safe, but the Hashalanth was bearing down on Laura. She didn't know what to do next and she looked down at Morgan who was still out cold.

Crying, and scared a young girl with her knees to her chest hid under a bed. To her side clinging onto a bear a young boy was bewildered by the events going on around him. The pair of them stared at the still body of Fr. Morgan. The boy was still inquisitive and he broke free from his sister's arms and reached out to touch Morgan's hand.

Morgan was still warm and it was if the touch had lit a fire within him as he stirred and found consciousness again. He looked up at the children and despite the cuts to his face he smiled warmly at them as he found his thoughts and painfully got back to his feet with his sword in his hand.

The Hashalanth was metres away from Laura as she backed away. The beast's arms were out stretched wide and the wings were showing their own full span. With each step Laura's options became less and she waited for the inevitable end and closed her eyes.

With nothing happening she opened her eyes and saw the black shape of Morgan leap out in front of the Hashalanth and block the incoming attack.

The Hashalanth was taken by surprise and stepped back but it was all that Morgan needed. He swiped with the sword, arced it up and around, around his head as he turned and pirouetted and gracefully the sword found its mark and with each slice the Hashalanth weakened and was beaten back.

Morgan was unrelenting in his attack and forced the creature backwards as it cried out in pain. But he had to defeat it, there could be no remorse or no feeling of guilt for taking another life. Morgan continued the attack and forced it towards the window where a final thrust caused the Hashalanth to fall back and out.

It cried out and Morgan was able to witness the demise of it as it impaled itself on the steel railing below. With its final breathe the Hashalanth called out and a lightning bolt cascaded across the sky illuminating it and the victorious shape of Fr. Peter Morgan standing in the broken window standing over his defeated adversary.

CHAPTER NINE

On the top floor of the Sunrise Corporations offices in New York Felix Masterson sat in his highback chair and stared out across the cityscape towards the sea and the Statue of Liberty. The sun was setting and long shadows of the buildings were drawn across the land. A golden hew filled the large spacious office and the low level classical music played through hidden speakers in the walls, floor and ceiling.

Masterson was deep in thought; as he had been for a couple of days. He had had meetings, PR exercises and press calls called off, and interviews and media attention withheld. His closest workers who had been with him from the outset of his business life had never seen Masterson become so withdrawn and distant, and they were becoming worried.

Masterson had sealed himself in his office and hadn't left it in nearly 36 hours. People would call but he ignored them; they would visit, but he would have them escorted away. He just wanted to be alone, and he needed time and space to think about the recent events.

This was not the usual Felix Masterson they had come to know and respect.

It would soon be time, Masterson thought, soon be time

for his visit. He was scared and nervous about the impending meeting, but he tried to find the strength inside himself to face up to this man. As he sat watching birds fly past his windows he thought back to the moment his life turned a corner, only a couple of days before.

Following his meeting with his science advisors and heads of departments, Masterson had headed back to his office for a meeting with a man he knew only as Victor. He thought the meeting was to discuss future research in a new virus but soon after sitting down with Victor he knew that the meeting was more serious.

He should've known from the moment he sat down and faced his visitor that it wasn't going to be an ordinary meeting. His guest called himself Victor and forgoing the pleasantries of the offer of drinks, he asked for the blinds to be drawn. Masterson obliged, clicking a button on his desk and as the blinds descended he surveyed his guest. He had pale white skin and a bald head, emaciated and thin, with sunken cheeks and sallow eyes, Masterson remembered thinking that the man needed as much sun as possible.

"I work for someone who will be using your global network of contacts for his own purposes." Victor said simply, missing the pleasantries. Masterson didn't like the wording of this. There were no questions, requests or suggestion of negotiation.

It came across more of an order and Masterson didn't like taking orders from anyone.

"Not without my permission and a decent price he won't!" Masterson snapped back. It was a bad way to start a meeting and Masterson disliked the man from the outset. "I thought this meeting was to discuss research?" he added.

"Mr. Masterson, this meeting is more than research, it far outweighs any business deal you have had before." Victor said. "You are a businessman, a very successful business man and a man in your position continually wants to have more and be the dominant player in every walk of life. My superior can allow that."

"Sunrise is positioned in the top 1% of all businesses and in all areas across the globe." Masterson said, quickly tiring of the meeting. "There is nothing that you can offer that I don't already have."

"World domination!" Victor said quickly and to the point.

Masterson chuckled and the final piece of evidence that this man was crazy fell into place. "I'm not a film villain, Mr. Victor. I don't want to control the world."

"No, but my superior does, and he will use your company and connections to do it." Victor said ignoring the remarks.

Masterson shook his head and smiled to himself. What the hell was this guy on about, he thought. World domination was a ridiculous ambition and one that was saved for the movies. He had better things to do with his time and he was eager to finish the meeting. But he sat back in his chair and looked over at Victor who sat silently across the table from him, although he had made his mind up about not continuing the discussion, there was still one thing he was intrigued to know.

"Why do you want me? Why Sunrise?"

Victor smiled and nodded. "Sunrise Corporation is a huge company with many facets we can use. Media, television stations, radio stations, newspapers and magazines. Medical research into cardiology, oncology, paediatrics, haematology, and numerous other specific areas are all well documented. Military research with contracts with the US department of defence, the UK Ministry of Defence and both the Russian and Chinese Governments. Your charities are extensively reviewed as the best in the world and they have connections with dozens of others. Your transportation systems, haulage, cargo ships and planes are continually growing, not to mention your holiday company, music production and stores. It is fair to say that your company has an impact on the majority of the world's population."

Masterson was impressed by Victor's recollection of all of his company's links. "Don't forget the IT development wing?" he added as a final boast of his success.

Victor smiled slyly to himself, "You are indeed ideally based to help us."

"I haven't agreed to anything yet, and I have to say, that I'm afraid I'm not interested in your offer." Masterson said.

"But you will be." Victor added. "You will meet with my superior and we will discuss this further." Victor stood and held out his hand.

Masterson looked at the pale bony hand. Despite his reservations about what he had heard, he stood and politely it. "I appreciate you coming by, but I don't think this is a project I can work with you on."

The pain shot through him like a lightning bolt. Masterson fell to his knees and with his free hand he clasped his temple. He didn't know what was happening but the images shot through his mind.

Skeletons, peeling flesh, fires burning through lava filled caverns. All images of damnation hurtled through his mind. In his mind he was travelling through the caverns dripping with blood with piles of bones and dismembered body parts strewn around.

Over the bodies he went, between demonic beasts whipping and beating the tormented souls who cried out in pain. He approached double doors with blood pouring over the edges and they opened automatically. Still on his knees Masterson clenched his eyes shut but in his mind he wanted to see the figure behind, he wanted to see the Prince of the Pit that awaited him on the other side.

The doors opened wider and he looked up at the towering figure of the Great Demon himself.

Victor let go of his hand and the images vanished as quickly as they had come. Masterson was gasping for air and looked up at the bald white face of Victor who leaned down to him.

"You will serve him, Mr. Masterson, and you will serve him well."

That was 36 hours ago and Masterson couldn't shake the images from his mind. He was never a religious man, but everything he saw was so real that he had to believe it. He couldn't find the words to tell people what he had seen and so had secluded himself from everyone around him. As it neared the time for the visit he found himself shaking with nerves.

He had never seen anything like it before and didn't want to see it ever again. The tension was unbearable and he closed his eyes to try and focus his mind, but the images of Hell flashed through his mind once more and he gripped the arms of his chair and opened his eyes gasping for air.

"Enjoying a trip down memory lane?" a voice said behind him. Masterson spun his chair round and saw Victor and a hooded figure standing quietly next to the intricately carved stone fireplace that sat in the middle of the office to give the sparse office a more homely feel. Masterson wiped the sweat from his face and tried to gather some composure.

"How - how did you get in here?" he asked approaching the two men.

"It is not for you to ask how, Mr. Masterson." Victor said. "This is my superior, Kronos."

Kronos was dressed in a thick black cloak with the hood pulled forward over his head. The shadows inside the hood hid his face and with a graceful movement he walked to the window and stared down. Masterson was mesmerised by him and as he moved he never saw Kronos' shadow cover the flowers, and he never saw the flowers wilt and die in less than a second.

"The world has changed so much," Kronos said as he stood at the window, "life has become so simple that people no longer fear what they do not know." His voice was deep, rich and almost soothing.

"My company works hard to make people's lives easier." Masterson said.

"And that is why we've chosen you." Kronos said.

Masterson tried hard to regain his composure and poured

himself a coffee. He had been in difficult negotiations before and needed to calm down. "Who's we?"

"You have seen where I come from Mr. Masterson," Kronos said turning to him, "you know all too well who we are."

"Well why do you want me?"

"Victor has already explained your company can reach around the world," his voice rumbled out, "with your lack of moral ethics you are ideally suited to assist with our domination."

Masterson stared at the hooded head. "What lack of moral ethics?"

"Your human experimentation in chemical and biological warfare, testing on human subjects. You have killed over 100 people to further your research and you did it without a second thought. It is that moral guidance that interests us."

"What are you planning to do?" Masterson asked.

"World domination." Kronos replied, proud at the thought. "We have agents in place across the globe already awaiting the attack order. For too long the world has been gripped by religious doctrine and now the time is right for a regime change and the Dark Lord is ready to lead them. You, Mr. Masterson, will play a major part in that plan as your company broadcasts our message and influences the people to our beliefs."

"What if I don't help?" Masterson asked backing away.

"You will help Mr. Masterson," Kronos said approaching him, "You will help or you will suffer the torture and torment that will bestow the rest of the population that does not join us."

Masterson backed away but he bumped into his desk and with the imposing figure of Kronos bearing down on him he had nowhere to turn. Kronos' cloak seemed to wrap itself around Masterson's legs and as the black figure lifted his arm a skeletal hand appeared from the sleeve and grabbed Masterson's arm.

Kronos forced it to the side and pushed Masterson off balance. With the forefinger of his other bony hand he touched the skin of Masterson's forearm. The skin burnt and sizzled as Kronos drew an elegant rune figure.

Masterson shouted in pain and fell to his knees but the grip of Kronos persisted as he continued to burn his skin.

CHAPTER TEN

The hospital was quieter now following the Hashalanth attacks. The male hospital workers had removed the remains of the beasts and were now clearing away the broken glass and tidying the wards.

Thankfully, nobody had been killed, but there were serious gashes and lacerations on a number of people. The chatter about the hospital was about what had happened, what the beasts were and more importantly about Fr. Morgan. He had shown unnatural skill for a man of his position and rumours were rife that changed by the minute. A nurse in the cardiology ward heard he was an angel sent down from heaven, while a porter in the basement was told that he was an American CIA trained operative intent on stopping drug cartels.

Only Morgan knew the truth and he sat in his locked office with his computer open trying to contact the Vatican.

In his own office in the bowels of the Vatican, Cardinal Conquezla sat and flicked through another book he had obtained from the extensive Vatican library. Intricate drawings and Latin text covered page after page of the 600 year old book but he was still no closer to finding any information on what was happening.

His office door opened and one of his assistants told him

there was a communication from Fr. Andrew Morgan waiting for him. Conquezla flicked on his computer and the black and white image of Morgan came on the screen.

"Andrew!" Conquezla exclaimed, "It's good to see you." Morgan smiled back on the screen. "Cardinal, it's good to see and hear you too." The images shuddered as Morgan adjusted the web-camera and then he focused on the screen.

"How is everything down there?" Conquezla asked.

"Not good," Morgan admitted, "Cardinal, last night we were attacked by two Hashalanth scouts. Nobody was seriously hurt or killed, but I had to fend them off."

Conquezla nodded, "Did anyone see you?"

Morgan knew part of his role was secrecy and discretion, and he regretted so publicly making his presence known. "The situation was such whereby subtly couldn't be used. Yes, people saw me."

Conquezla trusted Morgan and knew that if he had no option but act in front of people then the situation must have been serious. He asked Morgan to wait a moment as he left this office and entered the main office.

Banks of computers were spread across the wall, huge plasma screens showing maps of the world were on the main wall and priests worked silently on them with headphones and microphones.

The whole room was set up to detect transmissions and communications from around the world and gather information for analysis. On the big screen at the front Morgan's face appeared.

"Peter," Conquezla continued, "this isn't the only time this has happened." He picked up a file from the desk and read the brief notes on top. "Six days ago Fr. Stuart McKellen in Scotland was attacked and killed. Local police don't know what happened, but our liaison up there informed us that the teeth and claw marks were similar to a Quazon cat."

The Cardinal picked up another file "In Africa a documentary film crew and support team were slaughtered. Video footage we intercepted has been analysed and it looks like a Zyphon Eagle was responsible."

Morgan sat still and listened and then hung his head. "I thought this here was an isolated incident."

"No, these are the ones we know about and have concrete proof for." Conquezla said, "Attacks have been reported in Australia, Thailand, Siberia, Egypt, Germany, Canada, the US, the list goes on. But these attacks aren't verified as demonic beings, your report is the third one that confirms our unspoken suspicions."

"Have any of the other Knights reported in?" Morgan asked clearly shaken by the news.

"You're the first my friend. But I doubt you will be the last."

"Your Eminence," Morgan said using the correct title, "you need to get him to activate the Order. Before it's too late."

Conquezla nodded in understanding and had thought the same thing. "We need more evidence before we take that step. I need proof from the texts. At the moment we have random attacks across the globe and it isn't enough for his Holiness to give the order. But Peter," Conquezla's tone turned conspiratorial, "unofficially you may take whatever action you deem necessary to stay safe."

"I will your Eminence." Morgan said and he clicked a button on his computer and the screen turned to static.

Conquezla called for attention to his assistants and the priests turned to face him. "There is a change in priorities; I need all of you to research the records and any documentation that can shed light on the recent events. Get the trainee Knights to help if needed, but I want to know what is happening and I want to know within 24 hours." Conquezla watched as the men left their stations and headed off to begin their research.

He turned back and re-entered his office. "Hashalanth Scouts! What is going on?" he said to himself.

Morgan stood at his window and looked out to the court yard below. What was going on, he thought as his eyes shifted to the open window where he saw the Hashalanth enter to attack Laura the night before.

This was just the start of something and he feared that it could soon escalate out of control. He felt useless, feeble and inactive as he watched the people go about their work and occasionally look up at his office window. He needed to get away from here, he thought, the people he had worked hard to help over the years had seen a different side to him and none of them would understand his place and role within the church. He needed to head back to Rome where he could help wherever he could.

With his mind made up he quickly gathered a few of his possessions from the office and threw them into his bag, with a final look around the office he switched off the light and closed the door.

Within 10 minutes Morgan was back at his apartment but as he approached his door he saw it was open. Carefully he pushed it wider and Carlos Jimenez sat on his sofa with Laura making herself a coffee in his kitchen.

He closed the door loudly and made them both jump.

"Make yourself at home why don't you?" Morgan said dropping his bag on the chair.

Carlos stood up and faced the priest. "Padre, we could not find you and so we waited here."

"And what's she doing here?" Morgan said nodding to Laura

"She," Laura said, "wants to know if you're okay after last night."

Morgan looked away from them both and headed to his bedroom. "I'm fine, now you can both go."

"Padre, what happened last night? What were those things?" Carlos asked casting a quick glance to Laura.

Morgan stopped in the bedroom doorway and slowly

turned back to his two unwanted guests. "You wouldn't understand."

"Maybe not, but we know what we saw and we saw what you did," Laura said, "you know more than you're letting on and I think we have a right to know what the hell is going on!"

He didn't plan on explaining what had happened to anyone except Cardinal Conquezla, but she was right. They had witnessed the attacks, and they had witnessed his response, they deserved an explanation, but not the whole truth. "They were lost souls, forsaken by God and condemned to Hell." Morgan explained. "There have been attacks like these happening across the world for years." he continued. "Missing people, unsolved murders, sightings of mythical creatures roaming the mountains or coming up from the sea. But for nearly 2000 years we have kept them secret or they've disappeared into folklore. The truth is they are creatures from the pits of Hell."

Morgan wasn't in the mood to be questioned and he just wanted to get rid of them as quick as possible.

"They came from hell?" Carlos asked trying to follow what Morgan was saying.

"Yes, according to my Cardinal in Rome, they and a dozen others have attacked across the world these past few days."

Carlos crossed himself and said a quick prayer.

"That's impossible!" Laura said. "Hell doesn't exist."

In any other situation Morgan would've had a calm philosophical and theological discussion with her to discuss the possibility of Heaven and Hell's existence in reality, but after the previous night and his own desire to get back to the Vatican, he snapped.

"Why doesn't it? Because you believe it doesn't? Because you saying so, doesn't mean that everyone in the world should listen to you. To believe or not believe in something requires faith; it doesn't matter what type of faith as long as you have faith. You said you believe in science, well explain something to me would you please? Where in science have you ever seen anything like that

Hashalanth before?" Morgan had unknowingly stepped towards her and his voice was rising.

Anger was building up inside him at the continued ignorance of people who disregarded proof of what they had seen with their own eyes, the very ignorance that was being demonstrated once again by the woman in front of him. "Forget everything you've learnt and think, for once. Forget what society has taught you, forget what social influences and the media have taught you; use that scientific mind of yours for once to logically think about this."

The room fell silent and Morgan, realising he was standing over Laura backed off and went back into his bedroom and slammed the door behind him.

Carlos and Laura looked at each other and Laura could see that Carlos thought she was wrong. He was a devout catholic and she knew he would believe in heaven and hell.

"Do you believe him?" Laura asked.

"Si, Miss Kennedy, I do," Carlos replied, "but not because I'm Catholic, but because I know what I saw. I may not be as educated as yourself but I know that what attacked us last night was not of this world. All night I have thought about where it came from and none of the explanations I came up with were good enough. Now I have heard the Padre's explanation it all fits into place."

"Hell doesn't exist." Laura repeated.

Carlos looked at her hard in the eyes. "What if you're wrong? What if it does?"

"It doesn't!"

"Open your mind to the possibility that it does and then tell me if everything you've seen here suddenly makes sense." Carlos replied.

The bedroom door flew open and Morgan was staring at his mobile phone. He pressed a few buttons and waited for a ring tone but there was nothing there.

"Carlos, what's the best way to get to Mexico?"

"Mexico? Why do you want to go there?"

Morgan tried the number again. "What's the best way?"

"Fly is the best way, of course, but few planes go there." Carlos said, thinking quickly. "You can catch a boat and sail round or there are the roads."

His phone connected and he spoke loudly and clearly. "Jules, where are you?" he listened, "Are you safe? Are you okay? Jules?" It was a bad line and Morgan struggled to hear him. "Get to the airport... No... Mexico City Airport. The international one! ... That's right. I'll get a plane up and meet you there. Jules?"

The line went dead. Morgan looked at Laura and Carlos. "I need to go. I need to get to Mexico City as soon as possible."

"Padre, to get a flight so soon will be difficult. It may take a couple of days to get you there."

"Then work something out." Morgan snapped back. He went back into his room and threw clothes and documents in a bag.

"I can get you there." Laura called through from the living room. Morgan reappeared in the door and looked at her. "I can," she continued quickly, "We can use the Sunrise company jet and fly direct to Mexico and onto the States."

Morgan stared at her and stepped forward. "Thank you."

CHAPTER ELEVEN

So much had happened in such a short space of time, that Felix Masterson was still trying to allow his analytical mind to compute and understand the events.

He was so used to making snap decisions in the business world, from taking over flagging companies to buying stock in emerging businesses, that he couldn't cope with the events of the previous hours. His mind raced back in time to his initial encounter with Kronos and the images of Hell flickered in his mind once more as he stared at the open burning fireplace in his office.

He remembered all this as he headed the meeting to which the majority of department heads had turned up. With the windows overlooking Manhattan tinted to reduce the sun glare Masterson called the meeting to order.

"Thank you everyone for coming to this meeting so quickly." Masterson said as cheerfully as he could, but with the dark shadow of Kronos stood in the shadows to his side hidden from view, his nerves were starting to break. "As you all know certain activities and research within the corporation have been suspended for an undetermined period. This is due to an unexpected change in the company's vision and future direction."

He cast a quick glance at the shadow where Kronos was

standing and the wall seemed to move as one as the shadow peeled away from the wall and the hooded figure of Kronos approached the table.

"I have been approached to assist in a new project led by..."

"Myself!" Kronos interrupted in his reverberating voice. "I have reached an agreement with Mr. Masterson and with his blessing you will all serve me and my master."

Dave Holden, head of the broadcast media department raised his hand and spoke. "For what reason should we serve you?" he asked.

Being one of the senior members of the Sunrise board, and one of the most influential people in television, Holden was unused to being ordered around. "I've never met you before, so why should I suddenly change my allegiance to you?"

Kronos glided around the table as he spoke and the department representatives visibly stiffened as his cold shadow crossed their backs. It was as if life was being sucked out of them, all happiness, pleasure and joy was drained from them.

"You have never had a real master. It is time that you felt the power of a true leader; not this pitifully small man here," Kronos said indicating Masterson, "but a true leader who has been around for an eternity and shall continue to prosper in this Godless society."

The people around the table all cast a look at Masterson who sat head bowed in his seat; shoulders slumped, he looked dishevelled, beaten and exhausted. For everyone in the room it was the first time they had seen their commander in such a state; he was a broken man so different from the empowering persona they were used to seeing.

"I bow to no man" Holden said, "I don't care who you work for; I shall run my department the way I run it."

"Very well!" Kronos said facing him across the table. Holden never had a chance to react as Kronos reached out and a whip of fire lashed out from his hand reaching across the table and wrapping itself around Holden's neck.

He reached up to grab at it and struggled against it. Around the table the other members jumped up and backed away, screams and shouts echoed around the room as Kronos manipulated the fire rope and lifted Holden up from his seat and suspended him from the high ceiling.

The other department heads scrambled for the doors, but they were locked and there was no escape. Kronos levitated onto the table and looked down on them as the body of Holden fell limp and the flames from the whip engulfed his body.

"There is no escape!" Kronos exclaimed, "You shall all serve the army of the Dead. From the depths of Hell the Dark Lord comes and you shall serve him. You shall whisper his name to all you know and they too shall serve him. Speak his name and bring souls to our mission; speak his name and join our fight; speak his name... Lucifer!"

Kronos held his arms wide open and his cloak billowed open. From the folds balls of fire shot out and raced through the air, each hunted an individual who fell to their knees as the ball hit them in the chest and entered their body to burn their soul.

Kronos stood on the table and screamed in pleasure at the pain of the souls around him. With another thrust of his arms into the air the glass windows turned to flames.

The fireplace erupted in a kaleidoscope of colour as a whirlpool of fire and clouds formed into a vortex. From the centre, blood started to pour onto the marble floor and two glowing eyes, burning with the intensity of the pit it was creating, emerged from the flames with horns protruding from its forehead and neck. The movements were jagged and difficult, but finally the three toed foot and thorn covered leg emerged and set foot on the floor.

A foothold of hell on earth was created.

Masterson couldn't remember how long ago that meeting was, all feeling of time had been suspended and he sat on the floor of his once elegant office and overlooked the dying sun over Manhattan.

The new Sunrise Corps building was quiet, too quiet for a building that could hold nearly 2000 people. The mezzanine floors with coffee stalls and bakeries were deserted, the reception desks sat empty and the elevators hung silently on their steel cables.

Throughout the building, computers were switched off, coffee machines remained unused and offices were locked. Nobody was around. The most state of the art building on the Atlantic seaboard was deserted like a lost ship at sea. The captain of the ship hadn't been seen for days, but his influence was diminishing by the minute as the new commander sat at the top of the building and continued his master's plan for world domination.

Since his announcement and subsequent slaughter of the Sunrise senior staff, Kronos's forces had infiltrated each team and he was receiving reports of continuing demonic possessions of human souls and conversion of loyalty to the forces of the Devil.

With each new solider ordered to convert another, soon the whole of the world would be within the grasp of the Dark Forces. The effect could already be felt in New York, with a population of 8 million people there were now only 2 million left alive and half of these were under the influence of Kronos.

The media had reported on the state of the quiet streets, the increase in disappearances and recent murders, but with Sunrise media in control, the editorial content was more manageable and the rest of the country was still largely unaware of what had happened in the last 24 hours.

Kronos had recently had a report that a US Congressional Senator, William Riffkind, had been turned to the Dark Lord's cause and despite not showing emotion to his other minions, Kronos was pleased that a government official had been infected knowing that soon, the rest of the government would fall to their knees in front of him, and once the President does, Kronos thought, the country and world would soon follow.

Everything was going to plan, and Kronos knew that he would be well rewarded for his work once his Master arrived. Kronos walked around the wide expanse of Felix Masterson's office and in the corner he looked down at the cowardly shape of Masterson.

"You had an impressive empire," Kronos growled, "it is serving us well."

Masterson tried not to look up at Kronos, but there was an incredible magnetic force that made him look into the burning evil eyes. Kronos smiled at him, and reached down to stare at the man. "You look scared, and so you should be!"

The double doors to Masterson's office were suddenly flung open and a crook necked demon with a bald scalp, irregular bony legs, red eyes and sharp teeth like fangs hobbled in. Behind him dragged by a chain was an old man dressed in black. Blood had dried on his face from the gash on his forehead and his clothes had been torn and ripped from the rough handling he had endured.

Kronos stood in the middle of the room and looked down at the man and, as he looked up at the hooded skull of Kronos, the man revealed the white priest's dog collar around his neck.

"We found him in the street." the demon said quickly bowing down to Kronos. "He ran but the Hashalanth caught him."

Kronos looked at the pitiful man in front of him, kneeling down on the floor and then bent down so he was face to face with him. "Where is your God now?" Kronos asked.

"Who... who are you?" the priest asked through deep breaths that shot pain through his frail body.

"I am the true Messenger; the voice; the Dark Lord's servant." Kronos said removing his hood to reveal his head. The priest recoiled at the sight of the eye-less head bearing down at him. "What is your name?" he hissed.

"Fr. Joseph Riddell." he answered, his voice quivering with fear.

"Will you serve me Fr. Riddell?" Kronos asked standing back to his full height.

"I serve only God." Riddell replied will an edge of defiance in his voice; defiance, his heart did not truly believe he had.

Kronos walked away towards the fireplace and the demon

hauled on the chain and dragged Riddell to follow him. "You will soon serve two masters," Kronos said. "My army cannot penetrate the sacred soil of consecrated places of worship."

"Your evil army will never breach the church," Riddell said biting through the pain in his chest, "the walls of the church and the doors of heaven will forever be closed to you."

Kronos turned to him. "That day will come soon. All I need is someone to act on my behalf, someone who has served the church for most of his life... someone like you."

Riddell panicked and tried to move but a sharp lash of the chain around his neck from the demon brought him back to his knees. The priest looked about himself for help, but found none, he was alone, scared and forsaken by his own God.

In front of him the fireplace began to burn more brightly, flames danced from side to side and licked the stone walls. Around and around the flames circled until a vortex was created and a fiery burst of pure energy came forth and penetrated Riddell's feeble body.

He lurched back with his arms outstretched as the demonic pulse raced through his veins and entered every pore of his body. His brain became awash with images of hell and he shouted as the tormented souls that clawed for redemption and pleaded for help called his name. For years his mind and soul had belonged to God, but within seconds he could feel his heart blacken and his allegiances change. On his chest, the crucifix that his mother had given him on the day of his ordination glowed red and burnt into his skin and alighting itself into a ball of flame.

Riddell shouted out in pain and finally the attack ended and he fell to the floor gasping for breath.

Kronos knelt next to him and with a tight grip on his hair, lifted his head. "Who do you serve now?"

"I serve you," Fr. Riddell replied, "my Lord Kronos!"

CHAPTER TWELVE

Everything was a distant blur for Fr. Peter Morgan. From the moment he had agreed with Laura Kennedy to use her company jet to fly to Mexico, he felt like he hadn't stopped. He had quickly packed his bags and travelled with her and Carlos via her accommodation back to the hospital.

He didn't want to run and leave the children and families, but he knew they deserved an explanation. Carlos and the chief administrator had hastily set up chairs in a disused ward and those visitors and patients who wanted to come and see him were invited.

He didn't know what he was going to say in there to them, and trusted that God would speak to him. There was a hum of chatter about the ward as he entered and, as he reached the front, silence fell.

"Thank you all for coming," he said to try and ease himself in, "I realise there are questions surrounding what happened here last night. Some of them I can answer; some I can't; some questions I will answer and others I will not. I do not know why those creatures attacked here, or why they attacked us but for the moment we are safe. I can tell you that all over the world similar attacks have happened and unfortunately their casualties were worse than ours.

"Some were fatal." he said. "To try and get some answers I have spoken to my Cardinal in Rome and he has a team of experts researching these events. Because this wasn't an isolated incident I believe that more serious incidents will occur in the future and while I pledged my support to you all here, I am bound by my oaths to serve the church." Morgan paused for a moment as the 100 pairs of eyes watched him in silence. "I need to protect what I believe in, and I cannot do that from here. Miss Kennedy, whom some of you have met, has offered to take me to the US and from there I will travel to the Vatican where my skills and knowledge can be best used and where I can be the most help, not just for Rome but for every one of us here and for everyone around the world. This is a hard decision, but one I must make and it would help me do my job better if I had all of your blessings."

Silence.

Morgan could hear his own heart pounding in his chest and for long seconds nobody moved. He bit his lip and shuffled on the spot to leave when the father who had been grabbed by the Hashalanth in the ward stood up and spoke. "Padre, you saved my life and the life of my family. You have my blessing."

Morgan felt the emotion build up inside him and nodded in thanks to the man.

A woman two rows from the front stood up. "You serve a greater power and have demonstrated great skill that should be used to protect all mankind. Go and take my thoughts, prayers and blessings with you on your journey."

Morgan nodded in thanks and as a few more people stood and acknowledged Morgan's actions, he breathed hard to control the emotion that was building up within him. He thought that these people would judge him, cast him out and never look him in the eye, but as they praised him, he felt humbled by their response.

There was a slow rumble from the back of the room but the sound of applause soon erupted and shaking the chief administrator's hand he thanked the crowd. Morgan then left the ward with Carlos and headed to the airport to meet Laura and her company's private plane.

The private airfield was an hour from the hospital. The security guard let them through the gates and towards the small single storey building that doubled as customs, air traffic control, security and departure lounge. Laura met them at the rear of the building towards the runway.

"The pilot has filed his flight plan and we're set to go." she said. "We've got a stop off in Mexico City for re-fuelling and then onto San Francisco."

Morgan was impressed by the efficiency she displayed. The three of them headed towards the twin engine Gulfstream jet and at the bottom of the stairs Laura said farewell to Carlos and climbed the steps.

The co-pilot took Morgan's bags off him and followed her up. Morgan turned to Carlos.

"Thank you for all of your help over the past years." he said. Carlos had been a good friend and had smoothed the way for him to work closely with the hospital and patients.

"You have made a huge difference Padre." Carlos replied. "You have a calling and you must answer it. You will be missed, but you will be safe and you will return."

"I promise!" Morgan said. They hugged and shook hands and Morgan gave a final wave before the co-pilot closed the hatch and locked it.

With agonising slowness Carlos watched as the plane taxied away from the terminal and headed to the end of the runway. As the engines powered up the plane accelerated down the runway and the nose tilted up into the sky, Carlos waved.

With the wingtip lights disappearing into the distance, Carlos headed back to his car. As he started the engine gigantic muscular legs landed on the bonnet and razor sharp teeth ripped the roof off. Carlos looked up at the creature as the piercing scream of the beast ripped through his head. He covered his ears as the noise ruptured his ear drums and blood started to pour over his cheeks and neck.

He scrambled to escape from the car, but the arms of the beasts reached down, grabbed his shoulders and with what appeared to be no effort, his spine was snapped.

The plush comfort Morgan was in impressed him. He had heard of and seen in magazines the interiors of such luxurious private jets, but this was the first time he had been in such an aircraft. The large leather seats easily held him in comfort and the leg room was vastly superior to those of a commercial plane.

Maybe Sunrise Corps have their uses after all, he thought. With only 6 seats, three tables and a sofa the jet was sparsely decorated, with buttons on the arm rest Morgan found himself pressing them.

Laura re-entered the cabin and closed the curtain behind her. She sat down in the seat opposite him and watched him press the buttons.

"Be careful," she said warningly, "one of those activates the ejector seat."

Morgan smiled and stopped playing with them. He leaned back reclining the seat and looked up at the curved ceiling. "You have many questions to ask don't you?" he asked without looking at her.

"I have a few," Laura confirmed, "but I don't know where to start."

Morgan brought the chair back up-right and looked at her. "Let's start with me."

"Okay, who are you? You're not like a normal priest; I've never seen anyone do what you did."

"You're right, I'm not like a normal priest, although I still am a priest who conducts mass and hears confessions. I belong to a secret order; an order of priests dedicated to the protection of the church from all threats."

"Like what?" Laura asked.

"Like what we saw last night." Morgan replied. "The threats can come in many forms; ideological groups, political parties, teenage wannabe-terrorist groups, disgruntled parishioners."

"But that thing, that... Hasha-thingy wasn't a disgruntled teenage terrorist."

"No, the Hashalanth was one of the more extreme things we have to deal with." Morgan confirmed.

"Who's we?"

"We are the Order of the Vatican Knights. They were formed in 1245 at the first Council of Lyons by Pope Innocent IV. There have been many incantations of the Vatican Knights throughout history, but our main purpose is to serve the Holy See and act on instructions to protect the church from Evil." Morgan explained.

"Very few people, in fact, nobody outside the church knows about us, and very few inside know either."

"Then why tell me?" Laura asked, "I mean if it's so secret."

"It's hard to keep a secret when you've seen the proof." Morgan said. "Besides we have a long journey ahead of us and if I didn't tell you, you would keep on at me until I told you. And if the Hashalanths are just the start then our secrecy will be the least of the Churches problems."

"You think things are going to get worse?"

"I hope not, but it could." Morgan said once more leaning back in his chair. "Speaking to the Vatican, I've learned that other attacks are happening. Others in my Order are stationed all over the world and I imagine they have encountered similar things. While areas in the world are protected, the one place I'm needed is Rome."

"So why the detour to Mexico?"

"A friend of mine is stationed there. We're going to pick him up."

"Is he a Vatican Knight too?" Laura asked.

"Yes." Morgan replied simply as he closed his eyes and

listened to the drone of the engines.

Laura was about to ask another question but the heavy breathing of Morgan told her he had fallen asleep. Feeling the tiredness and exhaustion of the last day sweep over her, she herself lay her head back and thought about what Morgan had said.

If this is one secret the church has kept quiet, what else are they hiding?

CHAPTER THIRTEEN

They had been working for nearly 24 hours straight and the strain on the whole team was beginning to show. Cardinal Conquezla rubbed his eyes and sat back in his chair.

Around him were open books, files of photocopied pages and original 14th century texts with intricate drawings and illuminations drawn by monks of a bygone era. For hours Conquezla had read, researched, translated and searched for any references to similar events that had happened in the past. Despite the thousands of books held within the Vatican archive only a small fraction had been properly catalogued with indexes and topics.

He was determined not to be beaten and entered the main office to try and keep himself awake. A few of his staff members were asleep on the floor, others were slumped on their desks and one of the most loyal of his staff continued to read under the gentle glow of a desk lamp.

Scraps of paper, scribblings and notes were scattered across the tables. Coffee cups, trays of food and biscuit wrappers were sporadically cast and thrown on the floor. Conquezla was a man who wanted order, he hated untidiness, but these were extraordinary circumstances and he allowed the lapse in housekeeping this once.

Born in Paraguay in 1950, the young Louis Franco Conquezla was brought into the world in poverty. The third of seven children he never knew his father and together with his older brothers he worked from the age of nine to help bring some money in for his mother.

Needing money Louis took a job in a factory and given his diminutive size he was tasked to clear out behind the machinery as it slid backwards and forwards. For hours each day the continual banging, screeching and whirring of the machine bore into his mind as he scrambled across the floor on his hands and knees, swept away the debris and scampered back before the machine heaved its enormous weight back and the process started again.

In the four years he worked he never knew what the machine did, what it made, or the purpose for it, all he knew was that it had to be treated with respect. He was one of four boys who worked behind the machine and they all knew the dangers that were inherent to working in such a small confined and reckless place.

Never would Louis Franco Conquezla forget the day when a boy of six years old tripped over as he scurried away from the machinery as it backed hurriedly to its starting position, only for it to continue on its un-relenting task and with a sickening crunch the boy was crushed and killed. In shock the other young workers sat where they were and watched as the machine continued to pummel the now pulped body of the boy before one of them finally found their voice and screamed for help.

The adults in the factory were horrified by the scene and for only the second time in living memory did the factory not work during the week. The sight of the blood and the innards of the boy were forever etched onto mind of the young Louis Conquezla as he walked home.

Living in a small community the news spread quickly of the accident, but as he saw his mother's new violent husband standing on the threshold of the cramped house, he was met by a slash across the face from his vicious hands that had so often beat his mother, brothers and sisters. Fuelled by drink his stepfather continued to beat him and blamed Louis for the accident and death of the young boy.

Not one tear fell on Louis's cheek as he lay on the floor, so desperate was he not to show any emotion to his attacker. Finally the assault ended, either from guilt of attacking his step-son or more likely fatigue, Louis didn't care which as he felt the pain run through the bleeding wounds on his back, and the throbbing swelling pulsating across his face.

It was just another reason for him to leave, and after seeing the boy killed, Louis knew he needed to escape.

That night he gathered his few possessions together and kissing his younger toddler sister on the head he climbed out of the window and into the cold fresh night, away from the hellish life that had trapped him for so long.

He didn't know where he was going, or what he was going to do, he only knew that he couldn't spend another day in that house, or in that factory. Through the night he walked, mile after mile passed under his feet out of his town and onto the next, but it still wasn't far enough away.

For a week he walked, stealing bread and water wherever he could, on the seventh day of his escape he was finally too weak to continue and fell to the floor unconscious.

Awaking in a soft bed his eyes focused on a man dressed in black looking out of the window. The room was still, cool, fresh, but more importantly it felt safe. The man turned to face Louis and introduced himself as Fr. Juan Mitzi. It was on the steps of his church that Louis had fallen.

Louis slowly gained strength and through careful questioning by Fr. Mitzi he explained his story. Given the mistreatment, pain and misery he had suffered at the hands of his step-father he expected the priest, as he expected all men, to erupt in a fit of anger for abandoning his family and running away, but

Fr. Mitzi instead nodded slowly, listened to the words and said nothing other than telling Louis to get more rest. Louis gratefully accepted the offer and placed his head upon the pillow and quickly fell asleep.

After two weeks of comfort the moment Louis had feared came and it came knocking with a bang. Hammering on the church door stood Louis' step-father, seething with anger and clenching the fists that had done so much damage to Louis and his mother.

With a voice of thunder he demanded that Louis return with him, the roar of emotion and hatred from the man echoed around the church. Louis was shivering and hiding behind the front pew as he listened to the thunderous apocalyptic demands of his step-father.

Fr. Mitzi never flinched and never moved to allow him to enter the sacred building, but the non-combative approach of the priest incensed the tyrant further and Louis began to fear for the safety of his new friend. Against his better judgement he stood up from his hiding place and strode towards the door where Fr. Mitzi and his step-father stood.

As he stepped into the light pouring through the doors from the summer morning a new strength took hold of Louis and he put himself between Fr. Mitzi and his step-father. With an inner strength he never thought he could summon in the face of such an adversary he said he would never return home while his step-father was alive and would stay with Fr. Mitzi until that day came.

That moment when he told his step-father that he never wanted to see him again was the last time Louis saw the drunkard, he watched from the sanctuary and safety of the church as his step-father shuffled off without his prize.

Later that day Louis and Fr. Mitzi were walking through the gardens of the church, both barefoot and the old priest expressed his pride in the inner strength Louis had shown in facing his demons and standing up to the evil in his world. For the first time in his life Louis had found a father figure, and like other 13 year olds across the world he decided there and then that he would follow in his father's footsteps.

He studied hard and worked day and night for the good of the church. As his years of loyalty and devotion to the church continued, so it was noted by the Bishops and Archbishops who nominated him for the appointments and promotions throughout his career. However, unbeknown to his superiors, he had been recruited into the secret order of the Vatican Knights, by the then leader, Archbishop Carnegie.

Working within the Vatican, Conquezla was appointed a Cardinal, and subsequently as head of the Vatican Knights on the untimely death of Archbishop Carnegie under the Papal authorisation of the late Pope John III.

Quietly he walked around the office and was careful not to disturb any of his staff who deserved their sleep. He approached Fr. Stefan Jung who was still reading and making notes.

"Your Eminence," he whispered, although in the silence it sounded as though he was shouting, "I think I have something."

During the last day of research he had heard the same statement from other priests who worked for him. Everyone was eager to find the information and would approach the cardinal with their evidence, but after further research they discovered that the text was contradicted or refuted by another source. They needed definitive, irrefutable evidence before they could proceed. Conquezla sat down next to Jung.

"Have you slept yet?" he asked the young priest.

"No, Your Eminence." he replied, "I'll sleep when you sleep."

"You'll get some rest after this," Conquezla said, "You need it."

Jung nodded and moved the colourful decorated book so the Cardinal could read it. "This is a 16th century text quoting from an 8th Century source." he said quietly, careful not wake his colleagues. "Some of the writings are faded but from the sections I can make out there are descriptions and direct references to Hashalanths." Jung pointed to a faded section of the page that was open.

"Here it says 'Whence the winged creature with horned teeth lands, a massacre will unveil.' The following sections are faded and missing, but here it says 'The Hashalanth will be victorious on the eve of His return.'" Jung pushed the book away and produced another text in ancient Hebrew.

"If my translation is correct it states here "The days of darkness will return with the visit of the Mallakech.' I had read this before, but never put two and two together, until I remembered another text that Fr. Cespedes had quoted earlier, here." He pointed at a photocopy of a text in elegant swirling script from an 11th Century French monastery. "Here is says 'The Mallakech attacked and its brother the Hashalanth praised the Dark Lord as his deeds and wishes were fulfilled.' Your Eminence, I believe that this is the proof that this is the start of something!"

The previous 24 hours of no sleep evaporated from Conquezla's mind as he read the pages and made his own translations of the texts. Jung sat in silence and rubbed his eyes as the tiredness started to overtake him.

"That's it." Conquezla said, "That's it!" he called as his voice echoed around the stone room and his staff started to stir.

"I've a text on my desk that states a Mallakech is the torchbearer of the Lost Army of Deserted Souls." He stood up and everyone around him watched as he paced the floor thinking out loud. "A Mallakech and a Quazon cat are similar creatures, it could be that Fr. McCloud was wrong in his assessment of the bite marks on Fr. McKellen. It could in fact be a Mallakech that attacked; and with the unknown footmarks around the body of Fr. McKellen-"

Conquezla was thinking quick and he quickly scoured through some papers on a neighbouring desk and found what he was after.

"Yes... yes!" he was excited, "Here! A Mallakech attacks on the orders of his master. They don't attack on their own; they are vicious but obedient creatures and serve one master. Whoever was with Fr. McKellen was the Master and the creature was a Mallakech."

He turned to Jung. "Stefan, I want the next 5 minutes His Holiness has!"

Leaving his staff half awake and confused, Conquezla walked back into his office and closed the door behind him. At last he had answers; at last he had an idea of what was happening. All he needed to do now was convince the Pope that it really was happening and also urge his approval of the activation of the Vatican Knights.

He sat down in his chair and took a deep breath. There were still some members of the senior clergy within the Vatican who had no idea of the existence of his Order of Knights; he wasn't too sure if the Pope himself knew truth from fiction of what they were capable of. To activate the Order officially was a major risk for Conquezla as secrecy was his top priority. If persons within the Vatican knew they existed, he feared they would be interfered with. Conquezla knew of one particular Cardinal who would be displeased and frustrated that he hadn't been informed of the Knights existence.

It was indeed a risk, and if Conquelza was wrong about his assessment that these were the forces of Hell and it was all a case of genetic research gone wrong, then the future of the Order and his own role was in jeopardy.

His phone rang and he hit the speaker button.

"Your Eminence, His Holiness is in a foreign affairs briefing at the moment, but you may join him later for his afternoon refreshments." Jung said.

Conquezla thanked him and asked him to compile the information for him.

The Cardinal stared blankly at the wall. If this was a pre-emptive attack by the forces of evil, it was a major act of war against the church; one that he truly hoped his Vatican Knights could vanquish.

Cardinal Louis Conquezla walked briskly through the corridors of the Papal apartments with Fr. Stefan Jung at his side. Time had passed quickly since they had a worked out a working theory as to the incidents occurring across the world.

Their feet echoed down the marbled corridor and they quickly reached the private apartments of the His Holiness Pope Pius XV. The Swiss guards in their traditional Michelangelo designed uniforms stood to attention as they approached and one of them opened the door to allow Cardinal Conquezla to enter.

Fr. Jung stepped back and handed the folder to Conquezla and allowed him to enter on his own.

Inside, the private apartment was elegantly dressed with long draping curtains half covering tall thin windows. Murals adorned the walls and ceilings and intricately carved cabinets housed priceless religious artefacts.

Sat behind his wide desk was Pope Pius who beckoned Conquezla over and indicated him to sit. The Pope was on the phone and he covered the mouthpiece to speak.

"I'm on a conference call with the US President and the Secretary General of the UN." He explained, "Sometimes they don't know it's me speaking." He returned to the call and interrupted whoever was talking. "I understand that Mr. President, but until we have proof that these attacks are religiously motivated I will not publicly denounce them. I must go. Goodbye."

Conquezla was surprised by the abruptness of the Pope who was used to more gentle and serene pontiffs; however Pope Pius was in his early 60's and still had fire and determination in his desire to fight the leaders of the world to make the world better.

Pius turned to Conquezla. "Louis, it is good to see you," he said standing and pouring himself and his guest cups of coffee. "You look like you need this."

"Thank you," Conquezla said taking the cup. "It has been a long night for us."

"I heard," Pius said sitting down and taking a sip of his

own drink. "I understand that you were eager for this meeting?"

"Yes, as you know-" Conquezla started but was interrupted as Cardinal Philip Houseman, the Pope's advisor entered and took his place in the spare seat opposite the Pope. Conquezla re-focused after the interruption and continued. "As you know there have been a number of incidents occurring across the world in the past week. Some of these have been attacks against the church, others against the general population. Some of these attacks have been vicious attacks that have resulted in a number of deaths; the most noted so far being Fr. McKellen in Scotland." Conquezla passed Pius and Houseman a copy of his own file.

"Your Holiness, we have conducted research into these attacks and they can only be described as fulfilling a prophecy of the return of the Devil to the land of Man that was documented in several unrelated sources throughout history. Descriptions of beings walking the earth are described; names and places of attacks are also documented; all related and are confirmed by the recent reports."

"Is it a coincidence?" Houseman said quickly scanning the pages.

"No. I believe not." Conquezla responded. "One of the attacks in South America was thwarted by an individual and he contacted me and described the creature as a Hashalanth."

"A what?" Pope Pius asked looking up from his own file.

"A Hashalanth." Conquezla flicked through his file and pulled out a 16th Century drawing of the creature. "A winged beast with strong hind legs that allows it to stand at nearly 7 foot tall. Long protruding teeth at the front with an elongated skull. Two of these attacked a children's hospital in Venezuela."

Pope Pius and Houseman looked at each other. Conquezla could tell they were both shocked and Houseman asked the question they were both thinking. "How were they stopped? Who stopped them?"

"Was it one of your men?" Pius asked.

"It was." Conquezla confirmed.

"What do you mean one of your men?" Houseman asked looking between the two men. He didn't like being out of the loop and saw it as his role to have knowledge on all areas of the Vatican.

"Cardinal Conquezla's role within the Vatican is more than overseeing investigations into religious artefacts and proof of miracles." Pope Pius said, "He is also in charge of a secret Order who are tasked with the protection of the Church and its followers from the forces of evil and from attacks from the realms of Hell."

"What's their name?" Houseman asked rather suspiciously. The description of the order was familiar to him, but he couldn't explain where from.

"The Vatican Knights." Pius said bluntly.

"Preposterous!" Houseman erupted. "The Vatican Knights are a myth; a story from the ages. That Order has never existed, it is just the fabrication of years of whispers."

Pope Pius held his hand up. "I'll stop you there Philip. The Knights do exist and have existed since their first incarnation in the 13th century."

"I've never met one of them!" Houseman said, obviously frustrated that he was only just coming into this new piece of information.

"Their secrecy was for the good of the church and themselves." Conquezla explained calmly, ignoring Houseman's overt frustrations and annoyance. "There was no need to proclaim their existence to everyone, and it was on a strictly need to know basis."

"I needed to know this!" Houseman hissed.

"How would knowledge of their existence help you in your everyday duties?" Conquezla asked. "Would you knowing about them help with the planning of state visits to China?"

"Gentlemen please!" Pius said slapping the desk. "It should not matter who knew what when, just that we all know now. Cardinal Conquezla, you called this meeting for a reason."

"I did Your Holiness," He replied turning his attention away from Houseman. "I request that you formally activate the

Order of the Vatican Knights and extend to us your permission to protect the Holy Church and its entire people to the fullest extent of our ability using any and all necessary force."

Pope Pius stood up and slowly walked to his window that over looked St Peters Square. "When was the last time the order was active?"

"1751." Conquezla replied. "They were used to track a suspected messenger of the Devil across Europe."

"Your Holiness, using such untested means and symbolic persons such as these Knights is not appropriate. I urge you to reconsider and call on the people of the world to pray for safety and an end to this violence. Whatever these things are, surely a dialogue would be better than violence. The Americans have the largest armed forces in the world, perhaps we should assess how their methods of violence are effective in fighting these things." Houseman said standing.

Conquelza followed suit. "Prayer isn't enough to stop the soldiers of evil marching. We need decisive and proportionate action."

Pope Pius turned back from the window and looked at the two men. "I've already spoken to President Frost, and they have suffered significant losses and fatalities, not just in the US, but across the globe." Pius paused and thought for a moment, "Cardinal Conquezla, convene your Knights and activate the Order. I will address the people and urge tolerance and prayer."

Conquezla nodded in thanks, gathered his papers and exited the office leaving Houseman and the Pope.

"This is a mistake." Houseman said.

"Perhaps, but he has more knowledge of these beasts than us and I trust his judgement on the matter." Pius replied.

Houseman gathered his own file together. "Perhaps it would be wise if there was a liaison between the Vatican Knights and yourself? I would happily volunteer my time for this task."

Pius looked up at him. "Yes, please keep me informed of their duties."

CHAPTER FOURTEEN

"Mr. Masterson, how do you respond to the reports of your staff going missing?" The reporter thrust a microphone into his face as he walked from his limousine to Sunrise HQ.

He turned to her. "It is unfortunate that members of staff have disappeared, but it is not the fault of Sunrise Corps."

"What does Sunrise Corps say about the recent revelation that senior members of your staff have influenced media broadcasts?"

"The editorial policy of Sunrise has been altered to align itself with a new partnership that has been created." Masterson said pushing himself through the throng of reporters.

"What new partnership?"

"Who are you working with?"

Masterson continued to force his way forward. "A new era in this world is coming and myself and Sunrise will be at the forefront of it."

"Senior police officers are quoted as saying that 15 employees of Sunrise have been murdered in the past 3 days." A reporter called out. Masterson stopped on the steps of the HQ and turned to face the crowd. Cameras were pointed at him and bulbs flashed. "Do you care to comment?"

Masterson waited for a moment. "Those deaths were unfortunate but this company is not responsible for them."

"I never said Sunrise was, I just want a comment." the reporter shouted back.

"I've lived in this country all my life; worked in New York for 20 years and have travelled the world extensively. Never have I seen society take a nose dive as much as I have over the past week. Society killed those people; society killed the 13 year old boy on the East side last night. People die for no reason and when questions are asked no answers are given.

"I can't answer why these people were killed; but why don't you stand and ask the one organisation that revels in such situations; the one organisation whose business is dealing with the aftermath of these events? Why don't you ask the church why these people died? In these tumultuous times where is the spiritual leadership that the church says it has? Where are the figureheads that worship a god that allows such atrocities to happen?

"Ask them why these people died. I am a businessman not a priest, bishop, cardinal or the pope. If you want answers go and petition them and allow me to continue my work in making lives better by investing in things that people can practically use; not as the church does by using prayers and rituals that can only improve their own coffers and offer little hope for the people who believe in such myths!"

The reporters scribbled down the quotes and surprisingly, silence fell amongst them for a moment but then one raised her hand.

"Are you saying that the church..."

"I'm saying that the Catholic Church, after all of their preaching, speeches and dominance within the world should take some sort of account for the state of society." Masterson said. "If they want to make the world better then they should be more proactive and not tell people to be tolerant or pray. The church should give some of the vast amounts of money it collects each year; money given freely by people who need the most help, I'll add; back to the people and it should not focus on a belief of money for miracles."

The reporters erupted again but Masterson no longer listened to them. He had a free path to his office and he walked up the steps leaving his security men to deal with the reporters clambering for another quote.

He had done his job, he thought, he had used the sound bite quote Kronos had ordered him to say; Money for Miracles. With the press now riled up about his comments about the church he will be able to use his newspapers and TV channels to back up his statements and cause a backlash against the church.

TV programmes and documentaries were being hastily made condemning the church and its belief system. Masterson thought about the role he was playing in the downfall of the church as he crossed the deserted foyer under the watchful eye of a Quazon cat that lay hidden in the shadows.

After all he had worked for was this really what he wanted his legacy to be? Men had fought wars to defeat the church over the previous 2000 years but it had always stood strong; how was what he was doing any different he thought.

He had meekly raised these very questions to Kronos. He remembered the moment when the dark hood swept back to reveal the grinning skull look down at him. From the cavernous sleeve the fingers flicked out and Masterson watched as it reached up and touched his forehead.

"Each war uses whatever technology is available to them," Kronos growled, "The media is a new weapon and it will be used to control the thoughts of those people disgruntled with the Church. Once the foundations are laid the true war will break free and our soldiers will flood the earth. You, Mr. Masterson are not doing anything different from hundreds of people before you, only this time it is not man that is trying to defeat the church, but the Dark Lord himself. He will succeed and you will be rewarded!"

Standing in the elevator and pressing the button for the top floor, Masterson hung his head and breathed deeply.

What had he done, he thought, to deserve the honour of destroying the church?

The plane had been on the ground for an hour and Morgan watched the city speed past as the taxi fought its way through the bustling traffic. The rusting car ploughed forward and the driver sang whole heartedly along with a Spanish song on the radio.

He seemed distracted by the music and Laura flinched as she watched the oncoming traffic miss their taxi by inches. Morgan stared blankly out of the window and watched the grey clouds converge above them.

After a couple of more minutes they finally arrived at a traditional one storey stone built church, Santa Maria, the home of Fr. Julio Yegros.

Laura and Morgan headed through the gates and into the courtyard of the church where suddenly, serenity and calm descended on them as they left the hectic streets behind them. Morgan had visited Fr. Yegros many times before and knew his way around the city; but in all of his visits he had never seen the courtyard so deserted.

In fact, he noted, there was nobody around.

He banged hard on the thick wooden door and they patiently waited for an answer.

"It's a beautiful church." Laura commented looking at the paintings on the walls.

"It was constructed by the Spanish when they first arrived here a couple of hundred years back." Morgan said. "Unfortunately the town grew up around it and now it's almost lost amidst the jungle of the city."

Morgan banged on the door again and he looked around for any signs of life, but there was none.

"Wait here." he said and headed along the covered veranda and to the shock of Laura he jumped up onto a bench and used it to vault over the wall.

Morgan landed in the back courtyard, a private area where

the present clergyman could get away from the troubles of the townsfolk. In the shade and out of the heat Morgan walked across the grass to the grimy window set into the wall that looked into the sacristy of the church. Morgan wiped the glass clean and he could see cassocks, robes and books strewn across the floor.

Chalices and crucifixes lay on their side on the floor. The door to his side wasn't as strong or sturdy as the front door and after a couple of kicks the door was open. Morgan entered and from under his jacket he pulled out the hilt of his Celestial sword; it was attached to a shoulder harness so that it hung at his side hidden from view but readily accessible.

He carefully stepped across the threshold and found his footing between the disturbed objects that lay discarded on the floor. The lights were off and Morgan waited a moment for his eyes to adjust to the dimness. He headed for the curtain in the corner of the room that he knew led to the main alter at the head of the church. Carefully he peeled back the curtain and stepped out.

Emerging at the back of the alter Morgan looked about as he remembered the stone walls covered with murals; the tabernacle at the head of the alter covered in red velvet and surrounded by a large gold disc symbolising the sun. The rows of wooden chairs sat silently in front of him as he descended the alter steps.

He moved to the side wall of the church and headed to the confessional box that stood pronounced out against the cold stone walls.

The curtains were pulled closed on the centre vestibule but Morgan could see a pair of shoes protruding from the bottom. Carefully he stepped up to it and pulled the curtain back.

The face was pale, white, and devoid of blood and life. Dried mucus and blood stained the mouth and the skin was shrinking and pulling taut as rigor mortis took hold. The eyes were closed but Morgan knew the man was dead.

He heard a whisper in the air and instinctively ducked as a sword swept past his head and cut through the wooden frame of the confessional. In an instant Morgan had opened his sword and swung round to block another blow from his attacker.

The enemy's sword came swinging round and Morgan dodged it and then he saw the face of his adversary.

"Jules!" Morgan cried out, "It's me!"

Fr. Julio Yegros stopped his attack mid swing and his eyes filled with watery joy as he saw his friend. "Peter, you came!" He dropped his weapon and fell into Morgan's arms and sobbed into his chest. "You came, I knew you would!"

Morgan held him as his friend released the emotion, "Jules, what happened here?" he asked pushing Julio back to look in his eyes, "What happened to Fr. Alvero?"

Julio was crying but he tried to talk and between gasps for breath he managed to speak. "I saw him Peter!" he sobbed, "I saw him take over the mind of Fr. Alvero and torture him. He came at me and I had to defend myself I had to take his life. But it wasn't Alvero, it was him!"

He buried his face into Morgan's chest once more. "Who, Jules, who was it?"

"It was the Devil himself!" he sobbed and he fell to his knees dragging Morgan with him.

Morgan didn't ask any more questions as he knelt there with his friend in the middle of the deserted church. Morgan looked around himself and in the corner of the alter near the curtain he had entered he saw Laura standing there listening and watching everything.

In the adjoining house to the church Laura stood in the kitchen making a pot of coffee. Morgan was tending to Julio in the front room and after a couple of minutes he came in and took a drink off her.

"How is he?" Laura asked holding her own cup close to her.

Morgan took a sip of his. "He's fine. Shattered to say the least; I don't think he's slept for three days." He sat down at the kitchen table and looked at Laura. He knew she had a thousand questions burning inside her that she wanted to ask him, but he didn't know how to answer them.

Should he masquerade the answers, lie to her or just tell her the truth? He didn't know how to deal with them and he wouldn't until he was asked outright. After all she had seen and heard he didn't want to keep her in the dark.

If Julio was telling the truth and he had seen the Devil in Fr. Alvero then it was pointless in telling her lies when the truth was about to be exposed to all.

Unbeknown to Morgan, Laura was thinking the same thing. She did have questions, did want answers but she didn't know how to ask them. Would he laugh at her; shout at her; or completely ignore her questions? She didn't know but she needed to ask.

"Peter, that thing that Jules said, do you believe him?"

"Yes," Morgan replied instantly as if he was waiting for the question, "of course I do. But it's not because I'm a priest, it's because he's my friend and brother in arms."

"Is he a Vatican Knight too?"

"Yes, we were both stationed to South America at about the same time, but we were friends before we joined the Order."

"He said the Devil was here." Laura said finding the strength to ask the question, "Tell me the truth, is he real?"

Morgan looked at her from across the table. "You don't believe in God, you said so yourself. So if I told you what I believe to be the truth would you believe me?"

"I just want a straight answer!" Laura snapped. "I've been attacked by a creature you've said came from hell; and now I've heard a hysterical priest say he's seen the Devil. I just want to know if it is true then why the church hasn't told us it's real!"

Morgan smacked his hand on the table and silence fell on the kitchen. Morgan tried hard to control his emotions and his stare bore down hard on Laura who looked away from his eyes.

"When you first met me I bet you thought I was going to

be preaching about God, Jesus, heaven and Hell and how all of us are sinners and we'll be sent to hell. I bet that when you're out with your friends you've made fun of the church for its beliefs and what it stands for and I can almost guarantee that you've said somewhere that you think the church should shut up and let people live their own lives." he continued staring at her.

He knew he was right, and she also knew he was right. "You can't have it both ways Laura. You can't, on one hand, complain that the church preaches too much about good and evil and then complain when you aren't told about the existence of the Devil.

"What exactly do you think the church has been doing for the past 2000 years? Everything the church stands for, every homily a priest gives, every mass people go to is all part of a greater message that the Devil and Hell exists! We've been shouting about it for 2 millennia now; what more could we do to get the message out there?"

He didn't realise it but his voice was raised and he was standing up with fists clenched. He looked at his hands and white knuckles and sat down again. He couldn't have a continual argument with people about the existence of Hell if he was to do his job properly. "The only way to prove there's a hell is to show them Hell in all its glory. But to do that you have to unleash hell and all its demons and creatures on the earth. I'm sure you can understand that we have never wanted to do that and this situation we're in now is unprecedented and unimaginable. If this plays out the way I think it will it doesn't matter if you believe in God or not it will be the end of man-kind."

CHAPTER FIFTEEN

In the hours since Felix Masterson's comments regarding the church and society, there was a barrage of calls from media outlets asking for him to confirm his comments. Churches, cathedrals and chapels were all under siege from reporters desperate for a comment from members of the clergy to add fuel to the already explosive situation.

Kronos examined the TV screens as reporter after reporter continued to re-cycle the same information. On the channels funded by Sunrise a documentary was being screened examining the flaws in the church and how, over the years, it turned a blind eye to the crisis' that occurred over the world.

The Holocaust during World War 2 featured heavily and Victor smiled broadly as the transmissions travelled across the country. Unbeknown to the viewers of the programmes, subtle messages were being subliminally broadcast in the programme.

It was Victor's idea to manipulate a country dedicated to its television programmes and he watched as split second frames of banners, signs, burning crucifixes and destroyed churches implanted themselves in the minds of the population watching at home.

"You see Master," Victor said, "the hidden messages are

working, there are already people protesting at the churches. You should make your appearance now."

Kronos clicked and stretched his bony fingers, "No, I shall wait until the hysteria has reached its peak and when no answers come from the church then we shall reveal ourselves as the true saviours of the world." Kronos walked around the room and stood at the window that overlooked Manhattan.

Around him three Ukobach demons sat tearing the flesh off a bone that once belonged to a Sunrise employee.

Between 4 and 5 feet tall the Ukobachs had large heads, long noses, with wide mouths and short sharp teeth. The eyes bulged from their sockets and swivelled around so as not to miss anything happening around them. Their bodies were small and out of proportion to the size of their heads; similar in shape to that of humans they had an addition of a thin long tail that whipped about behind it as they walked.

Kronos turned back to Victor. "Increase the attacks. We need more wraiths to strengthen our forces."

"Where shall we attack sire?" Victor asked, getting excited about the prospect of the attacks.

"Everywhere," Kronos said, "wherever there are masses of people, summon the winged beasts to attack and destroy them. The time of his arrival is nearing and we should let the people see what is to come."

Victor bowed to his master, "As you wish."

Madison Square garden was alive with dedicated supporters shouting for their team. The two basketball teams jostled for the ball as it flew from one end of the court to the other. A team scored and the crowd cheered; the cheerleaders sprang up from the floor and danced in celebration.

The ball was thrown back into play and quick passes landed it in the safe hands of the star shooter. He leaped up into the air and released the ball at the optimum height. The ball sailed through the air, spinning and turning as it travelled up through a high arc across the court.

Opposition players jumped to reach it but were too slow as it missed their hands. 60,000 pairs of eyes watched the ball fly through the air as it dipped towards the ring and net. The shooter had thrown it too hard and it hit the ring and bounced up, everyone held their breath as it dropped again towards the backboard and directly into the net.

The shooter knew it was in the net and he punched the air, turned away and ran back to his team's side of the court. As he jogged back he stopped as nobody was cheering; the whole crowd was silent. He looked around but none of the crowd even moved. In the 6 years he had been playing professional basketball he had never seen a crowd so quiet, in such a small time frame.

He turned to his team mates but they, with the opposition, were stood staring at the backboard behind the net.

The shooters mouth fell wide as he saw the match ball pierced and hanging from a tail waving in front of the backboard. The tail belonged to a creature he had never seen before; sitting on the board clutching the top with its hind claws the creature had two sets of arms coming out of its body.

The head was large, with dark eyes, pointed ears and a short stubbed nose. It stared down at the star shooter standing solitary in the other half of the court. The tail flicked up and the ball was released and landed at the feet of the lone player. He looked at the deflated ball and then back at the creature. Unfortunately, neither he nor the other 60,000 people saw the other 50 creatures in the rafters jump from their hiding places behind the lights and land on the court. Standing nearly 8 foot tall on their muscular back legs the creatures roared and screamed as the huge hands reached out and flung the players up into the spectators.

Seeing the imminent carnage, people ran for the exits and clambered over each other to escape; but an invisible force flung the door shut and they couldn't be opened. The creatures leaped up and landed in the midst of the crowd and the sharp claws and razor like tails flicked and swiped at anything that moved. Body parts were cut off, blood sprayed and poured out and screams echoed around the stadium.

The creatures roared in delight as their prey ran and tried to hide; it would be a good nights hunting tonight and they would feast well.

It was a prime position, so the tourist information had told them, to see the evening spectacle of the Eiffel Tower glitter like diamonds with thousands of lights. At the top of every hour, the spectacle would begin.

Clare and Chris had managed to find time to sneak away for their secret rendezvous and had met, coincidentally they would tell people, on the platform at St Pancras station in London and had taken the high speed train to the continent. They hadn't taken long to find their hotel, and were even quicker to find the bed. They had made love frantically, and with the tensions of their individual home lives forgotten, they walked hand in hand across the plaza and stood and waited for the hour and the light show to begin.

"I'm glad you decided to come." Chris said, smiling and moving a wisp of hair from Clare's face.

Clare smiled back and held his hand to her face. "Thank you for asking me. With everything that's going on, I needed the break."

They kissed and embraced just as the clocks around Paris began to chime out and ring. Across the Seine the landmark tower lit up brightly and began to sparkle in the early evening; neither Clare nor Chris saw it, as their passion for each other dominated their senses.

Above them, bursts of flames streaked across the sky and crashed into the Tower, instantly melting the joints and bending the struts. The destructive noise was immense and jolted from their romantic moment, Clare and Chris looked across the plaza and river and saw the Eiffel Tower lean to the side and slowly crash to the ground. They felt the vibrations as thousands of tonnes of metal crashed to the floor beneath their feet and they held onto each other as the shaking almost made them lose their footing.

The buildings around them started to crumble as unknown objects crashed into them. People began running for safety, but Clare and Chris stood rigid to the spot, gripping each other in fear.

They stood in silence at the sight, but suddenly there was a piercing scream from behind them. The pair turned and saw a hunched figure, covered in rippling fur approach them. Chris had no idea what it was but his instinct was to put himself between it and his new lover. He carefully watched it, trying to guess its next move, but another shadow moved to the side of the first and he froze with horror as he saw another of the bear like beasts, and then a dozen more.

Each were identical, totally covered with fur, short noses and long teeth. The huge eyes reflected nothing and were just black holes on a black shape. The whole body looked powerful, beneath the fur Chris could see the muscles flexing and contracting as it prowled towards them. From the top of the scalp, running along the line of the spine ran a twin row of ten inch high sharp edged plates, similar to a prehistoric monster, with spikes protruding from its tail. The claws scratched on the floor and it focused its attention on Chris and Clare.

"What is it?" she asked, terror ripping through her voice.

Chris didn't get a chance to answer as behind them the destruction of the Eiffel Tower still crumbled to the ground, and the fire storm continued to rain down around them. The beast, a Quazon cat, staring at Chris flinched and suddenly pounced forward, swinging its claws through the air and catching him on the side of the face, snapping his neck.

Clare screamed in terror and tried to run, but from behind her an arm grabbed her around the waist, pulled her up into the air and across the Seine. She struggled to free herself and looking up at her abductor, she saw a face of fire looking down at her and it shouted in delight at his prey. The beast was a Mallakech and had outstretched wings of torn flesh, and while similar to a man, the body cavity was empty and the skeleton of the creature dripped blood and sinew on her. Clare screamed again as the fire beast turned suddenly and began to head towards the molten mass of the Tower.

In the last seconds before impact, she prayed that her family, three children and husband here safe.

Paris was in flames, the River Seine ran red with blood with body parts, heads, arms and legs that had been ripped apart and tossed into the river by the scavenging demons. The attack was still in its infancy, but the power and destruction of the city was almost complete.

The famous art galleries were burning bright, with no hope of saving any of the contents. Recklessly, the famous artworks of Da Vinci, Raphael, the old masters and famous Parisian artists were lost in the blink of an eye.

At the Louvre Museum, the tourists were running for their lives as the wraith demons, Hashalanths scouts, Mallakech demons and Quazon cats chased their prey with ever growing hunger. Light brightly shone up from the glass pyramid in the forecourt of the museum, shining directly into the sky like a beacon, but the light soon died as a shadow passed below the pyramid. The light started to dim and from beneath the glass structure a huge reptilian head emerged and smashed through the controversial architecture.

The twin headed reptilian creature slithered out of the museum, barely squeezing its huge body through the 35 metre wide hole. The two snake-like heads arched up and the fork tongues spat out from the huge mouths. The whole body was over 300 metres long and it curled around itself and slithered around, hunting its prey.

It snapped at the fleeing masses, grabbing men, women and children, nobody was safe from its attack and as the people fled, the snake followed them, finding new blood to feast on.

CHAPTER SIXTEEN

General Samuel Bailey stood and watched with admiration and pride, like thousands of commanding officers before him, as his soldiers climbed onto the troop carriers and prepared to head out onto the streets of New York City.

Stationed at Fort Bragg in North Carolina, he had been ordered to bring his brigade of 5000 men and women to the Big Apple to help protect the civilians from the attacks that had been taking place. He had received his orders from the highest authority, the Pentagon and the President of the United States of America, and as a career military man, he was prepared to follow them.

He had quickly attended a briefing with the other senior officers and then convened a meeting with his own company commanders to brief them. Their orders were simple. To stop the advance of the creatures; the use of force was authorised, but with a requirement to keep the collateral damage to a minimum.

Bailey had smiled to himself as he chewed on his unlit cigar as he heard that request. Obviously, he thought, the person asking it was a politician and civilian, and had never been in the theatre of war before. Nevertheless, he had made a note and passed the information on to his officers. If his soldiers chose to ignore that particular order, he didn't care less. He hated New York, he hated the populations arrogance and inbred innate hatred to anyone not born in their beloved state.

But orders were orders and as the last truck load of young brave souls headed from their secure compound and towards the bright lights of Manhattan, Bailey climbed into his own staff Humvee carrier and followed them. It may be a dangerous mission, but he was never one to let his men go alone into battle.

The streets were familiar but quiet as the 25,000 strong army slowly entered the labyrinth of New York. The parallel streets crossed at the intersections of the avenues, and ahead of them the large expanse of Central Park, the green oasis sat in the centre of the metropolis.

As they had advanced onto Manhattan Island, there had been a quick skirmish between the soldiers and their targets. Reports and rumours had quickly spread through the ranks that what they were hunting were aliens from another world. Descriptions of multi-headed creatures, with snapping jaws, tails of fire and blood that burned like acid were passed and whispered between the soldiers and whilst stating that the reports were "bullshit", deep down they wondered how true the reports were.

Intelligence reports passed to General Bailey had information that the creatures were congregating and gathering in Central Park. With a careful and professional eye he had assessed the information a thousand times. A as his soldiers slowly entered the boundary of the Park, he had a nagging doubt about the mission plan formulated by his own superiors.

He didn't like that there was too much cover with the trees for the creatures to hide in, and he didn't like sending near enough all the troops in there. He understood that they needed the firepower to tackle the enemy, but in a relatively confined space, with nervous soldiers and itchy trigger fingers, there was too much risk of friendly fire and unnecessary casualties. He wanted to send in only a small number of men to survey the situation. With no satellite imagery to assist them, due to technical difficulties, they were going in blind, and as a seasoned and successful commander, Bailey knew it was the wrong tactic.

In his Humvee, Bailey grabbed the chunky phone and pressed a button. Somewhere in the heavens the line was connected to his forward commander and he spoke quickly.

"Major, hold your line." He ordered. "Do not enter the park." He listened for the affirmative receipt of the order and then confirmed it with the Major. "That's what I said, fuck the orders, you keep our men out of that park!"

His driver looked at the General, almost in disbelief that his commanding officer was himself disobeying orders. He hoped General Bailey knew what he was doing.

The driver put the Humvee into reverse and began to pull the vehicle away when the radio crackled into life and the shouts of the soldiers filled the vehicle. Both the driver and Bailey stopped still and listened to the shouts and screams of the men, then looking out of the windscreen they saw six huge winged beasts with wide wings and sharp talons swoop down into the park.

The eruption of the gunfire could be heard and as Bailey ordered the Humvee into action, the whole vehicle was lifted from its wheels and almost thrown across the skyline crashing into the side of a building. The bricks and glass shattered around them, and the Humvee landed heavily on its reinforced roof, protecting the occupants.

Both occupants of the Humvee unbuckled themselves from their seats and climbed through the upturned contents of the vehicle and with a hard shove, the rear door opened into the night air. The driver led the way, armed with a submachine gun in his hands, and Bailey too stepped out, with his own side arm held up and ready.

Around them there was a strong smell of cordite and gunpowder in the air and the echoing gunshots around them filled their ears. Bailey looked around himself and saw a hoard of animal like creatures heading towards them. Growls of anger and shrieks of hatred erupted from the vile blood stained mouths of the beasts as they slowly approached the wrecked Humvee.

Bailey grabbed a spare submachine gun from the storage box, and stuffing spare magazines into his pockets, he indicated to his driver that he was ready to move out. They ran over to the shattered building with the weapons raised and found a concealed corner where they stopped to catch their breath.

"You okay?" Bailey asked the young soldier, seeing the blood seep down the side of his face.

The soldier checked the wound and said he was okay. They looked at each other, a General and a Private, both now equal on the battlefield. "Where shall we head?"

Bailey had to think for a moment as his mind tried to fade out the gunfire, the shouts, screams, screeching and terrifying roars from the beasts that he could now see traipsing towards the battered Humvee. Some of the creatures seemed almost human, and if he had to choose a word to describe them, it would be zombie. But his logical mind couldn't comprehend that. They had to be something else.

High above them, debris from a building came crashing down around them and looking up they saw a figure, a man, with wings protruding from his back at the shoulder blades. His body was glistening with blood and he looked down at the two soldiers. With a screech of glee the winged man jumped down and landed hard on the concrete before them, smashing the concrete.

Bailey depressed the trigger first and the burst of bullets ripped into the bloodied body, making him stagger backwards, but he didn't stop. The winged man looked at Bailey and the eyes narrowed, the teeth began to grow in the jaw, and the claws extended from the fingers. Bailey took aim again and he emptied the remaining bullets into the chest of the man until he fell backwards.

Bailey didn't know if it was dead and he sure wasn't going to wait around to find out. He loaded a fresh magazine into the gun and told the Private to head to Central Park, he had to find his men; he had to find reinforcements.

Major Parry shouted orders to his men to tighten the line on the left flank as another 6 two-headed spider-like creatures leapt over the tree line and began to scurry towards his men. They opened fire and the flames of rifles and machine guns zeroed in on them. The hot bullets found the targets and stopped the spider's dead.

Parry gave the order for his men to open fire at will, "Shoot any fucker that moves!" were his exact orders, and right now, his men were following it to the word.

He too opened fire on the incoming beasts, taking cover behind one of the armoured personnel carriers to reload just as the mangled body of a young Lance Corporal was thrown into the metal juggernaut.

Parry had never seen anything like it, the enemy were like a swarm of parasites, continually flowing and ebbing into the park area and attacking his solders constantly. There were so many of them that his men had no time to adjust positions, and the onslaught was continuous. There was no relenting in the assault and unlike other enemies he had faced on other battlefields across the globe, these creatures never needed to reload weapons, they were the weapons and with each monster they killed, there were another three behind it ready to continue the attack.

From his side, a corporal landed hard against the carrier, wiping blood and sweat from his face. "Sir, we're getting our asses kicked."

"Any report from the other lines?" Parry asked, quickly releasing a volley of bullets into the tree line.

"None sir. We're losing men like shit down a plug hole!"

Parry looked around him and saw the carnage, the scene amplified through his senses as the smell and sound of the battle crashed into his mind. Their position was too exposed and Parry knew it had them at an instant disadvantage. Depressing the trigger and emptying the remainder of the bullets into an oncoming dog-like creature, he made his mind up.

"Retreat." He said to the corporal. "Get the message out

to whatever men are out there. Whatever unit they're in. We're getting out of here."

The Corporal acknowledged the order and ran back into the heat of battle shouting the retreat order. Parry cursed himself for giving the order, he had never had to give it during his 16 years in service, but with the odds so severely stacked against him, he knew it was the right thing to do.

He thought he was relatively fit, but trying to keep up with the Private, General Bailey soon realised that he had spent too many hours and years behind a desk shuffling papers.

Both himself and the Private had managed to find an open door to hide in as the masses of blood thirsty pursuers chased them down. The door had led into the sanctuary of a church and as they burst through the doors, the terrified parishioners screamed at the sight of them.

The priest had quickly ushered them to the side and welcomed them to sanctuary. "I'm Fr. Riddle." The priest said, "Welcome to sanctuary."

Bailey accepted the welcome and introduced himself and the young private. "How is that you're safe, with those things just on the other side of the door?"

"This is a house of God," Riddle said, "out there is the army of the Devil. This is sacred soil and they can't cross the threshold. We're safe."

That was over an hour ago, and now Bailey and the Private sat in a corner quietly, away from the growing number of people seeking safety from the dangerous streets. As the only two soldiers there, they received sideway glances and looks, comments were heard under their breaths, but given what they had no doubt been through, Bailey ignored them and continued to chew on his unlit cigar.

To his side, the Private was clicking on the radio transmit button on his small portable device, but so far he hadn't found any unit replying. Bailey shook his head, and started to think what could've happened out there, beyond the walls. Were all of his men dead? Had any survived? Or had the Devil's Army, as Fr. Riddle called them, defeated them?

Bailey watched as the priest headed to the heavy door again, and let more survivors in. The General was interested to see what type of people had managed to escape. There were small families, immigrants, a cook and waiting staff, possibly from a high class restaurant somewhere. Wall Street bankers in their expensive suits were huddled together, probably, Bailey thought, thinking about their vast fortunes that were now worthless.

Children and elderly people of every colour were all sat in groups. Mothers tried to prepare food and drinks for the masses, and the fathers stood at the windows watching the scene unfold outside. The heavy door slammed shut and Bailey watched the newcomers enter and find their place amongst them. They looked like a young group, perhaps teenagers, hoods were pulled up over their faces and they walked with sunken shoulders. Definitely teenagers, Bailey thought.

The Private quickly looked up and caught Bailey's attention. "General, I've got something. A unit is in contact reporting to be about two streets from here."

Bailey ordered them to approach the church and they would head out and meet them. As the Private passed the order, Bailey gathered their equipment and weapons and they headed for the door. As the Private caught him up, Bailey watched as Fr. Riddle led the new group to the middle of the church and then shuffled off towards the altar.

"They're about a minute away sir." The Private said as he followed his commanding officers gaze. "General?"

But Bailey wasn't listening, he had taken a step forward and watched as the four new guests stood in the centre of the church, equidistance apart and they began to move in unison, swaying back and forth. He couldn't put his finger on it, he couldn't locate the feeling of impending danger, and he had learnt over the years that if something didn't look or feel right, then his instincts were correct.

It was unusual behaviour for the teenagers to be doing, and as he stepped towards them, he saw that they were in fact all wearing heavy cloaks.

The cloaked figures began to chant in unison and they raised their arms up above them, and from long thin fingers, they reached up towards each other's hands. As their fingertips inched closer together, sparks began to emanate from them.

Bailey turned to the Private, "Get that unit in here now!" he ordered, as he checked his weapon, un-latched the safety switch and readied himself.

Turning back to the figures, Bailey watched with terrified fascination as they levitated off the floor and in an instant the cloaks burst into flames, transforming into wings and the bodies were ablaze as they began to fly around the church.

The people around him began to scream and run for cover, and as they passed Bailey and the Private, the two soldiers moved forward and released small bursts of bullets at them.

The flying burning demons swooped and soared in the vastness of the church, reaching high up into the eaves, and then with great speed, diving towards the floor, grabbing the fleeing parishioners and killing them in their iron grips.

Bailey ducked down behind a pillar and reloaded his gun, just as the doors crashed open and the familiar face, although heavily bloodied, of Major Parry came running in. There was no greeting, salute, or exchange of notes, Parry and his men saw the danger and they all opened fire on the demons, chasing them around the church with their own stream of hot bullets.

Carnage began to erupt around them as one of the demons was downed by a severe barrage of assault weapons fire, and its remaining fire demons turned on the soldiers and dived down towards them.

With sweat stinging his eyes, General Bailey reloaded his last magazine into his weapon, and shouting an order to his men, he led the final charge.

It had been a hard battle, but these forces, he knew, were too strong even for the might of the US armed forces. They were defeated, beaten and would soon be enslaved to these things, Bailey thought, but he wasn't going to go down without a fight.

He shouted to his men to follow him, and with guns blazing, all of the soldiers with a fighting breath in them, followed General Bailey into the middle of the church and attacked the demons.

CHAPTER SEVENTEEN

In the cool dwelling of the living accommodation of the church, Morgan sat asleep in a comfortable chair next to the sleeping shape of Julio on the sofa beside him. Laura had been offered the bed further down the corridor and slept peacefully for a few hours.

After the heated discussion previously, Morgan had taken to answering her with one word answers. It wasn't in his nature to take offence or act in such a way, but he had limits with people who refused to believe something when the truth was directly in front of them.

He could accept that people didn't believe in things when all they have is just a person's word; but she had seen a creature that had never walked the earth first hand and yet she debated the existence of Hell. Before he went to sleep he had thought over the argument in his mind; could he have said things differently, should he have held his tongue?

Each scenario he thought through had him raising his voice at her and shouting her down. He never wanted to be seen that way, but sometimes he thought, it was the best way to get results.

Julio stirred and in doing so Morgan too awoke from his light sleep. They looked at each other and Julio was relieved that it wasn't a dream that his friend had come to him.

"You're still here?" he asked drowsily.

"Of course," Morgan replied, "How're you feeling?"

Julio slowly sat up and swung his feet off the sofa. "Better after that." he said stretching his muscles. "How long was I out?"

"A few hours. You just needed to catch up on sleep." Morgan answered.

"Peter," Julio said, "what I did; I had to stop him. I had to stop Fr. Alvero."

Morgan wanted to know what had happened, but didn't want to bring it up at the first opportunity. During his years of being a priest he had learnt that allowing people to direct the conversation is better than forcing the subject on them.

"What happened?" he asked.

Julio stared at the floor as the memories entered his mind's eye. "Fr. Alvero had come back from visiting a family a few miles away. He said that he had been attacked on the way back and from the look of him he had been. He had cuts to his face, arms, chest and back. It looked as though he had been set upon by a wild animal." Julio explained. "I cleaned him up the best I could but he didn't want it reported to the police. The next morning he sat on the floor there," he pointed to a spot on the carpet, "he was breathing hard and sweating. He scribbled things on a piece of paper in writing I couldn't understand and was speaking in a language I didn't recognise.

"He didn't pay any attention to me as I spoke to him and he pushed past me and headed to the church. I followed as he muttered his strange language. On the alter he had placed a gold communion dish and put the papers in it and gave a prayer of some sort. The papers caught fire instantly and it was like seeing a magician.

"He manipulated the fire in the air and moulded it into a ball of flame that hovered above him. He turned to me and spoke with a voice that penetrated my heart and soul." Julio paused as the memory ran through his mind once more. "It was pure evil, that's the only way I can describe it. He stood there and shouted at me and the flames above him stretched out and formed a sign."

Julio grabbed a pen and paper from the table next to him and drew a rune symbol. "I don't know what it means but at that moment I knew I had to defend myself. I managed to get back to the house to get my Celestial and when I went back into the church it was like he was waiting for me. We fought but he had strength not of this world. Fr. Alvero was nearly 80 years old, he could hardly stand up straight some days but here he was fighting me with the strength of 10 men. It was hard but I had to kill him. When the sword pierced his body he screamed out and a red haze erupted from his mouth, and it floated across to the altar. It took a shape, a shape I've seen so many times in books and scriptures. It took the shape of the Devil!"

Morgan sat quietly and watched as Julio sobbed into his hands. He couldn't imagine the guilt he was feeling for killing Fr. Alvero and there were no words he could say to make the guilt go away. Instead he moved seats and sat next to Julio and put a comforting brotherly arm around him.

"What's happening Peter?" Julio said. "What's happening to the world?"

Morgan shook his head. "I don't know Jules."

From the door there was a light knocking and Laura was standing there. Julio didn't want to be seen crying and moved away from Morgan and wiped his eyes.

"Sorry to interrupt," she said, "I've just had a phone call from a friend in New York that may answer that question." She crossed the room and switched the TV on to CNN international.

The images flickered but the signal was soon found and clear images of the attacks in Madison Square garden were shown.

"At the moment authorities are unable to identify the animals but it is understood that 50 were responsible for the attacks and murders of some 20 thousand spectators during the New York Knicks basketball game." The reporter continued. "This however is not an isolated attack with winged creatures being reported to have attacked shopping malls, pedestrians and schools all across the country. No explanation has been given but it's clear that the country is under attack, not from a foreign country but from elsewhere.

"Reports are also coming in that other cities, Moscow, Beijing, Munich, Berlin, London and Paris, as well as Sydney, Johannesburg, and Caracas have all suffered significant damage and attack from the creatures.

"Where these creatures are from we can only surmise but churches across the country are under siege as terrified people seek answers and refuge from what some are calling 'The Dark Army'."

Morgan and Julio sat watching the footage and couldn't believe what they were seeing.

"According to my friend," Laura said quietly, equally shocked by the footage, "similar attacks have occurred in Europe, Russia, the Middle East, Asia and Australia. Nowhere is safe."

The images on the TV changed and showed a crowd holding banners, shouting at the doors of a church.

"Similar scenes to these have been witnessed across the world with citizens demanding an explanation from the church. Worldwide criticism of the Catholic Church erupted after the CEO of Sunrise Corporation Felix Masterson told reporters to seek answers for society's breakdown from the church. So far the Vatican has declined to comment bringing further criticism from the public and politicians."

Morgan looked at Laura who stared at him open mouthed. "I have no idea what he's talking about." she said before Morgan could ask a question. Julio looked between the two of them confused.

"What's going on?" he asked.

"She works for Sunrise." Morgan said not taking his eyes off her.

Laura didn't like the way he looked at her and she turned away from him. "I tell you I don't know what Felix said."

Julio could feel the tension rising between them but his

mind was beginning to re-focus on the larger picture. "So what if she does work for him? We work for the church and it's under attack. We need to speak to Conquezla."

Morgan looked away from Laura at the mention of the Cardinal. He stood and switched the TV off shutting out the reality of what could be a disastrous scenario.

"I've already spoke to him." he said. "He's researching what's going on and I told him to activate the order."

"Has he though?" Julio said as his and Morgan's pagers vibrated on their belts. Each priest unclipped them and read the message.

The Order of the Vatican Knights was activated.

"Well that answers that question." Julio concluded. "We need to get to US soil and from there to Rome."

Morgan turned his attention to Laura who was still afraid to look him in the eye. "Laura can you get your pilot to file a flight plan for us?"

She nodded slowly but didn't fully acknowledge him. Morgan knelt down beside her and spoke softly. "Laura, I'm sorry, but I've been trained to be suspicious of coincidences. I know you have nothing to do with this Masterson chap and you are no way involved with what's going on in New York. But you are involved here and we need your help to get back to the US and then onto Italy. Can you help us?"

She smiled weakly at him and fought hard to keep the tears rolling. She pulled her mobile phone out of her trouser pocket and dialled.

Julio quickly went to pack a bag and Morgan switched the TV back on and sat on the sofa and watched the end of a recorded broadcast of a Vatican public relations statement to the world's media.

"Over the past few days there have been a number of unexplained attacks on people across the world. We cannot give a full explanation of these events until they are fully investigated. I call for all people in all countries to unite and pray for peace.

Unnecessary violence towards the Catholic Church and members of our clergy is unproductive in searching for answers. Please help us to help the world by allowing us time to research and investigate. Answers will be given, but in time."

Morgan sat back and shook his head. People won't listen, he thought, people want answers now and telling them to wait will only intensify the violence.

He knew the Pope was in a difficult situation, he couldn't say outright that the army of the Devil was walking the earth, but he couldn't turn a blind eye to the situation. It would bring more trouble to the doors of the church; trouble, Morgan thought, that he wanted to avoid until he was closer to Rome.

CHAPTER EIGHTEEN

The imposing 3 storey mansion stood in perfectly manicured grounds hidden away in the maze of Switzerland's Alps. Built in the 1600's the mansion was purpose built to house the headquarters of the Order of the Vatican Knights.

Secluded away from prying eyes the residents could train and hone their skills in the safety of the 'VK Schloss'; as students had come to call it. With a long winding drive way leading from the narrow road, the building was hidden from view by trees and bushes until the last moment when it was revealed to the visitors in all its glory.

With tall, white, thick columns guarding the entrance at the top of sweeping stairs that arched around to either side of an ornate fountain and met at the entrance door overlooking the grounds, visitors were forced to look up as they approached, and in doing so forced to face God and the one single sign that this building was used and owned by the Catholic Church; the insignia of the Vatican Knights carved from stone set into the very pinnacle of the facade above.

A long black limousine with two flags signifying the Vatican came sweeping around the driveway. The loose stones scattered in its wake as it turned and slowed to a stop. The dominating figure of Cardinal Louis Conquezla climbed out of the car and walked briskly across to the steps.

There was no ceremony, no fanfare for his arrival; he quickly climbed the steps and was met at the top by Fr. Stefan Jung.

"Your Eminence," he said "53 Knights have arrived so far and another 21 are on satellite hook-ups. We've had no word from the others."

Conquezla entered the mansion and his steps echoed off the marble floor as they quickly marched down the long corridor past art works of renaissance artists and sculptures. They headed towards a set of tall doors at the end of the corridor that opened automatically.

Inside they entered from the rear of the long chapel and walked down the aisle in between pews on either side facing each other. It was a long room with carvings and paintings by Raphael, Michelangelo and Da Vinci decorating the walls and corners. Above them a huge glass ceiling overlooked them and bathed the chapel in light.

At the head of the chapel was an altar and a large wooden carved throne for Conquezla. As he walked down the aisle the Vatican Knights in attendance stood to attention and bowed towards him.

It had been nearly 24 hours since Pope Pius XV had given his official authorisation of the activation of the Vatican Knights, and Conquezla and his team within the bowels of the Vatican had quickly contacted all of the Knights they could to attend VK Schloss.

Given such short notice only Knights from Germany, France, Denmark, Russia and across Europe had arrived; six African based Knights were also in attendance and with digital hook ups to those they had made contact with but couldn't attend, the Southern hemisphere Knights were sparsely represented.

While some of the Knights had already encountered and fought off wraiths and other beings from hell, others had not, and the media coverage they had seen had given them an inclination of what was to come, and what they faced.

Conquezla stood before his throne and let his Knights take their seats again. "My friends," Conquezla said, his voice echoed around the chapel, "thank you for attending at such short notice. For many of us it has been a while since we last saw each other; and I wish our meeting now was under more friendly and suitable circumstances."

He looked around at the men and he knew he had their complete attention. "In front of you is a copy of the official order signed by his Holiness activating the Vatican Knights. Our remit is to investigate these incidences around the world, interact if appropriate, and stop if necessary. All actions are sanctioned by the Vatican and all necessary means of action are acceptable."

Conquezla descended the three steps to the main floor and slowly walked along the aisle. "Gentlemen, evidence has recently been obtained that provides irrefutable proof that the forces of evil are walking the earth. Some of you have already had contact with these creatures, but for those of you that haven't we have had reports of Hashalanth scouts, Quazon Cats, Ukonbacks, Werewolves, Mallakechs, and Pyro Angels to name but a few.

"With the recent attacks in the US led by the Kallan'atak's in New York it is certain now that The Dark Lord is positioning himself to find a foothold on this soil." There was a murmur of voices around the chapel as this news sunk in.

"Our role is to protect the Church at all costs, even if that means losing our lives in the process. It is a sacrifice I am prepared to make and one you all swore an oath to uphold.

The Knights around him nodded in approval at his words. They had made an oath to the Church, to God and to the Order and Conquelza knew as he looked into their eyes that they would follow his orders to the end.

"This will be the greatest battle this Earth has ever seen," he went on, "good versus evil. God against the Devil. We must prevail, we must succeed. There are no armies in the world that can defeat them, we are the last line of defence for the Church, and for this world and we must not let them down."

He stood back in front of his throne once more and his voice quietened. "You will face opposition from the people. The Church has been criticised for lack of action and being at the front line you will be the focus of their distrust. But you have a job to do and you will all do it well." Conquezla outstretched his arms and brought his hands in to pray.

The priests in the chapel and across the world via satellite links also bowed their heads and joined Conquezla as he led them in prayer.

The men recited their prayers and Cardinal Conquezla blessed them. "We have a difficult task ahead of us, please rest and use the facilities available to hone your skills."

The Knights bowed again and moved off from their seats to the side doors. Conquezla watched them go and his eye was caught by Fr. Jung at the far end by the door he had entered. He approached the young priest looking more nervous than usual who quickly explained his worries.

In the blazing sunshine of the Swiss mountains Cardinal Philip Houseman stood breathing in the fresh air as he overlooked the fine gardens. From behind him Conquezla approached and stood next to him.

"I've always loved the fresh mountain air," Houseman said, "There is something about it that is so liberating."

Conquezla didn't bother answering, at that moment he didn't care about the fresh air, just why Philip Houseman was standing on the Veranda of his headquarters.

"What are you doing here Philip?"

Houseman was cheerful and smiled at him. "Louis, I am the Pope's closest confidant. I oversee nearly 800 people in the Vatican and I have the ear of the Pope. I don't take kindly to being kept out of this little secret of yours."

"Secret of mine?" Conquezla replied, "This Order has been

in existence for close to 800 years and during that time its work has gone unrecognised and without reward. Each man in there is dedicated to his role and they do their jobs for the Church. And the only way they can do that is by keeping their mouths shut."

"I need to know about this order."

"Why?" Conquezla shot back. He had clashed with Houseman before during meetings at the Vatican, some arguments he had won, others he had lost, and now as he faced Houseman on the veranda overlooking the gardens, he didn't appreciate the arrogance that the man now once more demonstrated.

"There were times in the past when such an order may have been useful in the defence of the Church." Houseman explained.

"They are not a private army!" Conquezla said. "Their roles are to protect the church against true forces of evil."

Houseman turned to him. "And how many times in the past have we seen attacks on the Church from religious extremists and governments?"

"Too many," Conquezla conceded, "but we are not talking about political motivations here, we're trained to deal with pure evil spirits and demons from the pits of hell."

Houseman wasn't a man to give up and he continued to dig for information. "How many Knights do you have?"

"I can't say."

"Can't or won't?"

"Won't!" Conquezla replied quickly. "You can say it's a need-to-know issue, but you knowing the number Knights doesn't help anyone except your own inquisitive nature. This is a closed order Cardinal Houseman and we do not take kindly to un-invited guests." Conquezla turned to head back inside. "Fr. Jung will escort you to your car and make sure you get safely back to the Vatican."

He turned to go but Houseman called after him.

"Cardinal Conquezla, I am here on the orders of His Holiness Pope Pius XV. I am here as liaison between the Vatican Knights and the Papal Council. I therefore need to know everything that happens here, including how many Knights you have. I shall report back to His Holiness and I shall direct you with his orders." He stepped towards Conquezla who stared hard at him.

In the 24 years Louis Conquezla had been in the order he had never had an outsider try to dominate the actions of the Order, like Houseman was now.

"I want it on the record that I am against this interference." Conquezla said, choosing his words carefully.

"Agreed." Houseman said calmly.

"I also want it noted that if you put any of my Knights in any sort of danger due to your lack of operational experience," Conquezla said forcefully, "I shall personally remove you from these grounds in the most undignified manner!"

"Well," Houseman said smiling and stepping past Conquezla into the Mansion, "we'll see about that."

With his bags packed Julio was ready to leave but the look on Morgan's face as he looked out of the window told him there was a problem.

There was a growing crowd on the doorstep of the church. Morgan had spoken to them earlier but they were now verging on an angry mob demanding answers and shouting questions at him. He had barely managed to close the door as they swarmed forward and continued to bang on the doors and windows.

"Is the pilot ready to fly?" Morgan asked Laura.

She nodded as she hung up the phone. He was ready and as soon as they were on board he would be airborne within minutes. The only problem Morgan thought was how to get to the airport.

Julio looked out of the window and saw the throngs of people shouting and chanting outside the church.

"We could go and talk to them again?" he suggested, but he knew it was a bad idea. With the media riling the public into a mad frenzy, the people outside wouldn't listen to logic or explanations. Morgan knew that those inside the church were going to have to force their way out.

Morgan was quickly striding from window to window trying to find a weakness in the crowd and then he saw it.

"Follow me." he said grabbing Julio's bag.

Laura and Julio followed him into the kitchen of the house and he carefully opened the door he had smashed down the day before. He turned to his companions.

"These walls on the left back onto the front of the church and the courtyard, however these other two don't. The far one there backs onto the street and this one here backs onto some waste land." He pointed to the walls in turn as he spoke.

"So we go for the waste land?" Laura said sizing up the wall she would have to climb over.

"The road," Morgan corrected, "we know it's flat so when we land we won't shatter our ankles; we'll already be in the right place to get a car and get out of here."

"You're stealing a car?" Laura asked.

"Borrowing one for the work of God." Morgan said smiling at her. Julio nodded in agreement and the three of them quickly skipped across the grass to the far wall.

Once outside the confines of the church, they could hear the chants and jeers from the people at the front and it unnerved them to realise how close they were.

But the chants and shouting were different now, gone were the individual calls for help and guidance. The voices were more uniform and there was conformity in their shouts for the priests blood and death to the church.

The three of them hunkered down next to the wall in the shadows but as they did they didn't see a long fingered claw creep over the top of the wall where Morgan had previously climbed. Elongated arms reached over and a long snout sniffing the air followed it.

With its thick rear legs it pushed off the wall and landed silently on the grass where it lay down and stared hard at the three partially hidden people by the wall. Known as a Zyphill Chameleon it followed its namesake and its skin began to change colour to that of the grass with darker hues to signify the shadow that fell across its back.

Between the three of them, it was decided that Julio would climb the wall first followed by Laura and then Morgan but the plan was shattered as a piercing scream ripped through the air.

The three of them turned to face the garden but couldn't find the source and as they stood there watching the empty space a man sprang over the wall and landed in a crouch beside the Zyphill.

He looked up at the two priests and his red eyes glowed at them. He smiled and revealed blood stained teeth and mouth.

"Those aren't humans out there!" Julio said reaching for his Celestial Sword. Morgan agreed and he too drew his sword.

Laura crouched down by the wall as the two priests flicked and extended the blades and began to circle the possessed man. He looked almost normal, but there was a pale blueness to his skin. The skin was beginning to hang loosely from the body, draping down from his face and arms. The hair was thin and there were clear blood patches where the hair had been pulled out.

Beside him the grass flickered and the spiky hump backed shape of the Zyphill revealed it's self.

"That definitely isn't a human!" Julio corrected himself.

"What is it?!" Laura screamed.

"A Zyphill Chameleon."

"A what?" she shouted back, backing away from the scene, edging closer to the wall.

"I'll explain later!" Morgan shouted, holding his sword ready for any attack that may come.

The Zyphill now held their attention and as they circled round it, the creature snapped its jaws, casting looks between the two priests, almost as if it were deciding which one to devour first. Morgan rotated his wrist, as if limbering up his limbs, allowing the sword to circle around in the air. The Knights were always taught to never strike first and defend second and it was with this mantra that both men waited for the attack.

They watched the Zyphill carefully and they saw it tense its muscles and leaped forward like an electrified frog towards Laura but the two Knights were ready; Morgan reacted first and the sword whistled through the air and sliced through the Zyphill's rear leg.

It fell to the floor and turned on him only to have Julio sweep down and carve out an arc on its back. The Zyphill screamed out the same piercing shrill they had heard earlier as it swung round with its front claw towards Julio. He stepped back and deflected the blow and as he did he swung the sword to his right and ripped through the arm of the demonised man who continued to advance on Julio as if not feeling the cold steel as it ripped through his skin.

Morgan took a step forward to protect his friend but a sharp kick from the Zyphill's able rear leg caught him in the chest. Julio though, still had room to manoeuvre and he tracked back and to the side to avoid the slashes and grasps from the man. The sword sailed through the air and caught the man and Zyphill on each swing, but they still advanced on him.

Julio was focused on the creature crawling towards him, the more dangerous of the two. The possessed man never saw the attack from Morgan who swung hard with his own sword and took his head off in one clean strike.

The body crumpled to the floor and a red mist rose from the wounds as the skin shrivelled and dried in the sun. The evil spirit inside him seeped away and floated over the wall to find another host body.

The Zyphill dodged another strike from Julio and lashed out catching his leg with a sharp claw. Julio cried out in pain and swung hard with his sword. The blade sliced through its foreleg and Morgan too struck down with his sword point first and pierced the thick skin of the Zyphill killing it.

Withdrawing the sword the green blood dripped on the

grass and as each drop hit the ground the blades of grass sizzled and dissolved as the acid eroded it. Quickly Morgan wiped his sword on the body of the possessed man and they rejoined Laura by the wall.

"We've got to go!" he said helping her to her feet.

Julio braced himself and Morgan stepped into his cupped hands and climbed to the top of the wall. Laura reached up and Morgan helped her and lowered her to the road on the other side.

Julio's bag followed but as he himself reached up to start his climb five more wraiths leaped over the wall and into the garden.

Julio saw them and turned to face them.

"Go," he said quietly. "I'll take care of these."

"Jules, no!" Morgan said forcefully, "We need to stick together."

Julio looked up at his friend. "I'll meet you at the airport. Go now!" he said as he grabbed Morgan's foot and pushed upwards causing Morgan to fall off the wall and into the road beyond.

On his own and outnumbered, Julio flicked open his sword once more and stood ready.

"Come and get it!" he said as he ran towards them and swung his sword skilfully.

On the other side of the wall Morgan was banging the wall with his fist.

"Jules no!" he shouted over and over again. Laura was at his side pulling on his arm. He turned to her and saw where she was pointing.

At the end of the street slow moving possessed demonic people were walking towards them. Eyes glowed red as they reached out ready to grab Laura and Morgan.

"We have to go!" Laura insisted, her voice cracking with fear.

"We're not leaving him!" Morgan said, "Jules? Jules?"

"Peter!" Laura snapped at him. He stopped and looked at her, fear and tears welling up in her face. "If he's anything like you he can handle himself, but I need your help! I can't fight off these zombie things." she pleaded with him. "Please! Help me and let's go!"

Morgan cursed himself silently as he saw the tearful woman almost breakdown from fear in front of him. He nodded and grabbed Julio's backpack and led her by the hand down the street. They turned into a narrow alleyway and down into the shadows to avoid the zombies, as Laura had so eloquently put it Morgan thought.

They ran through the narrow alleyways and roads. At each junction Morgan carefully checked around them to make sure the way was clear.

With the wraiths in their way they had to double back the way they came or wait several precious minutes before they could advance.

As they slowly crossed the city Laura had commented on how quiet the city was, so different from when they first arrived. Morgan agreed and hypothesised that the infectious bite of the wraith was spreading quicker than he realised, and that was how so much of the country and continent had been so quickly overrun.

Slowly they stepped into the shadows behind a steel dumpster and Morgan carefully inched his way to the corner and looked out. He scanned up and down the street and saw what he was looking for since leaving Julio at the Church.

A car with its engine running! He quietly called for Laura who joined him at the corner and he pointed it out.

"We'll borrow that." he whispered. "You head to the passenger side."

They counted to three and the pair of them ran out from the shadows and headed to the car. Laura reached the car first so eager and scared to be out in the open that she pulled the door open and threw the bag inside before slamming it shut and locking it.

She turned and saw Morgan reach the door a second later. She was willing him to move faster and get inside when a shadow crossed the windscreen and looking up Laura saw a wraith land on the bonnet. It bent down and the pale dried out skin pulled tight against its cheek bones as it smiled at her.

But it wasn't smiling for long as Morgan's sword sliced through its torso splitting it in two. Laura looked around and saw other wraiths down the street leaping through the air to get to Morgan and Laura as soon as possible.

"You drive!" Morgan shouted as he stood by the driver's door and waited for the wraiths. When they were only feet away the sword glinted in the sun and sailed through the air.

Smooth sweeps of the blade cut through the air, clothes, flesh and bones of the wraiths lay dead at Morgan's feet. He waited a couple of seconds before he climbed into the passenger seat and Laura pulled the car away from the kerb and headed off down the street at speed.

The whole of the city was now deserted with crashed cars scattered along the road. It was as if a war had taken place with bodies lying around on the pavements and in the buildings. Smashed shop fronts and burning buildings lined the streets, and the once busy city of 6 million residents was now deserted like a country village. Morgan and Laura travelled in silence apart from the occasional direction to the airport from Morgan.

Each of them were in their own thoughts with Morgan thinking about Julio and the destruction about them whilst Laura was thinking about her family in Boston.

After what she had seen and learnt so far she knew that a prayer may be the last option open to her and she quietly recited a few words to a God she was starting to believe in.

Ahead of them the airport came into view and they took a turning towards the private airfield. The gate was up and the security was missing as they drove onto the smooth tarmac and headed to the hanger.

Inside the pilot was patiently waiting by the steps of the

jet. Laura parked the car and she and Morgan strode across to the plane.

"It's good to see you Ma'am," he said. "The other passenger is on board."

Morgan and Laura looked at each other and their heads snapped up to the open door as Julio stepped out.

"What took you so long?"

Morgan broke into a huge smile as he skipped up the steps and hugged his friend. "How did you get here so fast?" he asked.

"It's easy when you know the back routes."

"Are you okay? No extra holes or anything in you?" Morgan asked checking his friend.

"I'm fine Peter." Julio said knocking his hands away. "Can we go now?" he asked the pilot.

The pilot shook his head, "We don't have clearance to take off."

"I don't think you'll get it anytime soon. Just get us in the air." Laura said, quickly stepping up the stairs to the plane.

Morgan, Julio and Laura entered the main cabin and the pilot once more closed the hatch and started his taxi run to the runway.

CHAPTER NINETEEN

The plane cruised at 30,000 feet and the weather was clear. They had just crossed into US airspace and continued on their arcing path across the country towards the East coast. The pilot had set the automatic systems and sat back in his confined space as his passengers in the main cabin stretched out in comfort.

In the rear cabin Julio had explained how he had defeated the wraiths in the garden and had fought his way through the crowd that had congregated behind the wall. The fight was hard, he said, people reaching for him from every direction and none of them seemed to be hindered as he sliced off arms, and legs of his attackers.

Finally he broke free and headed onto the main street where he found a motorbike lying in the road. He managed to start it and made his own escape, but using his better knowledge of the city he quickly found his way to the airport.

Morgan was pleased that his friend was with him and he smiled broadly feeling that they were getting somewhere at last. He was dialling numbers on his phone while Laura sat opposite him with her eyes closed. Julio sat on the other side of the cabin and looked at the clear blue sky above the wings.

Finally Morgan's phone obtained a signal and it rang, he

put it on speaker phone in the middle of the table and all three of them leaned forward. The crackly, but distinct voice of Cardinal Louis Conquezla answered the call.

"Cardinal," Morgan said, "It's Peter Morgan."

"Peter!" Conquezla said genuinely pleased, "Thank the Lord you're okay."

"I'm fine, I have Julio Yegros here too." Morgan added.

"It's good to hear your voice Your Eminence!" Julio said.

"Julio, are you okay? I heard there was an uprising in Mexico."

"There was," Julio confirmed, "there were a few incidents on the way out but we're heading back to US soil now."

"Where are you now?" Conquezla asked.

"We've just passed into American airspace and we're heading to New York to get a flight to Rome." Morgan said.

"That's good news."

"Gentleman," a new voice came over the phone, "How is it that you've managed to get on a flight? All international flights have been grounded."

Morgan looked at Laura. "We've been loaned the use of a private jet by an associate I was working with in Venezuala." Morgan explained. He knew the next questions and as much as he wanted to, he knew he couldn't lie.

"Who has loaned you a plane?" the man asked.

"Her name is Laura Kennedy and she works for Sunrise Corporation." Morgan said shaking his head as he said it.

"Sunrise Corporation?" the voice was getting tense and Morgan caught Laura's eye. "The very same Sunrise Corporation who's CEO went onto national and international television and denounced the Church and called for a rebellion against us? How could you be in league with such people?"

Laura broke the gaze she shared with Morgan and moved chairs to one at the far end of the cabin away from the priests and the conversation.

"Whatever the CEO has said has no bearing on the help

we are receiving now." Morgan said still watching Laura as she turned away from him. "She is independent of what's happening and has been an ally to us at this time."

"She's there now?" the voice asked.

Morgan didn't know who the voice was and was starting to get annoyed with him. "She is. But before we continue, may I ask who this is?"

"Certainly. I'm Cardinal Philip Houseman; private secretary, personal friend and close confidant to His Holiness Pope Pius XV. I am the newly appointed liaison officer between the Vatican Knights and His Holiness." Houseman said.

"Just the name would've sufficed." Julio said under his breath.

"Cardinal," Morgan said, stifling a smile, "I assure you that there are no issues surrounding our safety, despite the coincidence of them working for the same company."

"I am more worried for the safety of the Church." Houseman said.

Morgan shook his head. "So are we Your Eminence, that's why we're trying to get to Rome. Cardinal Conquezla, what is the current situation?"

Conquezla's voice came back over the speaker. "The Vatican Knights are activated and have been dispatched to protect their regions."

Houseman interrupted, "Seeing that you and Fr. Yegros have deserted your posts in South America your orders are to land in the US and limit the damage of these creatures in whatever city you land in."

Julio spoke up, "Surely Your Eminence that it would be wise to have as many Knights within reach of the Vatican, should any attacks by the dark forces be directed at the heart and soul of the Catholic Church?"

"That is a valid point, but the Vatican is well protected by the Swiss Guards and the Italian Government, and myself and His Holiness believe that will not be necessary." Houseman said.

"We've seen press coverage from the US and they're saying the military are ineffective and are under immense pressure." Julio said.

"What're you implying Father?" Houseman asked coldly.

Julio and Morgan looked at each other, "If the US military is struggling, then how confident can we be with the Italians and the Guards?"

"You have your orders." Houseman replied briskly.

"Cardinal Conquezla?" Morgan asked.

There was a pause as Conquezla thought about his answer. "You and Julio have your orders. You're authorised to follow Directive 32 at your own discretion."

Morgan and Julio looked at each other quizzically. "Can I confirm Directive 32? Three – two Cardinal?" Morgan asked.

"You heard me Peter." Conquezla said. "We must go now. God Bless and May the Lord keep you both safe."

The line went dead and Morgan shut the phone.

"Directive 32?" Julio asked, "What's going on there?"

Morgan nodded in agreement. "He wouldn't give that order unless something major was happening."

From the rear of the plane Laura turned back to them. "What is Directive 32?"

Julio answered, leaning back in his chair. "In the years that the Vatican Knights have existed they have always been under the control of one man. Currently it's Cardinal Louis Conquezla and he reports directly to the Pope. There has never been a liaison officer between the Knights and the Holy See. It sounds as though Cardinal Houseman has created a post for himself and positioned himself within the Order and is now trying to run things."

"And Directive 32?" Laura asked.

"Is an order stating that we should ignore all previous orders and get back to Rome as soon as possible." Morgan said. "Houseman isn't privy to our directives so will think that we're following his orders." he added with a hint of distaste.

"I get the feeling that you don't like this Cardinal

Houseman?" Laura asked rejoining her place at the table.

Morgan and Julio shared a knowing look. "I've never met him, but from what I've heard, Cardinal Philip Houseman is very ambitious." Julio said. "In the past 25 years there have been three popes. At each of the secret elections, called conclaves, where the College of Cardinals chooses a new pope, the rumour goes that Houseman was nominated at each of the last two conclaves. He didn't get through to the final round of votes.

"The reasons why he didn't, we don't know, but everyone knows he wants the top job more than anyone."

"It could be for that very reason that he wasn't elected." Morgan added.

"That's what I think." Julio agreed. "Anyway during the last conclave he was out of the running from the off, however a close friend of his was still in with a chance. A Cardinal Oskar Savasci, was a big name on the international stage, well respected within the College and Vatican and Houseman started to shadow him everywhere.

"Well, Savasci was finally elected pope after two weeks of debate and discussion and he became Pope Pius XV. To reward Houseman for his help and support, Pope Pius appointed him as personal secretary and he is using this new found influence to position himself to be elected Pope at the next conclave."

"I would bet large amounts of money that Houseman wasn't pleased to be left out of the loop with regards to the Vatican Knights," Morgan said, "only the Pope and the head of the Knights know of our existence. When he found out I could imagine him being rather perplexed and put out. Now he's muscled his way into the Order to try and influence things and show everybody he's a leader. Conquezla obviously isn't happy about it so hence the reason for Directive 32 and we'll head to Rome as we were going to."

Laura shook her head. "I can't believe how political it all is."

Julio smiled at her. "It's one of the worst political

cauldrons to be in Miss Kennedy, and we're now in the middle of it."

In Switzerland Cardinal Conquezla sat in his large office quietly staring at the manicured gardens outside across his balcony. It had been an hour since he had spoken to Morgan and he quietly prayed that no harm would come to him to or his other Knights.

Those Knights who had managed to attend the meeting had been dispatched to their assigned regions to protect as best as they could. He saw all of them as his sons and he had made a particular effort that day to speak to each one privately and discuss their fears, hopes and dreams.

They all knew that this was a dangerous time and for some they may not see the conclusion of the ensuing battle, so Conquezla listened to his children as they spoke about happier times and dreams and ambitions they had yet to fulfil. For some he took their confession and absolved them of their sins. Clean souls would lessen the burden on their shoulders, he thought.

One by one the Knights left the Swiss Chalet until only Conquezla and the few remaining Knights-in-training remained with the brash, bold and unwelcome presence of Cardinal Houseman.

Conquezla was frustrated that the Order that he was honoured to lead was being interfered with by Houseman. Thankfully, Conquezla told himself, Houseman hadn't been briefed on the training details of the Knights.

He wanted to keep some secrets and Conquezla vowed, as did all of the Knights, to take these secrets to the grave and beyond.

There was no knock on the door as Houseman entered the office. Lined with bookcases and colourful frescos the office reached up to the high ceilings on all side and the bare wooden floor echoed the footsteps of visitors to Conquezla's chamber.

"All of the Knights have gone?" Houseman asked briskly.

Conquezla turned back from the window slowly and

looked at the pompous man. "They have" he replied. "The last left 30 minutes ago."

"Good" Houseman said. "I also see you have received the authorisation of my attendance from his Holiness." He added indicating the letter sat in the middle of the large desk behind which Conquelza sat.

"I have."

"So everything is in order." Houseman said. "Any communications between yourself and the Vatican Knights will be passed through my office who will pass them to His Holiness." He paused for a second and Conquezla watched as the man's mind raced. "I would also like details of the training regime the Knights go through, the entry requirements for joining, numbers of members and where they are stationed." He looked down at Conquezla and smiled a practiced polite smile, but the hidden venom shone through. "Any time this evening will be fine."

Conquezla didn't answer and Houseman turned around and the feet echoed across the floor as he headed to the door. From his desk Conquezla picked up the letter in front of him and read out loud; his voice reaching every corner of the room.

"Authorisation is hereby given to allow Cardinal Philip Houseman access to the Headquarters of the Order of the Vatican Knights and to act as liaison officer between said Order and the office of His Holiness Pope Pius XV during this time of operational activity.

"All information gathered during said period will be passed at the discretion of the Head of the Vatican Knights to the liaison officer as deemed fit to limit the threat to the Vatican Knights." Conquezla looked up at Houseman. "Yes, Philip I have read this letter and nowhere does it say that you should have access to the confidential information such as our training methods and numbers."

Houseman stomped back towards the desk and snatched the letter from Conquezla's hand. "This is not what I drafted!"

"I know," Conquezla replied coolly, "your version had you

near enough taking my position and using the Knights as your own private army."

"How…" Houseman started.

"His Holiness contacted me after you sent your version and I reminded him of the decree passed in 1601 by the Congress of Bishops." Conquezla said standing up. "The Order of the Vatican Knights is a secret order and no persons unrelated to the order should be allowed access to headquarters.

"As you're already here I'll let that one pass, but His Holiness upheld my objection that as a liaison officer you should not be privy to the training methods countless men have kept secret for a millennia.

"This letter, sorry," Conquezla corrected himself with a sly smile, "signed letter gives me permission to pass what information I feel fit to give you. Anything more important that His Holiness needs to hear about I shall tell him personally, as it always has been and always shall be. If you wish to challenge this and change the procedures you will need the backing of the Pope and 100% of the College of Cardinals as stated in the records of the 1658 Congressional meeting. I for one will not back anything you put on the table so you've lost already."

Houseman breathed hard and read the letter once more. "I need to know what's going on!"

"No you don't!" Conquezla replied forcefully. "You may have bullied your way into your current position but it does not give you the right to know everything that is going on. I only see one man as having that role and he has that job until the day he dies!"

The two men stared at each other across the table.

A raw hatred had been brewing between them for years, and now it was coming to its peak. They locked eyes for a couple of minutes.

Conquezla spoke first. "You are not needed here, Cardinal Houseman and I kindly ask you to leave these grounds."

Houseman headed back to the door and opened it, turning

back to Conquezla, "You're Knights will fail. They are facing a greater evil than we can possibly understand. This Order will fall and I will be there to see it happen and when you come crawling back for forgiveness for failing the Church I will see to it that you are removed and excluded from the Church."

CHAPTER TWENTY

"Qualart-el-Manaton, Prysemply wasam-et -tutelm." Kronos chanted again and again as he stood at the newly constructed altar at the top of the Sunrise Corps building.

"The coming of the Dark Lord approaches and we shall serve gracefully for the rest of time. Bakalash tut flutchanta Qualart-el-Manaton!"

Felix Masterson was shackled at his hands and feet against a wall and despite the river of fear that ran through him he continued to watch the ritual. Over the last day he had seen Kronos's demons demolish whole sections of the headquarters building.

Support walls, joists and steel beams had been removed to create a cavernous 15 storey chasm in the heart of the building. Barely structurally strong enough to hold its own weight the building was now officially under the control of Kronos and his growing army of Evil.

He had begged Kronos not to destroy his building he had worked so hard to build, but rebukes about material wealth being worth nothing under the new order of the Dark Lord were directed at him from Kronos, much to the delight of his armed guards.

He now sat crouched on the floor mesmerised by the ritual

in front of him. He couldn't understand the language, but he knew that it was heavily reliant on sacrifice of whatever creatures or people they could get their hands on.

Masterson had watched in horror as a young lady from a department downstairs had been brought up from the recently constructed holding cells and tied down to the floor in the middle of a pentagram drawn in blood.

The chanting had intensified and the synchronised movement of the demonic congregation quickened as Kronos stood over the woman who screamed in terror as a flaming sword appeared at his hands and he shouted out in glee as the sword travelled down and pierced her chest.

Within the blink of an eye her whole body was on fire, but still she screamed, still she called out for help but none came as the crowd continued their chanting.

The ritual was now coming to the end and Kronos stepped away from the pentagram and sat back on his throne of skulls and bones. The chanting died away and gradually the fires that were lit around the room subdued as if being fed off the excited energy of the demons and hellish creatures around it.

The room fell dark and Masterson found he was holding his breath. He dared not let it out in fear of being reprimanded by Kronos.

"The time of His arrival is nearing," Kronos's voice echoed around the room, "he shall come and we shall welcome him. Bear witness Mr. Masterson, for the coming of the Day of Judgement of mankind that you helped create is upon us!"

Masterson shivered in fear as he heard the words. All he ever wanted to do was to help people, his business had only ever had one purpose to help make people's lives better, but there he sat in the shadow of an angel from Hell telling him that he was responsible for the destruction of mankind.

Masterson bowed his head into his arms and began to cry. He was meant to be a strong leader, a powerful businessman, he was meant to control things that were uncontrollable and make people do what he wanted them to do.

For years he had been a master of his world, of his business, but how had it come to be that he was now subservient, he thought. He wished he had been stronger, wished that he had more will and power to stop what was happening.

Was this his fault? Was he to blame? He tried not to think about it. To lose his company was one thing, but to be a part of the destruction of the world was too much for him to contemplate.

The Gulfstream private jet arced around in the sky over New York as the pilot once more tried to contact the air traffic controllers at JFK international airport; but for the 7th time there was no answer. The door to the main cabin was open and Laura and Julio were listening at the door as Morgan crouched on the floor to give them more space.

The pilot turned in his seat and addressed his passengers.

"There's still no response; I've tried all of the emergency channels and the standard frequencies, but there's no answer."

"What can be causing it?" Laura asked nervously as the plane banked once more and headed out towards the Atlantic Ocean before heading back inland.

"I have no idea," the pilot replied. "It's not atmospheric, there must be a problem on the ground."

Morgan and Julio looked at each other and gave knowing nods. Indeed there could be problems on the ground they both thought; but it was the cause of these problems that scared them.

The pilot flicked the radio switch and gave his call sign again but there was still no response. "I'll keep trying," he told his passengers, "I might have to do is an emergency landing without permission at JFK, but I'll circle it for while and see if there's any activity."

The passengers agreed with his plan but Laura asked a question they didn't really want to know. "How much fuel do we have?"

"About 45 minutes worth." The pilot responded checking

the gauges.

Morgan thanked him and the three passengers went back to their seats in the main cabin leaving the pilot to continue his efforts to contact air traffic control.

They sat down and faced each other across the cabin. "So what's the plan?" Julio asked. "We land, we refuel, we fly to Rome?"

Morgan nodded, "That's it. The sooner we get back there the better. I'll feel safer within the walls of the Vatican than I do here."

Laura looked at the two priests. "What about me?"

For the first time Morgan gave the question a thought. He was so determined to get to Julio and then to Rome that he never once gave Laura a thought. She had, after all, provided the transport of them both to US airspace and he was planning on using the company plane again to get to Rome.

Julio and Morgan exchanged glances. They both knew they couldn't leave her alone; they hadn't been updated to the full extent of events in the US or across the world, but they knew it was bad. To leave her would lead her to her demise and neither of them could live to face the guilt of doing that. The only safe and sensible option would be take her with them.

"You'll come with us, it'll be safer that way." Morgan said.

Laura sat back relieved that she finally knew where she stood in the mix of things. For the past 48 hours she had been following Morgan as he raced back to Europe and she only felt as though she was holding him back. Now she felt she could help in some way, now that she knew they would be sharing the same goal.

"So how…" she started to say.

The plane shook violently and the lights shimmered and blinked on and off. None of them were strapped into their seats and the plane tilted to a 45 degree angle. Julio fell out of his seat and hit the cabin wall hard. Morgan clung on to the seat but lost his grip and fell off the chair hitting the table.

Glasses, cups and other loose objects started to fall

forwards towards the cockpit; they were losing altitude fast.

The plane tossed again and the opposite wings dipped throwing the passengers across the cabin once more. Laura hit the wall and the wind was forced from her lungs as she rolled onto her back and quickly shielded herself from the broken glasses falling on them.

Morgan was tangled up on the floor of the plane but he managed to find a foothold to steady himself and eased himself up to look out of the window across the wing.

He saw two Hashalanth scouts flapping their wings next to the plane and taking it in turns to attack them. One came in close and its sharp claws ripped a hole in the wing and punctured the fuel tank. The scrapping of their nails on the steel caused sparks and the fuel ignited.

The plane dipped and rolled and headed down to the once busy streets of Manhattan. The pilot struggled for control, pulling on the controls, trying to bank the plane away from the attacks. The fire trail from its wing illuminated the night sky as the plane descended to the deserted streets. The Hashalanths gripped the plane, squeezing the fuselage and the claws tore through the fragile skin. The speed of the plane decreased as the attackers pulled the plane back, and like a toy, tossed it through the sky and down towards the streets.

In between buildings it flew narrowly missing the 40 storey skyscrapers. The pursuing Hashalanths continued their attack and forced the plane into a spin. As it quickly passed the 100 feet mark the wings clipped the road and were torn off. The plane flipped end over end with its tail crashing into a building and the other wing being taken off, sending the plane crashing into the street.

The speed was still enough to carry the plane forward, only the fuselage remained and it rolled and skidded through the narrow streets and headed for the river. As it entered a clearing the fuselage rolled onto its side and broke in two, the tail section breaking free.

The rear section rolled away from the river and came to a

stop, but the front portion continued its perilous journey and flew off the jetty and into the Hudson River.

Laura, with cuts and lacerations on her face and arms was horrified to see the water quickly rise inside the cabin. The nose of the plane pointed towards the surface and the water entered from the hole in the cabin below left by the rear section.

As they hit the water she saw Julio unconscious fall from his place under the seats and into the water and she had no idea where Morgan was. She scrambled up onto the fixed seats and tables and climbed as best as she could away from the oncoming water touching her feet at every step.

She reached the cockpit door and opened it but was met by the battered dead face of the pilot who hung from his seat. Above her through the glass she could see the surface of the river gradually get further away as the fuselage sank. She watched it go every second a little more out of reach. As she stood and stared at the darkening gloom above her she never saw the silver hand reach up from the water beneath and make a grab for her leg.

She never saw the silver skinned demon with pure black oval eyes glide silently beneath her as it dragged her down under the water.

CHAPTER TWENTY -ONE

It was an unusually dark night in Moscow as Fr. Petrov Badenski walked across the huge expanse of ground that was Red Square. He looked up at the towering walls of the buildings around him and at the elegant domed figure heads of St Basil's in front of him. How times had changed in his life time, he thought as a cold breeze stung his face. He had lived through the aftermath of the Second World War, the Cold War, the rise and fall of the Communist Party and the KGB. He had lived through so much, and he feared that his end was coming.

There was not another person in sight, although buildings were lit and the street lights were ablaze. Something wasn't right and from under his long coat, Badenski clutched the hilt of his concealed Celestial Sword.

Following the briefing he and his fellow Knights had had with Cardinal Conquezla they were all weary about the evils that were now amongst them.

He had trained for the majority of his life within the priesthood for a moment like this, but now he faced true evil he wanted nothing more than to be back at his parish reading bedtime stories to the orphaned children he helped look after.

He had previously served within the Soviet Army and as

he walked across the roadway that once was the parade ground of his country's military might, he thought back to his early days in the army and found solace and strength at the memories of the man he used to be.

Now, with his years nearing 60, Badenski could feel the end coming.

He heard the words of Cardinal Conquezla run through his head, he remembered the meeting he attended in Switzerland, and how his brother Knights could be facing their own end. He stood alone in Red Square, but in his heart he knew his soul was in the company of angels and his brothers already.

High in the sky the huge winged shape of a Hashalanth circled through the clouds. High above in the shadows of the night it banked round and missed the dome of St Basils by an inch. Its eyes were set on one man only.

Badenski only heard the rushing air at the last minute as he turned and faced the oncoming attacker. Claws sharpened, teeth dripping with blood, the Hashalanth silently swept across the cobbled square and with its talons grabbed Badenski from the street and with no effort from the muscular legs it ripped his torso apart dropping the remains back into the square.

The Hashalanth cried out in joy and swooped back down into the streets to find its next victim.

Fr. Alan Wythall swung his sword as one of the 6 muscular arms of the Hentexberg demon reached out to slash at him. The Hentexberg was 12 feet tall, with three arms on either side of its body. It had the ability to climb and swing across chasms, and as it chased Wythall up the steel structure of the Sydney Harbour Bridge, its dexterity was clearly evident.

The horned Hentexberg swung through the maze of the bridge girders, releasing its grip and grabbing onto the next steel beam. The muscular body, and double hinged jaw, snapped and salivated with anticipation at the thought of capturing its prey. Wythall ran as hard as his lungs and legs would take him.

He had fought his way through a hundred possessed men and women; he had cut down dozens who had tried to stop him; he was repenting his sins and praying to God for forgiveness as he was forced to make his escape up the bridge.

The Hextenberg screamed out as it swooped gracefully across the bridge, the noise was deafening and Wythall clutched his head as the noise pierced his ears.

He knew he couldn't outrun the demon, it was too strong, and he was too old. His lungs ached and burned, gasping for air as he took another step forward. In his attempt to escape the massed hordes in the streets he had sustained a laceration to his shoulder and leg.

Although at the time he managed to escape, the adrenalin was wearing off and the pain was creeping across the wounds and through his body.

Finally, he reached the highest point of the iconic bridge and looked out across the harbour. He had been up here a number of times and with each visit had looked out and stared in wonder at the scene below him.

The calm waters, the warm glowing sunset, the gentle hustle and bustle from the streets as the night life slowly awoke; he loved this city, he loved everything about it.

But as he stood there now looking at the crimson skies and storm clouds approaching, he dreaded the future. He had seen in a few days the whole of his city, the whole of the country and in fact the whole of the world slip under the spell and possession of the Dark Lord.

In those final moments of his time on earth, Fr. Wythall remembered how the infestation of the demons spread across the world so quickly that there wasn't enough time to react. He cursed himself for not having the foresight to react sooner.

Why didn't he attack those early demons sooner, he could've saved more lives.

Beside him a heavy weight landed on the walkway and Wythall saw the Hextenberg in front of him. The demon bore its teeth, each like a three inch nail glistening in the fading light. If it could smile, Wythall thought, it was smiling now.

Slowly Wythall found his feet and held his Celestial Sword firmly in his hand. He knew he couldn't win, but he wasn't going to let his demise be an easy victory. With his remaining strength he ran at the Hextenberg and swung his sword. The blade cut through the air and sliced at one of the demons arms.

A shrill erupted from the demon who swung another arm and caught Wythall on the chest. The powerful force sent the priest off the side of the bridge and down towards the turbulent waters of the Sydney harbour.

His body landed with a sickening crack on the waters and Wythall was barely conscious as the elongated silver snout, lined with miniature horns from the nose to the eyes emerged from the waters and snapped shut over his body.

Cardinal Conquezla stood in front of the banks of screens and watched as news reports from across the world flooded in around him. Every news outlet they watched in every language they could understand had the same story.

The demons of hell were rising.

China, Australia, India and Pakistan were all affected by the demons. No matter what religion there was, the demons attacked. Africa was literally on fire and fire and brimstones rained down on the dry plains.

The Middle East and the devout Muslim quarter of the world were affected. Conquezla shook his head as he saw the pain and suffering that billions of people were enduring.

Similar images of the reporters telling the stories while running for their lives as demons chased and killed them. Around the world religious fanatics were using the events to try and further their own cause.

"Bring down the church!" one protester was shouting on the monitor as a winged, horned fire breathing eagle came swooping from the sky and picked the protester up.

It was chaos across the globe.

In only a few short days the tentacles of evil had stretched across the world and humanity was fighting for survival against an enemy half of which never believed in. Most of the population didn't believe and belong to an organised religion, but that didn't matter now Conquezla thought. He turned from the monitors as Fr. Jung handed him a note. He read it three times before he looked up.

"I need to speak to His Holiness at once." he said, his voice rasping and dry.

Conquezla wasn't surprised to find Cardinal Houseman sat with the Pope as he entered. Formal greetings were passed and Conquezla passed the Pontiff a document. Houseman held his hand out for one of his own, but Conquezla ignored him and sat down.

"Your Holiness, media reports indicate that the attacks are worldwide," Conquezla said, "it's just not Catholics that are being attacked, Muslims, Jews, Hindus, Buddhists, atheists, everyone is subjected to the evil."

"How many are dead?" Pope Pius XV asked.

Conquezla thought for a moment, "It's difficult to say. We're monitoring all media from all countries, but it looks as though it could be in the millions, even an estimate of tens of millions would be low."

"And what about you're precious Knights? How are they fairing?" Houseman asked.

Conquezla knew that the question was coming, "We have suffered some losses." He said.

"How many?" he asked.

"Too many." Conquezla answered.

Houseman sat up straight, "So they have failed, as I said they would."

"Their purpose was never to fight a war, just to protect as best as they could." Conquezla said.

"Then what was the point of them? If they weren't going to stop these things then I really can't see the reason for them."

The Pontiff raised his hand to stop Houseman. "We are in the midst of a major incident Philip, such negativity is not helping."

"Your Holiness, I agree that these are grave times, but there has to be some sense of reality here. The US is over run by demons and if they can't defeat these things with all the weaponry and military strength they have, then what hope have we got?"

"Faith!" the Pontiff answered. "This is a terrible time but there are people across the world that will be turning to the church for support, help and guidance. We can only give that if we believe there is hope. Such comments like yours are not conducive to the safety of the world."

"I understand that, but so far the creatures are closing in on us here, we haven't had a direct attack here in the Vatican, but it won't be long before there is one." Houseman said, "What are we going to do when they come knocking at our door? Prayer and hope won't help us."

Conquezla was shocked by this response. "And what would you suggest?"

"Conversation. Open a dialogue with these things and try to come to some sort of truce."

"A truce!?" Conquezla almost shouted. "A truce is only useful when there's a stalemate and each side is making no advance. Look out there Cardinal, watch the news, we're on the back foot and we're losing ground quickly."

"Cardinal Conquezla," Houseman said calmly, "We have tried your approach and it hasn't worked, we are praying everyday but nothing is getting better, the only avenue we haven't tried is diplomacy and discussion. Let us forego your Knights and try the road of discourse."

"Discourse and discussion cannot help when there is no dialogue with the opposition. We must fight to defend." Conquezla retorted, agitated at the overt calmness of Houseman.

Houseman smiled at him, but it had no sense of warmth,

only malice. "That is not our way."

It was too much for Conquezla to hear and he gathered his papers and with no grace and civility stood and stormed out of the office, slamming the door behind him.

Houseman slowly folded his papers away and spoke to Pope Pius. "Such actions are unbecoming of a Cardinal. His position should be brought into question, as should his role as head of the Vatican Knights."

Pope Pius spoke quietly, "I agree, but he is passionate about the protection of the Church."

"As am I."

"As we all are," Pius countered, "but his knowledge about these beings is needed. He shall remain in post and we shall continue to use his Order. For if you disagree with their actions and necessity, I believe they are aiding and assisting our efforts."

In his private suite of rooms in a newly completed infirmary Pope Pius knelt before the alter that sat in an alcove along the wall. A golden cross, intricately decorated with jewels sat at the centre, with small candles burning slowly around it. He was in the medical facility having an annual heart check-up, a condition he acquired from an illness he had as a small boy. It was nothing serious but his doctors insisted on a complete physical each year.

Unfortunately, whilst he was in the new wing which was attached to but not yet a part of the sanctuary of St. Peter's Basilica, he was not protected against evil forces as afforded to all other Catholic establishments throughout the world. This would only happen when the new infirmary was officially consecrated later in the year.

Pope Pius had seen the news reports on the television and had been reading the information supplied to him, and it scared him. The images he had seen raced through his mind and with millions of people being attacked across the globe, they were all turning to the spiritual leaders for help.

The churches across Rome were packed with people

praying and asking God for help. However St Peter's itself was empty, they had reasoned that it was too dangerous to have such a centre piece filled with a congregation. Pius had reasoned that should anything happen and the walls of St Peters were breached, they would merely be offering the bodies and souls of those trapped within the Basilica to the creatures.

They all wanted questions answered, they all wanted guidance, but what could he tell them? Was everything going to be alright? Could he really tell them that? Would God intervene? If He was going to, why hadn't He?

Pope Pius truly wanted to help, but as he knelt before his altar he felt no guidance, no inspiration.

He felt helpless and he began to weep.

With his head bowed as he recited the prayers that trickled through his mind, a cold wind blew across him and the candles were extinguished. He looked up and around him, and couldn't see the source of the airflow, but as he crossed himself and stood, he caught a glimpse of a shadow in the corner.

"Who's there?" he asked. "Show yourself!"

He fixed his attention on the shadow and watched as it glided out and across the floor.

"I am the darkness," a voice whispered, "You are the light."

Pope Pius looked around himself for the source of the voice, but there was none.

"We are opposites, we serve different masters," the voice continued, "the day comes soon when you will suffer, and the Dark Lord will dominate this world and you will perish."

"Who's doing this?" Pius asked.

"The banished angel." The voice replied.

Pius watched as the shadow slowly moved towards him, and he backed away.

"Who?" he asked again.

"Lucifer!" the voice said as the shadow covered Pope Pius's feet and gradually covered his legs, his waist and body, and finally his head.

Pius tried to shout for help, but the shadow wrapped tightly around his chest and constricted his movements. He fell to his knees as the shadow moulded itself to him and seeped into his skin and with a spasm and frantic shudder Pope Pius lay still on the floor, possessed by the Dark Spirit.

The new medical wing was as modern as any hospital. Modern equipment adorned the walls and the bright lights reflected off the floor and immaculately clean surfaces.

At the far end of the corridor the double doors burst open and a hospital gurney came crashing through with nurses and doctors jogging alongside as the patient was assessed.

Pope Pius had his robes unceremoniously opened and heart monitors and blood pressure machines were hooked up to him as the gurney was pulled to the side and into another private room, emblazoned with the seal of the Vatican.

Following behind the bed were Cardinals Conquezla and Houseman, both as anxious and nervous as each other as they watched with the other dozen people who had followed the gurney, the Pontiff being assessed by the doctors. They were about to enter the room, when a stern looking nurse ordered them all to stay outside and the door was shut closed on them.

Houseman shook his head, deep in thought and as he walked past Conquezla he muttered, "Where's your precious Knights now to stop this?"

CHAPTER TWENTY-TWO

Fr. Peter Morgan slowly opened his eyes and managed to look around. He was in an alleyway, tall buildings reached up high towards the grey sky around him. He sat up and gently touched his head checking for serious wounds. He was cut and bruised, but thankfully nothing seemed to be broken.

Very carefully he got to his feet and leaned against the wall as the dizziness hit him. His mind swirled and span as the memories of the last minutes inside the plane replayed themselves.

He remembered the Hashalanths, the plane being out of control and he remembered the tail section being ripped off and falling away towards the city streets. He looked around and found items belonging to the plane; the plush cushions, seat belts and the chairs, and there at the end of the alleyway was the tail section itself.

Morgan stumbled down the alleyway towards the tail, and as he shifted he suddenly realised it was snowing.

So numb was his sense of touch, that he didn't feel the ice cold flakes fall on his face. The cold wind brushed across the city, wrapped around his cheeks, but he felt nothing. He looked up at the sky and saw the thick clouds above him but there was something else there, something that made the whole scene more sinister. He watched the sky for a moment and then he saw it. There was a flash behind the clouds but there was no noise. Again and again flashes in the sky illuminated the clouds, showing the true colours of crimson red and black. It was as though a thunder storm was closing in, but whilst there was lightning, there was no thunder.

The whole city was quiet, not silent, but deathly quiet. There was no traffic, no hustle and bustle that he had experienced the other times he had visited New York. The whole place had a different feel to it but Morgan couldn't quite place what was missing, or what was different.

It could've been the shock from the crash, the near miss of hurtling through the air and surviving, or it could've been the lack of sleep and cloud of tiredness that was finally creeping up over him.

As he climbed to his feet he stumbled and crashed hard into in a steel dumpster. Pushing it against the wall, the crash echoed along the alleyway. Further down the alleyway Morgan saw some movement, shadows at first, but then those shadows became distinct shapes and they moved towards him.

They moved slowly, but steadily towards him, and through the pain pacing around his body, Morgan could see that their movements were jagged, difficult and very familiar. They were the poor victims of the wraiths, and they were coming for him.

Morgan backed away from them, trying as best as he could to keep to the shadows. He moved away into the silent city, but the cries of the wraiths following him nipped at his heels as he stepped out into the street and the bitter wind awoke his still drowsy and drained mind.

The streets were deserted and Morgan moved quickly across the road, around a corner and into a shattered shop front. The windows were smashed, the door broken off; the vandals had had fun, Morgan thought.

He stumbled through the deserted streets, and at each intersection waited and watched for any sign of movement. There was no traffic, the remnants of the destruction of society evident as the crashed cars littered the streets. Shop windows and store fronts were smashed and the contents sprawled everywhere. It wasn't a riot, it wasn't looting, Morgan thought, it was carnage and the evidence in front of him told him that this army wasn't interested in material personal gains.

Ahead of him a group of wraiths approached crashing through the streets. Morgan carefully fell back into the shadows and into a shell of a store. He watched as they came closer and then, one of them stopped.

Morgan looked at the man, apparently a former police officer from the look of his tattered uniform. The wraiths skin was pale and tight over the bones, seeping with blood at the edges as it peeled away from its eyelids. The eyes were glazed over, grey like an approaching storm cloud.

It seemed to be smelling the air, almost like a hound tracking its prey with disjointed movements, the wraith entered the store front and began to prowl, and hunt for Morgan. The other wraiths outside the store had noted the divergence and they too began to enter the store.

Morgan had the hilt of his sword, he flicked the blade out and readied himself ready to strike.

He was about to jump up and attack when a hand clasped down onto his. He turned and saw a man reaching out from under a pile of clothing. He was dressed in camouflage fatigues and he signalled for Morgan to be quiet.

He wasn't a wraith, and as Morgan tried to gather his breath at the sight of the man, he saw other movements around him. To his right another camouflaged man appeared, and further along, a woman emerged from under a table.

They were all armed with guns, and Morgan watched as they professionally moved forward and at the same instant they proclaimed their presence to the wraiths and opened fire.

The persistent chattering of the machine guns filled the air with burnt cordite and Morgan saw the spits of fire from the barrels of the guns spatter bullets into the bodies of the wraiths.

Within seconds the carnage was over and the soldiers stood proudly over their prey.

The first soldier pressed his voice-mic and spoke, "Echo one, four Tango's taken down." He listened to the reply over his earpiece and then turned and looked at Morgan. "Copy that. We also have a civilian here sir. Looks like he's been through a lot – Copy that. You're coming with us." he said to Morgan.

Morgan followed the soldiers as they ducked and weaved through the derelict buildings. Flanked either side by an armed man, Morgan didn't ask any questions as they led him across the city and down into the subway.

They passed empty ticket stalls and passed through the barriers, stepping over the remnants of bodies and decaying corpses that had been attacked and destroyed by wraiths. They descended the steps towards the lower tunnels and emerging into the flicking lights of the remains of a subway station, the soldiers and Morgan climbed down onto the tracks and began to follow the rails deep into the darkness.

His eyes were becoming accustomed to the low light and he was beginning to make out the shape of the tunnels and the small alcoves that were built into the walls. After 10 minutes of walking the soldiers stopped and stood in the darkness in silence.

Ahead of them, Morgan saw torches flicker and dance off the walls and floor and as they stood there, the lights came closer and soon Morgan was facing 6 more soldiers, each equally armed with the leader of this group flashing his torch in Morgan's face.

"Is this him?" he asked.

"It is."

The leader looked at Morgan, sizing him up. He nodded at one of the other men who stood in front of Morgan and indicated for him to lift his arms up to be searched. "What's your name?" the leader asked as the soldier ran his hands over Morgan.

"Fr. Peter Morgan."

The soldier found his Celestial Sword and showed it to his

superior. "And what's this?"

"A tool." Morgan said simply.

The two men stared at each other in the glow of the torches, and Morgan could guess at the conclusions the man was coming to. He wanted to know where this priest had come from, and if he was really a priest. After a minute the man turned and ordered his team to bring Morgan with them.

They had followed side tunnels from the main subway line and eventually passing through a metal door set into rock face, the soldiers and Morgan entered a large expanse where Morgan estimated about 100 people were busy rushing around.

Some were soldiers, sitting at radio transmitters and checking weapons, others were clearly civilians, scared and crying into their neighbours shoulders. As he was led through the bodies Morgan saw a man near the far wall, reading quietly to himself, immersed in his bible.

The soldiers took Morgan to a small ante room and inside there sat a powerfully built man, short grey hair, hardened face and eyes of passion and determination that could only come from fighting on a battlefield.

The insignia on his shoulders had him at the rank of General, and as he stood up to shake Morgan's hand, Morgan felt the strength in his grip.

This man is ready for war, Morgan thought.

"Father, I'm General Samuel Bailey. I hope my men didn't scare or offend you?" he said, indicating for Morgan to sit down.

Morgan gladly accepted the seat. "Not at all General. It's good to see friendly faces."

Bailey smiled and ordered a medic to attend and see to Morgan's wounds and for drinks to be brought to them. "It's not very often we find someone like you walking the streets. My men conduct patrols everyday, and you Father, are the first man we've come across who hasn't been attacked by those zombies."

Morgan smiled to himself. The word zombies was an appropriate description of the wraiths, popularised from the media and movies. He thought about correcting the General, but figured that at this time of despair, the last thing he needed was a patronising priest to correct him.

"How did you come about to be here?" Bailey asked.

Morgan took a breath. "Our plane crashed." he said, "Myself and two friends were travelling back from Venezuela to get to Rome when we were attacked by those things. It brought us down and here I am."

"You survived a plane crash and walked away? Jesus, you must really have God on your side!" Bailey said laughing loudly. "What about your friends?"

Morgan had no idea what had happened to either Laura and Julio and he shook his head, saying he presumed them to be dead.

"That's war." Bailey said. "In war there're casualties."

Morgan winced as the medic cleaned his wounds on his face and he turned to Bailey. "I need to get to Rome."

"Rome?" Bailey said, "Not likely padre. There're no flights anywhere. All commercial and military flights have stopped. It's chaos."

Morgan's heart sank and he fractionally slumped into his seat. If there was no way back to Rome, then there was no way he could protect the Vatican. Morgan looked around himself and watched as the men and women continued to carry out their duties. They appeared to be coping well, given the circumstances, Morgan thought, but maybe it was the military training that was allowing them to hide their true feelings.

Despite their professionalism, he could still sense their fear, their doubts, their anxiety and trepidation.

"What's happened here?" Morgan asked.

Bailey stood up and began to pace around the room. "I command, I used to command I should say, just over 500 men. We were tasked to counter the offensive moves of these things and with every military capability available to me we pounded their lines and held them off. With attack helicopters buzzing them we sent nearly half a million rounds of ammunition into them, yet they still kept coming. The bullets stopped them, but there was always another 3 behind them waiting to attack.

"They moved quickly, some of those creatures leapt from building to building, and those things with wings would come down and pick my men off the ground and just toss them aside." Bailey stopped and looked around him, "Needless to say we were outnumbered, and they soon overran our lines. We fell back and dispersed into the streets, but being stretched so thin, we lost more men.

"We needed to regroup and finally we all convened down here and execute guerrilla tactics on them, taking the zombies out whenever we can." Bailey sat down again and leaned forward. "Father, you say you need to get back to Rome, I don't think you'll be safe there. I don't even think we're safe here."

Morgan sat in silence and ran his hands through his hair. He was tired, and he needed sleep, but there was still too much to do. "How many of you are there?"

Bailey looked around him. "Out of 500 men and women under my control, we now number 23. With the 76 civilians out there, we're not an easy group to keep hidden for long." Bailey leaned forward and his voice dropped low, almost to a whisper. "Father, I'm not a religious man, but I can see that those people out there don't need a military leader, they need a spiritual leader. There is a priest among them, Fr. Riddell, but, if you'll pardon my language, he's fucking useless. He just sits reading his bible all day and doesn't help. You say you need to get back to Rome, I think these people could do with your help more."

Morgan remembered the old man sat near the wall and he nodded. It did seem strange that despite everything that was going on, he would be so immersed in the book, perhaps it was a coping strategy. "I've been called back to Rome." Morgan said, "Believe me, I can do more help for these people and the world by being there."

Bailey nodded, but didn't really believe Morgan. "And this

will help you?" he said holding up the collapsed Celestial Sword.

"Yes." Morgan replied accepting it as Bailey handed it over. "It's come in handy."

Bailey watched as Morgan took the item and held it in his hands. During the past week he had seen some of his best and strongest men fight fiercely to the bitter end, and even though those who survived denied it, he knew they were scared. He could see it in their eyes and in the subtle movements of their hands and fingers that shook uncontrollably with nerves and adrenaline.

He could see the same effects in the civilians that his team were now protecting; but as he studied Morgan, he couldn't see these same signs.

"You're unlike any priest I've met before," Bailey said, "you're very calm."

Morgan smiled at him, "I've heard that before," he said, thinking back to his conversation with Laura, "but in these times, calmness and clarity of thought is needed."

Bailey smiled back, the creases and age in his hard battled skin clearly seen. "A sword wielding priest is calm?"

"We have our moments." Morgan said.

From the door, a young soldier, heavily dirtied and battered from days of fighting came rushing into the room and stood to attention in front of his superior.

"Sir," he said, out of breath and trying to stay calm, "we've reports of heavy movement and activity at the Sunrise building."

"More than usual?"

"Yes sir." The young officer replied.

Morgan sat and listened as the officer explained the reports, and as he spoke, Bailey quickly filled Morgan in. Their intelligence seemed to believe that the Sunrise building was the epicentre of everything that was happening. It appeared that the wraiths and demons were all being summand to the building, and the only conclusion they could give was that something big was about to happen.

"There's also another report." the young soldier said,

casting a quick look over to Morgan, "Our spotters have seen two people being taken into the building. A woman, and a man; he looks like a priest."

Bailey looked over to Morgan who was suddenly sitting up. "Your friends?"

"They could be." Morgan said, his mind beginning to fill with hope as he stood up, "I need to go to them. I need to help them."

Bailey stood too and followed Morgan as he left the room, heading the way they had come. "Father, if our intelligence is correct, then that place is a fortress. There is no way anyone can get in there, and with those things ready to kill anything that crosses their path, as soon as you're discovered, and you will be discovered, then they'll rip you apart."

Morgan stopped and turned to him. "Then let them try!"

"Father -"

Bailey reached out to grab Morgan as screams filled the room, and from the far wall, people began to run and scatter. Bailey and Morgan both pushed through the crowds to try and see what was happening, as did Bailey's soldiers, with their guns at the ready.

Against the wall, the old man, the priest, Fr. Riddell, was crouched down, like an animal ready to strike. The soldiers shouted orders and information to Bailey, and in the commotion, Morgan managed to pick out that the man was possessed and attacking people.

He appeared to be a frail old man, but as the soldiers advanced on him, his true abilities were demonstrated as he leapt up and clung to the wall like a spider and as the guns tracked and opened fire on him, the man sprang away from the wall, landed in the midst of the soldiers and with abilities beyond his years, he attacked them.

He clawed at them, pulling them back, ripping at their bodies and armour, tossing them around like rag dolls. The priest seemed immune to their attacks, almost revelling in the barrage of rifle butts and kicks, but still he wouldn't be subdued.

With an almighty lunge, the priest reached out and effortlessly snapped the arm of one of the soldiers before hurling him into the others, sending them scattering across the floor. He was out of breath, and in the poor light, his animalistic behaviour was more threatening.

Morgan watched the scene unfold as his mind flicked back to the description Julio had given of Fr. Alvero attacking him in Mexico. It was happening again, and he found himself with his sword in his hand. A second later he advanced on Riddell.

They faced each other, and neither wanted to strike first, but the temptation for Riddell was too much and he leapt forward. Morgan anticipated the attack and ducked, keeping the sword between him and Riddell as the blade cut through his attackers leg. Riddell fell to the floor and rolled up onto his knees ready to attack again.

Bailey had grabbed his own gun and was helping his soldiers, pulling them back from the scene. He was about to join Morgan in the fight, when Morgan shouted and ordered him to stay back.

Riddell smiled, showing his blood stained teeth as he prowled the floor, circling Morgan. This time it was Morgan to attack first and the sword sailed through the air, missing Riddell, but quickly cut across to the side and sliced through the retreating priests arm, sending him howling in pain. Morgan didn't relinquish his attack as Riddell countered the melee and kicked out and slashed across Morgan's chest.

Morgan fell back and regained his position as Riddell pounced forward and arcing through the air, Morgan span, fell to his knee and thrust the sword up and into the abdomen of Riddell who fell to the floor.

Morgan waited several seconds for any sign of movement from Riddell, but none came. With Bailey now at his side with his gun aimed and ready to fire, Riddell was rolled face up and the bloodied face looked up at them both.

"You're world," Riddell coughed, "will end soon."

The dying priest shouted out in pain and convulsed as he arched his back and from his mouth and eyes, a grey mist seeped out, and travelled across the floor, to the wall and dispersed into the cracks of the mortar, leaving Fr. Riddell's corpse behind.

Bailey led a small team through the tunnels, with Morgan close behind them. All of the soldiers around him were armed and keeping a careful eye on the walls and shadows for any sign they were about to be attacked.

Finally they started to ascend from the tunnels and carefully they emerged into the subway station. Soon they were stepping out into the dying sunlight that cast an orange glow over the New York streets.

The small team quickly found a hidden position where they could observe the street, and as they ducked down low, Morgan's attention was caught as he watched wraiths emerged from around the corner and slowly staggered across the street away from them.

After he had defeated Fr. Riddell, Bailey had agreed to Morgan's hasty request that he try and find and infiltrate the wraith lair, if anything to try and help Laura and Julio.

Bailey had at first refused, but as he thought about the skill Morgan had demonstrated. He concluded that perhaps it was worth a try. With a diminishing number of soldiers available to him, it wouldn't be long before his small resistance unit would be defeated. He had looked the priest in the eye and said, "So we either die now, or die later. Bring it on!"

Now as they waited in the shadows, Morgan was humbled by the sacrifice that Bailey and his men were about to make, just to give him a slight chance to get into the lair.

They carefully moved position and darted from shop fronts to alleyways, to collapsed buildings and against crashed and burnt out cars. Eventually they saw the glass frontage of the former Sunrise Headquarters.

The burning night sky flashing with a kaleidoscope of

colours and patterns spanned out above him. Morgan looked up in amazement at the sight, never before had he seen such a ballet of colour and magnificence. Bolts of lightning, fingers of power cracked and ripped across the sky, all in the same direction, all pointed to the same place.

Morgan followed the line and saw the pinnacle of the Sunrise Corporation building towering high above the city scape of New York; the lightning forking towards it, the blood red clouds gathering around it.

Around them, as if gathering from all across the city, wraiths, Hashalanths, Quazon cats and Martex Solders, standing over 12 feet high with abnormally long arms and long faces with sunken eyes, were making their way to the building. Pyro Angels, Hextenbergs and Zyphill Chameleons all passed before them and all of them were in some sort of trance.

Morgan stayed still in the shadows and watched from across the street as the creatures from hell approached and surrounded the glass frontage of the former Sunrise Corporation HQ. He could see that the building was, previously, a magnificent piece of architecture.

The glass and steel construction, elegantly gliding upwards into the city was standing proud against the other skyscrapers of New York City.

But now it was a hive of activity of evil forces that were wandering the planet. The tentacles of pain, misery, and death reached out from this central hub, and as he crouched down Bailey and his men readied their weapons.

The plan was simple, Morgan would disguise himself with a cloak they had found on the corpse of a wraith and he would join the throng as they approached the building. As he neared, the soldiers would emerge and open fire on them, hopefully distracting them and allowing Morgan a chance to get into the building.

A crowd of wraiths were approaching made up of former citizens of the city, still dressed in their city uniforms. A police officer, office workers, a tourist. Their clothes ripped and tattered, their faces slashed and bleeding and their skin pale and white.

The eyes of the wraiths were blank and empty and with no thoughts behind them. They staggered and stumbled along the street, with the only thought in their minds, to reach the hive and await the command from the master high in the tower.

They stumbled past Morgan and he took his chance with a final look of thanks to Bailey. With his hood pulled across his head and face he fell into step with them. They ignored him and he walked with them into the growing masses of the crowd outside the building.

The masses continued forward and into the building and into the atrium with the mezzanine floor above them. The smell of rotting flesh hit Morgan hard in the face and with his face hidden he could feel himself heaving, wanting to be sick.

He was looking around, trying to find a path, but with the masses of wraiths and demons cramming into the building, he couldn't move.

Suddenly there was the distinctive sound of gunfire and the demons and wraiths turned and shouted. The pressure around him was released and he was free to move as the wraiths and beasts cried out and began to confront their attackers outside. Morgan broke free and headed to a door he guessed led to the stairs.

He pushed and stumbled through the crowd and towards the door. He opened the door and slipped inside and indeed there were stairs leading up. He threw the cloak hood off and began to climb the stairs, in his hand he held the Celestial Sword.

Kronos stood at the shattered window on the top floor of the Sunrise Corporation building. His heavy black cloak danced around him as the wind blew through the window.

He stood and watched the scene below as his army approached and he felt pride in what he had achieved in such a small space of time. His forces had infiltrated the human race, commandeered bodies, spread their disease of evil and hatred and now they were about to launch an attack on the ultimate goal; The

Vatican.

His wraiths now populated 80% of the world; there wasn't a country on the planet that hadn't been touched by his evil and poisoned finger. His army's numbers were great and mighty and it was more than enough to take into battle against the meagre population of 800 people within the Vatican City.

The fight would be swift, he thought. Once done and the Pope had bowed to his power, then the Dark Lord would appear and sit on the throne of mortal men, laughing at God.

It would be a good day, and he would be well rewarded for everything he had achieved. But it was still to come and he had to focus his attention on the immediate future and the task that lay before him.

He turned from the window and faced the two people who had been brought to him. Wraiths held them both tight by the arms as they knelt on the floor, covered in blood and entrails. Laura Kennedy and Julio Yegros looked up at the imposing figure of Kronos. Terrified, shocked and shaking with fear they watched him, watched him closely and watched as he carefully picked up Julio's Celestial Sword.

"An elegant weapon." Kronos said. "A weapon I haven't seen for many, many years. A weapon used by only the most skilled of swordsmen, and the most loyal to the church."

He handled the sword carefully and examined the intricate detail on the hilt. Julio watched as the towering figure turned the collapsed sword hilt around in his hands.

During the training to become Vatican Knights, the recruits are taught a technical skill in how to activate and collapse the sword. It required a subtle flick of the wrist, a gentle extension of the arm and the flick of a hidden switch on the hilt to extend the blade. It was a technique that allowed the sword to be covertly concealed and carried with ease but activated and used quickly when necessary.

The technique was also a security measure so that no unauthorised persons could activate the sword should it ever be lost or stolen. Julio didn't say anything and watched silently as Kronos slowly rotated it.

With a quick flick of his wrist, the near silent sound of the metal blade extended, Kronos had opened the sword.

Julio flinched at the sight of the sword fully extended and the blade reflecting the flickering glow of the fire. The blade was perfect, the edges where the sections of metal joined were smooth, crafted by skilled sword-smiths from years of tutoring and training, with knowledge passed down from generation to generation.

Kronos looked at the blade and then at Julio. "A very elegant weapon." he repeated.

The wraiths holding Julio pulled him to his feet and forced him roughly towards Kronos and, in front of him pushed Julio to his knees.

"The forces of Hell are walking this earth. They are reaching out into every corner, in every country. Everyday more people are succumbing to our power and soon we will have under our control the very seat that you have sworn to protect. But you will not see it. Instead you shall feel the cold blade of your own sword." Kronos said.

Julio struggled against the grip of the wraiths who held him and pushed him forward.

"No!" Laura shouted, struggling against her own wraiths hold. "You can't! Let him go! No!"

Kronos turned to her and bared his teeth in what was almost a smile. "And why can't I?" he asked as he swung the sword around through the air and the blade cut through the exposed back of Julio's neck, his body falling limp and his head rolling forward towards the broken open window and fell out towards the street below.

Kronos laughed loudly at the sight. "You see?" he shouted to the assembled wraiths and demons. "Even in death, he wants to run! Where is your God now, Vatican Knight? Where is he now?"

Still laughing he walked towards Laura and her wraith guards pulled her forwards and pushed her to her knees.

"Do you believe in God?" he asked her.

Laura was choking with fear and tears streamed down her face. "No - no I don't!" she said honestly.

Kronos snorted and ran a bony finger down her face. "You should really. Not that it would do you any good now, but belief is good, it focuses the mind, allows you to see the bigger picture. But it's too late now!"

Kronos stepped back and swung his hand out, the blade of Julio's sword glinting in the light and like a flash it sped towards the back of her exposed neck, slicing through the air.

Laura closed her eyes and waited for the strike but it never came as the clash of metal on metal echoed around the room.

She looked up and saw the two wraith guards sliced dead on the floor beside her and a cloaked figure with their own sword above her neck, blocking the incoming sword of Kronos.

She could see the determined eyes of Fr. Peter Morgan staring and burning hard at the sight of Kronos above her.

CHAPTER TWENTY-THREE

Cardinal Houseman walked briskly through the corridors of the Vatican apartments. He was contemplating his next move, pausing at a high window that was looking out across St Peter's Square.

The Holy Father was incapacitated, possessed by an evil spirit, there was no leadership within the church; there was no leadership within the walls of the Vatican. He loved the church, loved his religion and loved his God; he therefore needed to try and step up and take control of this situation.

His beloved Church was under attack, and Houseman wasn't prepared to stand by and watch as the forces of evil take control and destroy everything that he believed in and worked so hard to protect.

The Church needed action.

The remaining people within the Vatican needed leadership, and the devout people taking sanctuary within churches across Rome and the world, needed to see there was still hope. His mind was made up and he continued down the corridor towards his private offices.

Conquezla stood at the foot of Pope Pius's bed within the infirmary. The repetitive regular beep of the heart monitor was the only sound that filled the room. The Pontiff was still, helpless and, in Conquezla's eyes, feeble. He looked so different from the strong leader that he knew and respected so much, and he turned away, not able to look at the bed ridden figure anymore.

He stepped out of the room and closed the door behind him as Fr. Jung approached him.

"Any change Your Eminence?" He asked, worry clearly seen in his face.

Conquezla shook his head. "No, no change."

"I shall pray for The Holy Father." Jung said, crossing himself. Conquezla nodded and patted the young priest on the shoulder. He admired the dedication of the younger man, but also found his optimism too much to bear. There was only so much prayer could accomplish, and in that it only gave the person praying an inner sense of well-being.

Conquezla himself had been through and seen so much during his years of being a priest that he no longer truly believed in the power of prayer.

He did however believe in the power of man and, should any obstacles be put in their way, it was man's will and strength of being that accomplished what seemed to be impossible.

"Your Eminence," Jung said, walking beside Conquezla, "you've had a message from Cardinal Houseman's secretary."

Conquezla stopped himself from cursing the man. "What does he want now?"

Jung checked the note in his hand. "He requests that all Cardinals available to attend a special conclave in the Sistine Chapel at 3pm to discuss Article 27. Does that mean anything to you?"

Conquezla took the note from Jung and read it himself. "Yes it does." He said, reading it again walking quickly for the exit.

"What is Article 27?" Jung asked, as he strode to keep up.

"Article 27 is a special clause within the minutes of the Congress of Bishops from 1651 that allows a vote to be taken should there be any reason why the Pope can't complete his duties. Houseman wants to vote on electing a temporary Pontiff while His

Holiness is incapacitated." Conquezla responded.

"But that's good isn't it? In this time of peril we need leadership." Jung added.

Conquezla turned to Jung as they walked. "It is, if the chosen person is the correct person for the job, but who do you think Houseman is going to nominate, and do you really see him resigning if we get through this alive?"

The Sistine Chapel was as magnificent as ever. Painted partly by Michelangelo, some consider the Last Judgment fresco one of his greatest accomplishments. The intricate detail of the paintings was magnificent and Conquezla was always in awe of them. But as he entered now and approached the papal throne at the far end of the Chapel, he took no notice of the works of Raphael, Bernini or Botticelli that adorned the walls.

There were 200 Cardinals within the College of Cardinals, and they would all attend the Vatican during the election of a new pope. However as Conquezla strode down between the pews set against the side walls facing each other, there were many vacant seats with only 56 Cardinals in attendance.

Ahead of him, standing at the far end next to the papal throne stood Houseman.

"Cardinal Conquezla," Houseman said, "good of you to join us, at last." He strode across the floor, gliding like a phantom as he stared intently at Conquezla. "As you know," he continued addressing the small congregation, "the Holy Father has fallen ill and our very best doctors are monitoring and caring for him. But the world is under attack from a deadly foe that is infecting the population with evil and death. The highest levels of government across the globe are polluted by these beings, and all attempts to negotiate a truce have been futile so far.

"The people of the world are scared and are looking for leadership, and nearly a billion pairs of eyes and hearts are looking at the church for guidance and spiritual strength. His Holy Father should stand up and give the masses reassurance, but his poor health will make that impossible."

A murmur of chatter broke out amongst the Cardinals. Conquezla was not one of them. He continued to stare hard at Houseman who waited patiently for the noise to quieten down. He could hear some questions being asked.

What should happen? Who should stand up and talk to the world? Is negotiation with the attacking forces an option?

They were questions that Houseman hoped to be raised, and as a consummate politician and statesman, he was ready for them, ready with his answers, ready to lead.

"My Brothers," he said, raising his hands to quiet the room, "these are difficult times. We need a proposal and we need a decision." The nods of approval spread across the sullen faces of the men. "It is for this reason that I have called you here now, why I have done some research, and why I make this proposal to you all now."

Conquezla shifted uncomfortably in his seat. He looked down at the note in his hand, summoning him to the Sistine Chapel. He knew the writing and knew it was in the hand of Houseman himself. As he sat there now listening to the man talk about the good of the Church and the need for leadership, it suddenly struck him.

The note was a pre-emptive disclosure to Conquezla of his intentions. None of the other Cardinals would have any idea of what was coming, what was to be suggested. It was a sickening ploy by Houseman to show how influential he thought he was in front of the College of Cardinals, but it was also a way of embarrassing Conquezla.

"My Brothers, I propose to you now that we enact Article 27." Houseman said proudly. There was silence in the Chapel as the suggestion was absorbed. Houseman looked around at the men, but the faces of shock wasn't the reaction he was hoping for. "We need a show of force from the Church, and this is an option we need to consider."

An elderly French Cardinal spoke up, "Article 27 is a

drastic step to take. It was written at a time when disease and the fear of the Black Death was rife. It was intended to be used when the current Pope was in such an incapacitation that he would never recover. His Holiness is still with us, and still may recover."

"Yes," Houseman said, "you chose the correct word. He may recover. Whatever evil the Pope has fallen under, we don't know if or when he will recover. And if he does, do we know what sort of cognitive functionality he will have? If he can't act as the leader of this Church, then we have no leader."

Conquezla stood up and entered the aisle. "Cardinal Houseman, if your suggestion of enacting Article 27 is approved, by the small number and small proportion of the full College of Cardinals here this evening, who do you propose be selected as the temporary holder of the Keys of St Peter? And for how long would they be in post?"

Houseman gave a slight smile as he faced Conquezla in the aisle. They faced each other like gunslingers in the Old West.

"Those are good questions, and as this is a dire emergency, I feel that we need someone who is ready to stand up and take charge of this situation, someone who won't put all their hope in a group of useless marauders wandering around slicing and dicing anything that moves. We need someone close to the Holy Father who will bravely continue his vision for the church."

"I have no intention of putting myself forward."

"And why should you? You don't hold the respect of your fellow Cardinals like others."

"Like you?" Conquezla asked.

Houseman smiled and looked around at the other Cardinals, watching the two men. "Are you nominating me? I graciously accept." Houseman spun around and headed back to the front of the Chapel. "My Dear Brothers," he called out, "I accept the nomination of Provisional Holder of the Keys of St Peter, as put forward by Cardinal Conquezla. Are there any others who wish to stand against me in this perilous time?"

A silence fell upon the Chapel, the old men looking at each

other for guidance, but none was forthcoming. "Then with one nomination and no objections, we shall vote." Houseman announced.

CHAPTER TWENTY-FOUR

Fr. Morgan continued to face down Kronos who had stepped back after appearance of the Vatican Knight. The wraiths around him were seething and baring teeth at the priest, all wanted to leap forward and attack Morgan, but the over bearing power and presence of Kronos held them back.

Morgan could feel a deepening sense of fear and despair dwell inside him, there was a sense of abandonment and helplessness etching away at the back of his mind and with the imposing figure of Kronos, Morgan could only guess that being there in the central lair of the enemy was sapping all the inner strength from him.

Morgan risked a quick glance over at Laura who was knelt on the blood soaked floor. She was crying hard, whimpering and shaking with fear.

He himself was scared of the situation they found themselves in, but he found it hard to imagine how she felt. As a confessed atheist the whole experience of coming face to face with demons from hell, and creatures she had admitted to not believing in must've been overwhelming to all her senses. With the sight of seeing Julio executed in front of her, the trauma must have been unbearable, and in that instant Morgan knew he had to protect her at all costs.

He had just emerged on the top floor as the blade came slicing down over Julio's neck and he watched with terror and anger at seeing his friend killed. There was nothing he could do for him, but as he saw Kronos advance on Laura, Morgan felt the urge to fight back, and now he stood facing him.

"Another Vatican Knight?" Kronos said, "I thought you were all destroyed?"

Morgan didn't answer and continued to stand up against the demon, sword at the ready. The glinting edge of the blade reflected the low light emanating from the fire and the electrifying skies above them.

"Stand down, soldier." Kronos said. "Your battle is over and the war is lost. Stand down, drop your sword and you shall not suffer the same fate as your friend."

Morgan angled the sword up towards Kronos. "You may have found a foothold on this world, but you shall not be victorious in your master's quest for the destruction of the church. Faith will vanquish you and send you back to the pit that you came from."

The deafening laugh from Kronos reverberated through Morgan's chest as it shook the walls. The Wraiths around them joined in the mocking. "Faith? Faith you say? Faith has no place in the world now. Faith was the last resort of a desperate man who had no solid proof of the existence of the Supreme Being. Here we stand now showing the world that we do exist.

"And where is your God to rebuke us? Where are his angels to fight us off? What sort of God still hides when his beloved creation of man is threatened? What sort of God allows such suffering? A coward does, a charlatan does, a weak and feeble being that is too scared to face his opposition on the battlefield does."

"He will show himself." Morgan said.

"When? And to whom? Your history has been strewn with vague stories of devout people seeing possible sighting of God.

Burning bushes, apparitions, ghosts, all were signs that God supposedly exists but with no solid proof. Well here we are, my dear Knight, proof that the dark side exists and we shall not hide anymore!" Kronos said, taking a step forward, starting to circle Morgan and Laura.

Morgan followed him, not taking his eyes off him. Deep within the back of his mind he knew what Kronos was saying was true.

The Devil had indeed played his hand, showing his strength and ability to infiltrate all walks of life on Earth. His forces were marching freely across the land with no opposition, nobody standing up to stop them.

Reports had been made of some military forces trying to battle against the onslaught of the wraiths, Hashalanths and demons, but their mortal weapons were no match for creatures that were already dead. The number of creatures they were facing was too great for even the might of the American and Chinese armies to combat effectively and they too had soon succumbed to the supremacy of Lucifer.

Many armies had been infiltrated from above, from the higher ranks, and from there the evil filtered down. It was a carefully planned, controlled and co-ordinated attack for maximum widespread destruction of the population.

Morgan carefully watched Kronos as he continued to walk around him. "The Church will not fall." He said as defiantly as possible.

"It will fall, fall to its knees and beg my master for mercy. But no mercy will be given. Not today or any day until the end of time." Kronos said, "Stand down little man, and join me as we watch the Church fall under our control."

Morgan tightened his grip on his sword and took a step closer to Laura to protect her. "No! I will fight with every ounce of strength in my body. I will fight whatever you throw at me, I will fight until the end of time, but I will not let this continue."

Kronos gave a wry smile and lowered his sword. "Very

well, little Soldier. Hath mak!" he shouted.

Within a split second, two wraiths had engulfed Laura, holding her by her neck, forcing her to the floor. Morgan tried to reach but he suddenly felt the claws of a Hashalanth grab his arms, pulling him backwards and wrapping him up in the enormous wings.

He thrashed and struggled, swinging his sword to try and attack, but there was no effect as hands began to crawl all over him, pinning his legs and holding him down.

He was in a thick cloud of dark smoke, the breath in his lungs compressing out of him, forcing him to gasp for air. He opened his eyes and could only see darkness and grey wisps of smoke; the limbs of the wraiths reaching up and entangling them around his arms and legs. Kicking and thrashing out Morgan managed to free his leg, but was quickly restrained again by an unknown and unseen foe.

His heart was pumping hard and the rage inside him was rising. Finally with burning lungs he managed to grab a lungful of air, but the putrid smell and taste of rotting flesh and death filled his senses and lungs. He coughed up as the foul odour penetrated his skin and eyes.

Taking another lungful of rancid air he managed to shout out in pain and the claws began to rip into his skin in his arms and legs. His strength was leaving him, he was tiring, but he knew he had to continue to fight. Morgan could still feel the familiar hilt of his sword in his hand and he clung onto it, using it as his one hook of hope.

As his mind began to fall back in on itself, Morgan tried to blank out the pain that was consuming every nerve ending. The sword in his hand made him think back to his early days within the church, his training as a Vatican Knight and subsequent deployment to South America.

Morgan had experienced an eventful life, leaving school at 17 he had his heart set on joining the military. He finally decided on joining the Royal Marines and following the intensive training courses he was posted with 40 Commando Unit. While there he enjoyed the lifestyle of any young Marine, the hard work of training, marching, and exercises, and the excitement of deployment to foreign countries for mutual training sessions and simulated warfare.

When on shore leave, he would join his comrades in the local bars, drinking to excess, meeting the local women, and having encounters that would surely be frowned upon within the church.

However, when on an operation in a politically unimportant African country engulfed in a civil war, so his superiors put it to them during their briefing, Morgan's unit had come under heavy gunfire.

His men fought well, holding their position, keeping the high ground, but a well-aimed grenade from the opposing forces caught them off guard and shrapnel ripped through Morgan and his team. Two of his men suffered the majority of the blast and Morgan was pierced through the leg by the flying metal.

They had no choice but to call in a helicopter to evacuate them out, and after another 6 hours fighting they were safe back in the makeshift base the peacekeeping force of NATO had constructed.

Morgan was incapacitated for months and slowly his will to live and desire to get back on his feet was slipping away. It was during this time that he was visited by the Brigade Chaplain and their daily discussions turned to God. Day by day Morgan began to feel a need to help people, a need to serve a greater purpose, a need to serve God. While still in the infirmary he began to research the processes of becoming a priest, and with the help of the chaplain he began on the long road.

During his studies, with some being in Rome, Morgan was introduced to Cardinal Conquezla and during their conversation, Morgan talked about his sudden inspiration and calling while serving in the military. Conquezla took an interest in Morgan and remained in contact with him throughout the remainder of his studies and subsequent ordination. They became friends and when

Morgan was finally ordained Conquezla was there and soon offered him a position that wasn't normally open to new priests.

He offered him the chance to join the Vatican Knights. With his military background, Conquezla saw potential in Morgan, and Morgan jumped at the chance to become a part of such a secret sect within the church.

The training at the Knight headquarters in Switzerland was intense. Martial arts, hand to hand combat, and swordsmanship were all taught by some of the most talented and skilled men and women in the world. From China and Japan, America and Europe, the instructors were all dedicated in their teachings and were eager to show these young new recruits how to face and fight any number of enemies.

However given the secrecy of the Order the teachers never knew the true purpose of their being there. They were well paid and well looked after, and for some that was all they wanted.

Three years later Morgan had finally completed his training, two years ahead of the rest of his class. When offered his choice of assignments, Morgan quickly jumped at the opportunity to work in South America, and so it was that he was sent to Venezuela.

These key moments in his life flashed before his eyes as he continued to struggle against the clawing and slashing hands. His face was wrapped up in some sort of cloak and the sensation of flying was suddenly upon him. Fear began to grab at him and tear at his soul as he tried again and again to shout out and call for Gods help.

But he was helpless and couldn't do anything.

For what seemed like an eternity he struggled against the hidden attackers but then it all stopped. No hands were upon him; no claws cutting at him. He was alone in darkness, falling. His heart beat harder with every passing second that he fell, and he mentally counted the seconds and guessed that the impact would come soon. But it never came.

With the rushing wind blasting in his hair he suddenly

found himself lying on a stone path and the mists of darkness slowly clearing.

Morgan shook his head and tried to clear the dark cloud from his mind. His senses were still tingling with over stimulation and slowly they began to reach out and find any sort of information about the new environment he was in. Somewhere in the distance he could hear a female voice calling his name, and as he forced his eyes open he could see a blurred image of a woman, a woman he recognised.

It was Laura.

Laura called out to Morgan and managed to reach him, pulling him close to her. "Peter, thank God you're okay." She said.

Morgan tried to speak, but his voice was coarse and hard. "Where are we?" he finally managed to ask.

Laura looked about herself, shaking her head and saying she had no idea. Morgan could see clearer now and he saw to his surprise that they were sat against the frontage of a shop. They were on a street, but somehow it was a street he recognised.

Painfully he stood up and saw a street sign, Via della Concillazione. With a buzzing and blurred muggy head, Morgan stumbled into the street and looked around him with Laura close by and there at the far end of the street was the final stronghold of the Catholic Church.

The Vatican, St Peter's Basilica soaring high up into the sky stood before them. But to Morgan, more horrifying was the mass of thousands, probably tens or hundreds of thousands of wraiths and demons standing on the cusp of St Peter's Square, all waiting for the final attack.

CHAPTER TWENTY-FIVE

Morgan shook his head to try and clear the memories of his previous life, and looked at the sight of the forces of evil, literally on the doorstep of the Vatican.

Wraiths, Quazon cats, Zyphon eagles, Zyphill Chameleons and above them Hashalanth Scouts circling around the dome of St Peter's, the list of other demonic beasts that had grouped at the periphery of the Vatican boundary was too long for Morgan to register, but he could easily estimate there were over 750,000 of them, all waiting to pounce on the opportunity to attack the Church. He leaned against a pillar as he suddenly noticed that the whole street was full of the creatures, and many more he hadn't seen or recognised before.

As the mass of creatures began to shout out at the Vatican, there was a disturbance behind them and the crowd began to part. Morgan turned towards the commotion and saw Kronos walking proudly down the formed aisle. He stopped at Morgan and Laura.

"Bring them!" he ordered.

Both Morgan and Laura were grabbed from behind, pushed out and followed Kronos to the front of the crowd. The demon's eyes as they passed them were filled with evil and hatred and both Morgan and Laura could sense that they all wanted to pounce on them, kill them and rip them apart, but it was only the ironic saving grace and presence of Kronos that stopped them.

Neither Morgan nor Laura could look at any of them as they felt their souls filled with terror and hatred. Mouths snapped at them, razor sharp teeth glistened dripping with blood, and claws reached out to grab the new fresh blood that was paraded in front of them now.

Laura moved closer to Morgan who put his hand around her shoulder and pulled her closer. He watched the crowd close in around them as they neared the front. With the ever imposing building of St Peter's Basilica becoming clearer, Morgan felt a shard of hope enter his mind and heart.

He pulled Laura close and whispered to her. "They can't cross the line into St Peter's Square. It's sacred consecrated ground. If we can get through and into the Square we'll be safe."

He didn't know if she had heard or understood what he had said, but he hoped that merely hearing his voice, she would be able to find some inner strength to hold on a little longer.

Kronos strode proudly towards the front of the crowd and finally he emerged at the peripheral edge of St Peter's Square. Ahead of them was the large expanse of the square, edged by large columns and in the middle a tall obelisk. Behind that at the top of stone stairs was the multi entranced façade of St Peter's. Morgan had been here many times and each time he was always amazed at the size and architectural scale of the Basilica.

Kronos turned to Morgan, "From here you will see the final destruction." he said. "He will come soon, and when he does, we will be able to cross the line and advance towards victory."

As he stood, holding Laura close to him, Morgan suddenly realised that he no longer had his Celestial Sword. With a free hand he searched his body, but he didn't have it.

"You were disarmed during your transportation here." Kronos said, watching as Morgan searched himself, and pulling Morgan's sword out from his own cloak. "Do you think we would let you come anywhere near the Dark Lord armed?"

Morgan looked up at Kronos and with steely determination and strength he spoke. "To disarm me before your master arrives is mere proof that you are afraid of me. Scared of what I could do, and scared of the power of the Church that still faces you. You haven't won yet."

"You chose your words well Little Soldier" Kronos said, "We have indeed not won… yet!"

The crowd closed in around them and using the movement, Morgan carefully shifted position and moved closer to the line that marked the edge of St Peter's Square. The baying calls of the wraiths surrounded them as they shouted insults towards the Vatican. The sheer excitement of the crowd was palpable as the pushing and shoving grew harder and stronger. But the wraiths that held them both stopped Morgan and Laura from breaking free and getting to mild salvation.

The whole atmosphere began to change and looking above them the Hashalanths circled, squealing and screeching, calling out to the demonic army below. Their wings, outstretched with the claws snapping, cast shadows as they swooped and glided across the sky in front of the fading sun and around the iconic dome.

"He is coming." Kronos said, watching as the beasts looped above them once more. The skies were darkening and the power of the sun was weakening as the clouds closed in above them. The shadows that draped across the buildings, the roads, and the faces of Morgan and Laura, became entangled and merged into one grey mass. All colour from the world seemed to be being absorbed into the clouds.

Laura held onto Morgan's hand tightly and he squeezed it in return. There had to be a moment, he thought, a time when they could both break free. All he had to do was wait, he told himself, but then the question was wait for how long.

It took only a few more seconds for Morgan to get his answer, as above them the clouds began to circle and form into a tornado funnel. But there was no wind. The Wraiths all cheered and called out to the coming of their own Lord and in doing so they released their grip on their prisoners. Morgan jumped up and pulling Laura behind him they ran across the threshold and onto Vatican soil.

Neither looked back as they ran across St Peter's Square, past the two fountains and the obelisk and onwards, towards the steps of the Basilica.

As they ran up the stairs, Morgan finally risked a glance back and saw the angry mob shouting at them. Above the demonic wraiths he saw the funnel grow larger and slowly inch its way towards the earth. He knew there wasn't much time left before Lucifer found a foothold on earth, and the final seeds of doubt that the end was near slowly began to creep into his soul and mind.

It wasn't the grand affair that Houseman for years had dreamed of, but his ordination to the position of Pope was still official. Who needed the pomp and elongated celebrations, he thought as another Cardinal came forward and kissed the gold ring on his finger, pledging their loyalty and devotion to him.

Houseman thanked each of them in turn and as the next Cardinal approached he sat proudly and shifted on his throne awaiting this particular Cardinal's pledge.

Conquezla slowly stepped forward and looked up at the man he despised, now sitting in the seat of power of the Church he loved so much.

Houseman smiled to himself as he watched his once equal opponent now step forward.

"Don't worry Louis," Houseman said quietly, "I'm sure nobody will think any less of you for forgetting your beliefs so quickly."

Conquezla looked up at the outstretched hand and then at the smirking face of the Pope.

"You don't deserve to be sat there." He said, locking eyes on the man above him. "You've stolen the seat of St Peter on false pretences and you have no idea how to defeat this evil. For your own selfish reasons, you will bring destruction to this church."

Houseman leaned forward, "Maybe, but here I sit, head of the Church. Now – will you pledge your allegiance to me?"

For a moment the two men stared at each other. Silence fell upon the chapel as the other Cardinals present sensed the animosity and hatred fester between the two men, they had seen it before during other meetings and they all anticipated the moment when Conquezla would kiss the Fisherman Ring, a traditional sign of the Pope, cast in gold for each new Pontiff, on the Pope's finger. However given the speed of the unexpected election of Houseman, a copy of the Ring was borrowed from the Vatican Museum and given to Houseman. They all watched as Conquezla stood motionless in front of the throne.

"Show your allegiance and loyalty and I will show you how the church will defeat this evil." Houseman said.

Conquezla stood up and turned his back on the Pope, leaving the ring untouched. He strode off past the line of Cardinals who separated and formed a path before him.

Houseman stood and shouted after him. "To turn your back on me, is to turn your back on God. I am the last hope we have and to abandon us now is to abandon the will of God to stand and make peace with these things."

As Conquezla reached the doors they opened and he came face to face with Fr. Peter Morgan.

Morgan strode into the Sistine Chapel, with Laura close behind him. Morgan acknowledged Conquezla who had stopped and was now watching as his student purposely strode into the centre aisle of the Chapel. Laura followed him and as they walked towards the seated Pontiff, she could feel the eyes of the Cardinals on her.

"You can't make peace with these creatures," Morgan said, his voice echoing around him, "they come for war. We can't negotiate with them, we have nothing they want. There'll be no reconciliation as they now want power. They come here to destroy the world, they come to wreak havoc; they come to obliterate, annihilate and raze the church to the ground."

He continued and stood before the Pope.

"You seem to have an intimate knowledge of these things, Father-?" Houseman asked, standing up and allowing himself to stand high and look down at the congregation.

"Fr. Peter Morgan, a member and dedicated servant to the Order of the Vatican Knights." He answered, standing up straight, despite the pains cascading through his body.

Houseman smiled and descended the steps and faced Morgan. "Ah, a Vatican Knight, one of Conquezla's flock. The group of men that were destined to save us from these beasts and in whose shadow we now stand as they fail and bring us to destruction. And who is this?" He asked, nodding towards Laura.

"She is a victim of this situation who has helped me. She deserves protection and security." Morgan said.

"And you can give it her?" Houseman asked, beginning to circle them, like a prowling animal.

Morgan instinctively began to move and put himself between Laura and the Pope. "I can protect her better than some people can by trying to negotiation and open dialogue with a group of beings who only want to literally tear the head off the church. And with that I'd hate to be in your shoes at the moment Cardinal."

Houseman stopped and stood up to Morgan. "Do not talk to me in such a manner!" his voice crackled around the chapel. "Pope Pius may be incapacitated, but I have been elected Pope in his absence and you should address me as such."

"You may have been elected pope, but I do not recognise you as such. Until His Holiness Pope Pius dies, he is the one I will pledge my allegiance to." Morgan retorted.

"You shall pledge your allegiance to whoever sits upon this throne." the Pope said.

"I shall pledge my allegiance to the rightful heir of that throne, to a man chosen by the Cardinals who were guided by the Holy Spirit, not by lack of choice." Morgan shot back.

Houseman stared hard at Morgan and slowly climbed the

steps and stood next to the seat of power. "I see you have inherited the acid tongue of your tutor. Cardinal Conquezla, please take this – this insolent man away from here. I have no need for either of you, either of your services. And I announce and proclaim that from this moment on, The Order of the Vatican Knights is hereby disbanded and any reference to their existence and duties shall be met by excommunication from this church."

The whole chapel was silent and as he stood facing the Pope, Morgan felt a movement to his side. He turned and saw the aged face of Cardinal Conquezla.

"Your Holiness," Conquezla said, trying to keep solemnity in his voice as he spoke, "The danger we face now is nothing like we have faced before, or ever shall again. Discussion and discourse are not the way to approach and deal with an army that is camping on our doorstep and prepared to kill us all."

"Do you honestly think that your one Knight will stand and defeat that army?" Houseman asked. "If that's what you think, then by all means, let him go out there and face them alone. He is your last Vatican Knight, use him well."

Houseman turned away from his congregation and with brisk footsteps echoing around them he left the Sistine Chapel quickly with a line of Cardinals following close behind him ready to serve their new master.

CHAPTER TWENTY-SIX

Within the basement of the Vatican, Conquezla stood behind his desk. He was pouring three glasses of scotch for himself, Morgan and Laura.

Following the outburst in the Sistine chapel, Conquezla had ushered Morgan and Laura away to the relative safety of his department. He tasked Fr. Jung to take Laura to get freshened up and find her some clean clothes and that now gave him a chance of a private meeting with Morgan.

"I'm sorry for the outburst." Morgan said, swilling the drink around his glass.

Conquezla smiled at him. "Your words were reflected in my soul, Peter. That man is not the rightful heir and he is leading us on a collision course that will destroy us all. But tell me, what's it like out there?" he asked, taking a sip of his drink.

Morgan shook his head, "It's literally Hell on Earth. The news reports don't do it justice. There are Wraiths walking around everywhere, people are being killed everywhere and those who don't succumb to the deeds of the Devil are subjected to God only knows what."

"Unfortunately God doesn't know."

Morgan looked up at the tired face of his Master. "How is the

Pope? Pope Pius I mean."

Conquezla finished his drink as Laura re-entered. She was showered and wearing a tracksuit that Jung had found for her. "Fr. Jung?" Conquezla said, "Join us. These are hard times and you have served us well."

He poured a drink for the young priest and Jung timidly took it from the Cardinal and shuffled back into the corner.

"Pope Pius is not well." Conquezla said. "He is under the power of a demon and his heart grows weaker. He's dying. The doctors can barely stabilize him, but with such a powerful force acting against them, it's difficult."

Laura spoke up, "What's wrong with him?"

"He's possessed by a demon," Conquezla said, "his mind, his heart, his soul is under the control of a demon."

"I thought you said those things couldn't come onto Vatican soil?"

Morgan looked up at Conquezla, and both had the same response. "No, so did we. But what it does mean is that the threshold has been breached and those beasts out there can now cross the line into the square and attack us." Morgan paused as he swilled the drink around his glass. "Whatever has happened has happened, however His Holiness became possessed, it's happened, what we need to do now is figure out a way to reverse it. Have you tried -"

"We've tried exorcism," Conquezla said, "we've tried every version we could find, but nothing seems to do anything. With that demon in him, on these grounds, it is merely a foothold for the Devil to walk straight in here."

"Parasite." Jung said under his breath.

Morgan stopped examining his glass and turned to the young priest. "What did you say?"

"Nothing." Jung said nervously. "Just that it's like a parasite."

Morgan smiled. "Exactly. Your Eminence, there may be a way to release his Holiness from his demon, and save us."

Conquezla led Morgan, Laura and Jung down into the crypts below the Vatican. Hidden, carved tunnels that had been used for hundreds of years as the final resting place of those Popes gone before them.

In little alcoves there were altars where small private masses could be held for groups of pilgrims visiting the centre of their faith. Laura glanced across at them, seeing now a smattering of nuns and young priests knelt before the crucifixes that adorned the walls, each praying for salvation and strength.

The four of them continued through the tunnels until they reached a heavy metal door set into the rock face. Conquezla pulled a key from under his cassock and unlocked the door, letting them all in, and locking it behind him.

"Over here." he said, indicating the far wall.

Morgan slowly stepped over and saw a large stone altar, battered and weathered by years of use. The lighting was dim in this stone room, dampness was etched in the air and the temperature was cold.

Conquezla walked to the other side of the altar and removed a long dark wooden box from a hiding place within the altar table and placed it on top. He turned the box to Morgan and nodded for him to open it.

Morgan looked at Laura, then at the box and carefully he unclipped the clasps and eased the lid open.

Inside was lined with fine velvet, and the smell of incense filled the air. Lying in the box, perfectly wrapped in a delicate silk shawl was an object that was as long as the box.

"It's only right that you should take ownership of this now. There is no better time for it to be needed." Conquezla said as he watched Morgan carefully pull back the silk cover and reveal a sword.

"Is this -?" Morgan started to say, but the words couldn't come out of his mouth.

"It is."

"I thought it was a myth, a rumour, a story made up by

theologians centuries ago." he said, gently running his fingers along the sharp blade and down across the hilt and the handle.

Laura stepped up and looked at the sword. "What is it?"

"The Sword of Gethsemane." Morgan answered, not taking his eyes of the weapon.

Conquezla reached over and removed the weapon from the case. It was about 20 inches long with a thin blade that widened nearer the tip before reverting to a piercing point.

"The Sword of Gethsemane, Miss Kennedy." Conquezla said, weighing up the sword in his hand. "Forged from the very blade used by St. Peter to attack the Roman soldier in the Garden of Gethsemane on the night of Our Lords betrayal; gilded at the tip of the blade from the remains of the spear that pierced Christ's body as he died on the cross, and the handle swaddled and wrapped from the scraps of cloth that were discovered in His tomb after His resurrection."

They all stood in silence as they looked at the weapon, and even Laura, the least devout believer, could sense the importance of the weapon.

"There were stories of it," Morgan said, "being lost at sea as St. Paul travelled the Mediterranean but they were just stories."

"It is one of the most important relics we have, and given the grave situation that we now face, Peter, I entrust it to you to use against that army of darkness that quickly advances on us." Conquezla said, handing the sword to him.

Across the wide expanse of St. Peter's Basilica, Morgan led Laura and Conquezla to the main doors that would soon open up to the evil forces gathering in the Square beyond.

Their steps echoed around them as they approached the doors, but their way was blocked as a row of a dozen young priests walked in front of them. The three of them stopped and Conquezla stepped forward, knowing each and every one of them.

One of the priests stepped forward and addressed him. "Your Eminence, we request that you allow us to join Fr. Morgan in his protection of the Church."

They were Vatican Knights in training, some more advanced than others, but all dedicated to their calling. Conquezla had chosen each of them personally, as he had chosen Morgan, and he knew the strength of spirit they had and knew they would fight until the very end, but he couldn't bring himself to give the order to send them to what he believed to be their certain deaths.

"I cannot send you out there." he said, "I cannot give the order."

"Then let us go of our own accord."

Morgan stepped forward and faced them. "Are you prepared to stand and fight the very essence of Evil? Are you prepared to give your lives, every muscle, every bone, every drop of blood for the church?"

They all answered yes, and Morgan turned to the Cardinal.

"They're ready." he said, and turning from Laura and Conquezla, he walked to the heavy wooden doors and opened them, leading the Knights to face the demons.

Like thousands of men and women who had themselves faced certain death as they entered the Coliseum 2000 years before them, and only a few miles from where they now stood, Morgan looked out across Piazza San Pietro, beyond the Vatican Obelisk that stood proudly in the centre, and at the end of the curved colonnades stood the mass of the Army of Darkness, eager to attack the Church.

The 13 Knights walked down the steps and forward towards the demons. The chanting and baying calls from the wraiths roared in their ears.

"Follow my lead." Morgan said quietly, "Don't strike first; show restraint."

The Knights walked across the plaza and beyond the obelisk and forming a line, to give each man room to move, they spread out to create a weak defence.

In his hand, Morgan gripped the Sword of Gethsemane

and he looked down along the line of young inexperienced Knights. They were nervous, he could tell, scared and no doubt terrified. He felt the same, but he had to show no fear.

Each Knight drew their own Celestial Sword and with a flick of their wrists, the blades extended.

He took a step forward and looked either side of them. They were indecd ready, he thought.

From across the plaza, Morgan saw Kronos shouting calls to him, waving Morgan's own sword back at him. He didn't know why, but Morgan smiled at Kronos, and holding The Sword of Gethsemane high he shouted out.

"For the Church!"

He ran forward and the Knights followed him, shouting too, swords raised and ready for battle.

CHAPTER TWENTY-SEVEN

Conquezla and Laura stood at the foot of the Pontiff's bed. The rhythmic beep from the heart monitor was the only sound in the room, with the distant screams and shouts muffled, but still slightly audible.

"We can't do this," Laura said, "we can't stop his heart."

Conquezla stepped to the side of the bed and gently touched the unconscious Pope's forehead. "We have to try and save him. Stopping his heart should release his soul from the control of whatever demonic being is inside. Once free, as Morgan said, we can restart his heart and then as leader of the Church he can oust Houseman and perhaps we'll stand a chance to survive. Doctor?"

A doctor approached, his white coat flowing behind him.

"Doctor, we need you to do something for us."

Conquezla explained their proposal, but the Doctor flatly refused.

"Absolutely not Your Eminence. I am Doctor and I have given a vow to keep my patients alive. I will not stop his heart and effectively kill him. Have you spoken to Cardinal Houseman about this?"

"He is preoccupied."

"I imagine he is busy. I must ask you to leave now."

Conquezla took another step towards the doctor. He was never a confrontational man, his position was one of dignified restraint, but there were times when the cardinal had to use more bullish tactics.

"Indeed the army of darkness is on our doorstep, doctor. It is my sworn duty to protect this church and all those within its walls from the destiny of eternal damnation, but I need the Head of the Church beside me."

"Stopping his heart and restarting it, while in such a fragile state could cause more irreversible damage. I will not be a part of it."

"Then step outside doctor."

The doctor turned from the cardinal and heading back towards the desk he grabbed the phone and dialled for security.

The blades of the Knights flashed through the air, crashing into the blades and bodies of the wraiths before them. The laborious movements of the wraiths made it easy for the Knights to strike them down, one after the other the demonised soldiers were cut down, the last remnants of life evaporating from their bodies and shrivelling up into balls of skin.

Morgan led the Knights forward into the mass of demons. They held a line across the expanse of St. Peter's Square, stretching from one of the delicately carved fountains, in front of the tall obelisk in the centre, to the other.

The Knights were stretched thin, but they had enough room to manoeuvre as they continued their defence of the Church. Each Knight knew that they were outnumbered and outmanned, but as the fight continued, they managed to hold their positions.

The weaker demons, the pawns, were sent forward first and the Knights easily cut them down.

High above St. Peter's Square the darkening reddening clouds, swirled and slowly descended, hovering above them like an eagle ready to strike. The Pyro Angels sent a cascade of fire balls raining down onto the square, carelessly striking anything that moved, demons, wraiths, humans, nothing was safe from the onslaught.

The cries of the Hashalanths circling around them pierced their minds. A younger Knight grabbed at his head as the screams ripped through his mind.

Morgan saw him fall to the floor and as he himself dodged the incoming blade of a wraith, he swung his sword and sliced his attacker in two. At pace Morgan ran to the Knight, quickly and skilfully cutting through the air any wraiths that got in his way. As he ran he saw the Knight being mauled by the wraiths, their hands scratching and pulling his skin away from his face. The Knight shouted out in pain and with blood pumping from his wounds, Morgan knew he was too late, but he continued to run forward.

Only feet away, Morgan lifted his sword up and shouted in anger and hatred at the beasts attacking the Knight. He held his sword high and gripping the handle he swung down, the blade slicing through the robes and flesh of the Knight.

Morgan stood with the dead Knight at his feet, the wraiths closest around him stopped in their attack. It was a difficult decision to make, but Morgan knew that to cut down the Knight himself would save his soul from the torment of being possessed and dragged into hell.

The wraiths were advancing and Morgan could see that they were about to be over run. They needed a tighter line, now one man short and stretched thinner they needed to retreat back towards the steps of St Peters.

He shouted the order and the Knights followed him back to the edge of the oval plaza at the foot of the steps. As they retreated the wraiths pounced forward and grabbed two more Knights who were fleeing back with Morgan.

Morgan stopped, swung his sword and displaced three wraiths in one move. He saw the unlucky Knights pulled back into the hoards of demons and watched their feeble attempts to escape as a Zyphill chameleon slinked around the group and showing its true form of wide mouth, razor sharp teeth, blood seeping from the pores in its skin, the creature ripped into the body of the helpless priest.

Houseman adjusted his white robes and sat on his seat in the Sistine Chapel as the black cloaked figure strode down towards him. The other cardinals had been dismissed back to their rooms and the new Pontiff had only two loyal assistants beside him as he greeted the representative of the evil forces into the sacred chapel.

A single seat was situated at the bottom of the three steps that led up to Houseman, his attempt to try and show that his elevated position meant he was in charge.

The figure seemed to glide across the floor, his face hidden by a hood, his hands tucked into the sleeves across his chest. He stopped short of the steps.

"I come bearing a message from my master." He rasped, his voice echoing around the chapel.

"And which master is that?" Houseman asked, not standing to greet his guest.

"There is only one master," the hooded figure said, "the One you fear, the One who was there at the beginning, the One who stood up against your God, the One who will return and take this world for his own."

"So what is your message?" Houseman said dismissively.

"Surrender. Surrender now and mercy may be passed to you and those within these grounds."

Houseman stood up and stepped towards the figure. "Remove your hood, I wish to see the face of the man who makes demands of this church. What is your name?"

The figure pulled the hood off, "I am Victor. A loyal servant of the Morning Star, the Fallen Angel, the one you call Lucifer."

Houseman was taken aback by Victor's features. They were human, but barely. Gone was his bald head and pale skin, instead his face and head was heavily scarred with lacerations that appeared to be inflicted by an animal. Patches of skin hung from his neck and cheeks, the blood, thick red was coagulating at the gaps in his face.

Houseman cleared his throat and spoke, "You should not come in here and demand the surrender of the Church. This Church has stood for 2000 years and fought many enemies, we shall not surrender." Calmly, Houseman lowered the tone of his voice, making it more persuasive, "But we can offer a truce."

Victor laughed, blood catching and gurgling in his shredded throat. It echoed around the Chapel, "A truce? Look outside your window! In a matter of a week our forces have trounced and overrun every town, city, country and continent we have set foot on. Millions of people have joined our cause, millions have been killed, and outside now there are a million soldiers of darkness ready to crash through the doors to pillage this sanctuary.

"I could stop it happening, I could end it all now and let you live. But you must surrender now. To wait for His arrival, you will not be offered this chance, or this promise to be unharmed again. He will soon walk among us, and he will have his vengeance against this church and against you. For too long he has been captive to your Gods punishment, and now the time of his rule is over and my Lord's rule will begin."

"This is Holy ground," Houseman said with a sly smile on his face, "no forces of evil can cross the threshold without being destroyed. So let your Lord come, let him cross the Holy line, and let me watch him be once more vanquished and sent to the depths of Hell."

There was silence between the two men, and finally Victor spoke. "His arrival is imminent. What is your decision?"

Houseman stood erect and spoke. "Our answer is no."

Victor nodded in understanding and turned away. He walked back the way he had come and Houseman watched him leave.

"Tell me, Your Holiness," Victor said, calling over his shoulder, "you say that no evil can survive on Holy ground, yet how does that theory work, if evil was invited?"

Houseman stared at Victor as the words sank in and there

was a sudden understanding, a sudden realisation, and a sudden terror that gripped him.

He had invited this envoy into the inner sanctum of the Vatican, and he had therefore opened a door for evil to enter. "YOU ARE BANISHED FROM THIS HOUSE OF GOD! LEAVE, LEAVE NOW!" Houseman shouted, but it was too late as the high windows above them smashed instantly and Zyphill chameleons began to crawl through them and onto the wall, changing colour to match their surroundings.

One of the aides ran to the Pope, and the other ran to the doors, calling for help, calling for the Swiss Guard.

The security guards were pulling Laura and Conquezla away from the bedside of the unconscious Pope Pius. For an older man, Conquezla put up a good struggle and managed to thrown one of the guards off his back and managed to reach over to the other guard and pull him off Laura.

"Get them out of here!" the Doctor shouted.

"No!" Conquezla retorted, "We're the only chance to save the Pope!"

"Get them out!" the Doctor repeated.

The two guards regained their composure and advance on Laura and Conquezla who backed up towards the Popes bed.

Around them, the floor started to vibrate, the windows shudder, and the walls shake. Everyone looked around themselves and at each other and then at the limp body of the Pope in the bed.

His breathing was becoming heavier, longer, deeper. His chest was rising and falling at a quicker pace and as his fingers, hands and legs twitched, his eyes were clearly moving.

"He's waking up!" Laura said with a twinge of hope in her voice. But Conquezla slowly took her arm and pulled her back away from the bed.

The Doctor had grabbed his stethoscope and leaned over the Pope to listen to his chest. A smile crossed his face and he looked up at Conquezla, as if to boast that his diagnosis and course of action was correct. He was about speak when the hands of the Pope shot up, grabbed the Doctor around the head and neck, and with a sharp twist, the Doctors neck was broken.

Laura screamed and tried to hide behind Conquezla who watched in horror as the possessed Pope arched his back and with straining tendons bulging in his neck, he spoke in a coarse deep voice.

"It is time!"

The main doors to the infirmary shattered and splintered and the two guards turned to face the Hashalanth that entered, its wings outstretched, its claws ready for a fight. The two men ran forward, guns raised, but the razor sharp claws ripped through their clothes and skin, killing them.

Laura had instinctively dropped to the floor for protection, and she watched as Conquezla reached under his cassock and pulled his own sword hilt out and flicked it open, extending the blade and heading for the Hashalanth.

Morgan stood half way up the steps to the doors of St Peters and with the Sword of Gethsemane in his hand, he and the remaining 3 Knights continued to defend their church.

The Quazon cats and Zyphon Eagles had joined the wraiths in their attack, and Morgan knew that it was only a matter of time before they would be defeated. He heard a scream and a shout to his side and saw one of the younger Knights fall to his knees with a rusted sword piercing his chest.

High above them the spiralling cloud funnel had reached the plaza floor and with a crash of thunder the ground violently shook. Morgan, the remaining knights, and their own enemy stopped their fighting and turned to watch as St. Peter's Square was ripped apart.

As if a knife had jaggedly sliced through the ground, a gaping chasm formed, sending rocks crashing into the earth. Those Wraiths and demons standing in that area fell into the pit, falling towards the centre of the earth, once more to their eternal damnation.

Those shouts and screams of the wraiths and demonic beasts that were calling out for deaths of the remaining Knights were drowned out by the crescendo roaring growl that emanated from the chasm.

All beings, good and evil, turned to the source of the noise, and with sweat dripping off his face, Morgan watched as putrid sulphuric smoke billowed from the crater. Molten rocks erupted from the earth's core and shot upwards, crashing down into the plaza, killing the wraiths they landed on.

Morgan stood breathless, watching the chasm, not flinching as the rocks shot up and out, scattering sparks and molten debris all around him. He stood and watched as the red glow of fire and the earth's core illuminating the plaza was dimmed as a shadow could be seen cast on the rising smoke.

At the edge of the chasm, the glinting razor edge of a cracked long claw could be seen gripping onto the ledge, digging into the ground, tearing up the surface as the Beast pulled itself from the pit of Hell.

Houseman cowered behind his throne and looked out once more as the whipping tails of the dragon-esque creatures crashed through the pews and cracked through the air, ripping the plaster and marble from the floor and ceiling. The intricate artwork of Michelangelo, Botticelli and Perugino were destroyed in seconds, and the debris from the ceiling fell all around the chapel.

Houseman watched in horror as the few Swiss Guards who rushed to the calls of help from his aides, fought off the demonic attackers. Being professional soldiers they were well trained in combat skills but as they clashed with the whipping tails, they were obviously no match for the forces of Hell.

From the far end of the chapel, Victor called out in delightful glee, "He has come. HE HAS ARRIVED!" He pointed at Houseman who was trying to crawl away from the carnage around him, as his final surviving aide was ripped in two by the creature.

"You are your God's representative here on Earth!" Victor shouted. "You shall meet the Dark Lord and you shall be his first trophy!"

At a window a winged Hashalanth sat perched, and at the order of Victor, its immense wingspan opened and swooped down towards the terrified Pope, grabbing him in its claws and carrying him upwards, and out of the chapel.

Conquezla wielded the sword with a gentle but effective touch as it blocked and parried the swipes and attacks of the Hashalanth. He hadn't handled his own Celestial Sword for nearly 15 years, but when he saw the dreaded path that the world was descending into, he had retrieved it from his private offices at Schloss VK.

He could feel the skills that had been drilled into him through hours, days and years of hard training begin to find their balance once more within him. The muscle memory of holding the sword at the correct angle, the repetitiveness that he hated during his own training was now beginning to ebb through him, and manoeuvres and positions that he had long thought lost and forgotten were now resurfacing as his mind remembered how to fight.

The seven defensive positions of the sword were perfectly placed and deflected the razor claws that came swiping across at him, and, as he pivoted and sliced the sword through the sinew and muscle of the Hashalanth, he found the target point he had waited for and the glinting edge of the blade pierced the armour of the creature and killed it instantly.

Laura looked up from her position beside the Pope's bed, and saw the heavily out of breath cardinal head to her.

"We don't have long." He said, between heavy gasps for air. "We must still try."

Laura was still doubtful that the plan they had come to the infirmary to carry out would succeed, but seeing that the whole world was descending in chaos, and their own lives now had limited options, she reluctantly removed the tube from the Pope's mouth and flicked switches on the machine next to his bed. The gentle repetitive tones ceased and they both watched as the Pope struggled to breathe on his own and finally he took his last breath.

Morgan watched as the one he knew as Lucifer crawled out from the pit. His expectations of the beast had, like many others, been skewed and manipulated by the representations and imaginations of those artists and theologians who had described the Devil.

To Morgan, he appeared to be human like, but with the traditional wings of an angel protruding from his shoulder blades. The wings and feathers were burnt and the tendons with them were exposed and broken. The skin was scarred and lacerated, red and burnt, blistered and tortured. The arms were strong and the clawed hand that gripped his fiery sword had talons that flicked out as Lucifer flexed his fingers.

Morgan was transfixed on him as he walked towards the steps of St. Peter's. As he approached, the wraiths parted, allowing a path to form. Morgan could see two tails whipping out from either side from his tail bone as he approached; each one appeared to have a life of its own and its own curse as it reached out and grabbed wraiths, and sucked the life out of them.

High above them a screech from a Hashalanth called out and Morgan looked up to see the creature glide down and deposit the white robed Houseman on the steps. Morgan stayed where he was, not wanting to weaken his position but the remaining two Knights ran to their Popes side and checked he was still alive.

As Lucifer approached, Morgan continued to stare deep into his burning eyes; the thin almost skeletal face, sunken cheeks, and flaying skin.

Morgan found himself wondering how normal Lucifer looked, but then his mind recalled the story of how Lucifer had once been a loyal angel of God. But when God made man and called them his greatest creation, Lucifer refused to bow down to Man as he saw angels as the higher being. Following this there was a battle for heaven that saw angels with allegiances to Lucifer fight against those loyal to God, led by the Archangel Michael. Lucifer's forces were outnumbered 3 to 1 and they ultimately lost the battle and were cast into the eternal pit of damnation to be subservient to God and all of Mankind.

Despite the near normal angelic appearance of Lucifer, he still carried a putrid air of command, evil and death about him, and the wraiths backed away as they sensed their Master among them.

Only feet away from the Pope, the tails of Lucifer whipped out and pierced the bodies of the two knights and flung them into the crowd of waiting wraiths who dived onto the fresh meat and began to devour them.

Morgan had to act, he knew it. He couldn't stand by and watch this beast, this fallen angel kill the Leader of his Church. He gripped his sword tightly and began to focus his mind, but what could he do, he thought.

Lucifer looked down at the white robes and spoke. "If you are His servant, and your master is not here, then I shall have my vengeance on you!"

Lucifer raised his flaming sword high above his head, and calling out with a scream, with anger and hatred filling his eyes he swung the sword down hard towards the helpless Pontiff.

Morgan's sword blocked the blow and he stood between Lucifer and Houseman. Lucifer took a step back at the sudden appearance of Morgan standing defiantly in front of him, staring down at the priest as if nobody had ever stood up to him before.

"I swore an oath to protect this Church," Morgan said, "if you want to get in here, you'll have to get through me first!"

Lucifer smiled and then laughed loudly.

The wraiths around him followed their master's lead and laughed too, the whole plaza erupted in a barrage of calls and shouts for Morgan's death.

"I bow to no man!" Lucifer said.

Morgan knew his chances of survival were small given the numbers he was facing, but he was never one to give up without a fight. He wasn't prepared to sit back and let Lucifer destroy everything he believed in, not without giving his own life first.

With the grip on his sword firm, Morgan moved quickly and swerved the blade of the sword through the air aiming directly to Lucifer, who didn't flinch. Morgan's sword came crashing down and impacted on his Celestial Sword held by the grinning Kronos.

CHAPTER TWENTY-EIGHT

Seeing his own sword face back at him made Morgan feel uneasy and sick to his core, for he knew what the weapon was capable of and what damage it could do in the hands of a skilled swordsman.

Morgan and Kronos faced each other, each sword ready to strike, but neither wishing to make the first move. Out of the corner of his eye, Morgan saw Lucifer lean down to the unconscious Houseman and he could just hear what was said.

"I can sense you are not the true representative of this Church," Lucifer said, "I don't sense the Holy Spirit within you, or in this church. You are all unprotected."

Lucifer stood up and faced the baying crowd who cheered him as he held his arms aloft with the flaming sword high above his head. "My brothers in arms," he shouted out across the plaza, "tonight we will take our revenge, our revenge we have waited too long for. No longer shall we sit in shadows, tomorrow as the sun arises, we will be the dominant force on this world, and we will prove to Jehovah that we cannot be beaten!"

The crowd shouted again and Lucifer turned to the doors of St. Peter's and with his powerful sword, he swung at them, crashing through them, sending splinters and debris across the steps and creating a gaping hole in the façade of the Church.

Morgan ran towards the entrance and with his sword held high he swung at Lucifer, but Kronos was too quick, he blocked the sword and quickly attacked Morgan. Morgan lost his balance and as he was forced back into St. Peter's, he wildly swung his sword to try and protect himself from the incoming melee from Kronos.

Morgan scrambled across the floor backed away, trying to find his feet, balance, and some space that would allow him to attack Kronos, but the demon pivoted and span, aiming his own sword at Morgan. His heavy black cloak swept around and up creating a veil of confusion for Morgan who only reacted at the last split second as the glinting edge of the sword missed his head by an inch and impacted hard into the marble pillars.

Momentarily subdued, Morgan moved away from Kronos, wiping the sweat from his face and then faced him ready. Morgan could tell Kronos was a skilled swordsman from his balance and elegant movements, unlike the wraiths outside, and he knew to face him now in the expanse of the Basilica would take all of his skill and nerve.

St. Peter's Basilica is a huge cathedral, some 220 metres in length, 150 metres at the widest point, it is an art gallery in itself with priceless works of art and sculpture on show throughout the nave and side chapels, taking 120 years to build and complete.

Statues of founding saints, chapels, altars and monuments to past Popes ran along each of the walls, every corner and every crevice was dedicated to a saint or Pope.

Like many churches throughout the world, the Basilica is a cruciform shape with the nave leading from the main entrance door up the longest length of the cruciform to where it meets the intersection directly beneath the great dome that stretches nearly 140 metres into the air.

When not in use for official occasions, the Basilica is free from pews and chairs, and Morgan was glad of the space as he blocked Kronos's sword, swivelled on the ball of his foot and lashed out at him, catching the demon's leg, cutting him, but not mortally wounding him.

"Hic ego sum, stand in domo tua, veniat ubi es coramme." Lucifer was calling out. *Here I am, standing in your house, but where are you to come and face me.*

Morgan only momentarily heard the words and barely translated them in his head as Kronos attacked him once more. Through the vastness of the Basilica the swords clashed and echoed around them. Sparks flew from their blades as Morgan backed away towards one of the columns that had a monument to Pope Innocent XII at its base.

Using the column as a protective shield, Morgan dodged the incoming blade and ducked as it crashed through the monument and penetrated into the marble column.

Morgan used the opportunity and attacked Kronos, but he was too quick and lashed out with his skeletal arm and caught Morgan in the chest sending him 20 feet through the air landing heavily on his side, sliding across the floor, his own sword falling from his hand away from him.

With his side hurting and head burning with pain, Morgan still managed to ease himself up to his knees. Kronos was pulling his sword out from the column, but it was Lucifer that Morgan was focused on.

He was walking, arms aloft, his tattered and destroyed wings on his back held out wide, heading to the Papal Altar directly beneath the Great Dome, and itself directly above the tomb of St. Peter himself. The altar was designed by Bernini. It is covered by a 95ft high canopy of four twisting columns and an intricately designed cover. Only the Pope himself used this altar for celebrating mass.

"Pulsus sum vobis, ut ego feci omnia serviunt tibi laudes." Lucifer called out. *You banished me, when all I did was serve you and sing your praises.* "Et proiecisti me depostia tandem fronte, ubi amor aeternam?" *How dare you cast me aside, where was you eternal love for me?*

Morgan turned and saw Kronos run at him and jump through the air, sailing down towards him with his sword aimed at

Morgan's chest. Morgan rolled away as the blade hit the marble floor, but the enraged Kronos continued to kick and lash out at him as Morgan scurried away trying to find his own sword.

Laura looked at Conquezla as she readied the defibrillator and it slowly reached its charge.

"What if this doesn't work?" she asked nervously as she held the paddles in her hand and looked at the bare chest of the Pope.

Conquezla shook his head, "I don't know." He said simply.

If he was honest, he didn't know what would happen, or what he hoped to happen. The Pope he had vowed to serve was lying in front of him now dead, the army of darkness was inside his church, his sanctuary, and there was no sign of the God he had given his life to serve coming to their rescue.

In all his years serving the Church he always felt there was someone he could turn to, someone he could talk to, someone who would listen to his fears and worries and not judge him for his thoughts, but now, knowing that his death was imminent, he felt alone. He really didn't know if what they were about to do would help anything, but part of Conquezla maybe wanted just someone he trusted to listen to him one last time, and forgive all of his sins.

He nodded to Laura and she pressed the paddles onto the chest of the Pope and pressed the buttons.

The limp body convulsed and fell back to the bed.

"Try again." Conquezla said.

Morgan had found his sword, but not his balance as he was sent spiralling across the floor again into the centre of the nave. Kronos was smiling broadly as he looked down at his prey, and Morgan slowly edged away.

His face was heavily bloodied and lacerated from Kronos' attacks and he spat blood from his mouth as the stinging sweat in his eyes blurred his vision.

"At least you put up more of a fight than Fr. Yegros." Kronos said, "He died begging for mercy, on his knees!"

"He wouldn't do that!" Morgan shouted back.

"No," Kronos said, "he died in fear!"

With no warning Kronos swung down and missed Morgan who rolled away and onto his knees. Kronos had over reached and lost his balance and Morgan used his mistake to attack him.

The Sword sliced through the thick cloak, but if Morgan had hit any flesh, he didn't know.

Kronos kicked out and caught Morgan in the knee, buckling it and sending him crashing to the floor. Morgan looked up and saw Kronos leap up and land on top of him, his nails and finger like claws scratching and ripping into his arms and hands.

Morgan scrambled to free himself, defending himself in any manner he could and found himself rolling towards the Papal altar, and towards the crypt steps below.

Despite the commotion of them fighting, Lucifer had calmly walked up on to the Papal altar and was standing on the marble table looking high above him at the canopy.

"Vigilate, ut ego tuum Ecclesiae cadens ad genua et factus novum!" *Watch as I bring your Church falling to its knees and I become the new God!*

In a flash, Lucifer's whole body turned to fire and the explosive force reached out and destroyed Bernini's masterpiece canopy. Levitating up above the altar and towards the dome, Lucifer continued to burn bright, with every rising second his whole body grew and expanded in size.

Within the dome itself, Lucifer once more erupted with a ball of fire and the dome that was constructed by the greatest and best minds the world had ever seen was destroyed. The heavy metal cross that sat at the very pinnacle of the dome came crashing down onto the papal altar.

Outside, the wraiths called out and screamed as they saw the glow of their master arise like the fallen angel he was through the dome of the Church that was at the heart of their hatred. As they screeched and screamed, the skies above them flashed with lightning and the noise of the crack bellowed around them.

Morgan and Kronos had barely fallen through the crypt entrance when the remains of the dome had come crashing down onto them. Both of them were covered in debris and in the confines of the crypt they faced each other again.

Their swords clashed as they attacked and blocked each-other's blows. The confined space of the crypt, with the low ceiling and many columns made it difficult to manoeuvre, but seeing Kronos stumble and weaken, Morgan was revitalised to continue his attack.

He found new energy as he ducked and dived behind the stone columns and being light on his feet he almost pranced around the disorientated Kronos. It was as though being in such proximity to the tombs of the deceased popes of years gone by, had intensified the power of the Holy Spirit within the crypt, and this in turn weakened Kronos, but invigorated Morgan.

Morgan's sword swept upwards slicing through the thick cloth of the cloak, and the severed hand of Kronos fell to the floor. Not finishing the move, Morgan sliced down and again finding his target, the sword embedded in the clavicle of Kronos who fell to his knees.

Morgan pulled the sword out and kicked out at Kronos who fell backwards. Kronos was laughing, "You may have defeated me, Vatican Knight, but my master is still -"

The sword cut through his neck and cleanly removed Kronos' head. Morgan didn't want to hear another word from the vile beast and he felt no emotion as the sword cut through and killed him.

The lightning cracked again and Lucifer continued to rise upwards towards the clouds. The fire emanating from his whole body was lighting up the whole of Rome. He arched his flaming head up and smiled as he knew he had won, but looking up he saw the clouds part and the white light pulsate down towards him.

Laura pressed the buttons on the paddles again and the body writhed and withered. She knew it was too late now and there was no way they could bring the Pope back, he had been without oxygen to the brain for too long.

"Once more." Conquezla said quietly.

Reluctantly Laura pressed the paddles again to his chest and pressed the buttons.

Like feedback in an amplifier, the defibrillator sparked and exploded next to her, cascading sparks across the room. Other electrical items too exploded as a sudden surge of energy filled the room.

The body of pope began to glow white and he slowly raised up off the bed, eyes wide open. He looked paralysed and terrified as his head arched back and from his mouth, nose, eyes and finger tips, pure white energy erupted from him and shattered every piece of equipment around them.

The white light hit Lucifer and forced him back down to the Papal Altar as he writhed and struggled to free himself from the force that had attacked him. The flames had been extinguished and he lay prone on the marble table as the white energy continued to attack him.

Morgan slowly emerged from the crypt and shielded his eyes from the bright light. He looked up at the source high above him and he fell back, arms out to his side. The light flowed out and across the altar down towards Morgan, hitting him directly in the chest. The light filled his body with such power that his whole body erupted with light and the pours in his skin glistened like diamonds.

As the light surged past Morgan it began to fill the whole of the Basilica with brilliant white light.

Like a wave sweeping over a sandy beach the white energy

swept down the nave of St Peters Basilica, cascading across the floor, rolling around the pillars and arcing up across the walls.

It flowed around the altar and swirled like a whirlpool as it entered the crypt and washed across the marble floors. The body of Kronos evaporated instantly as the wave washed over it and as the energy surged around the chambers, the headstones of the past Pontiffs illuminated with dazzling light. There was a build-up of pressure within the crypt and suddenly there was an explosion of power that shattered the stone columns, and erupted upwards, destroying the altar above it and sending the tormented body of Lucifer upwards, through the shattered Dome towards his Maker once more.

The wave crashed through the doors of St Peters and was met head on by the forces of evil. The wraiths screamed in terror as the energy pulse washed over them, evaporating them and turning them into dust. There was a scramble to escape from the oncoming onslaught, but the masses were too crowded and they were caught in the torrent as it crashed over them.

The chasm in the middle of the plaza was washed over and filled up to the brim with the positive energy, but the wave didn't stop there.

Onwards and outwards it flowed, following the course of the streets throughout Rome, the energy wave found its own route and like the demons at the Vatican, any creature it touched was destroyed.

Across the oceans, deep into the troughs of the seabed, to the tip of the highest mountains, the white wave flowed. Across America, like a tsunami it enveloped everything it touched, destroying everything that the demons had touched, leaving no trace behind. The Pacific was cleansed, the Asian continent, from the biggest cities to the smallest islands, everywhere was touched by the energy wave.

In New York the wave raced through the streets of Manhattan, finding its way through the linear streets and swept away the carnage that had unfolded there.

The Sunrise Headquarters began to fill with energy, the mezzanine floors were wiped clean, the windows were repaired, and each floor that had been ripped out by the wraiths was replaced.

On the top floor, Felix Masterson still sat, slumped on the floor, chained to the wall. He stirred from his slumber as he saw the pure white light approach him. It terrified him as it slowly neared and encircled him and paused, almost surveying and judging him. He shouted at the top of his voice for help but it never came as the wave washed over him, dissolving the chains from his wrists, healing the wounds he had suffered and he fell back and let the energy cleanse him.

In the subway system beneath New York, General Bailey and his last remaining men were crawling and staggering away from the counter attack of the wraiths. They were feeling their way along the dark tunnel as the light poured across the station platforms and onto the tracks, following the curved walls. The light took Bailey and his men by surprise, and they turned to face it, shielding themselves from the light as it came crashing through the darkness and wrapped around them, pushing them off their feet. The tidal power of the energy was so immense that the soldiers were carried away down the tunnel and to salvation.

The whole world was being purified, the whole world was being saved from the evil hoards, and within minutes the whole planet was calm once more as the energy wave slowly dispersed and evaporated into the air.

CHAPTER TWENTY-NINE

Laura Kennedy walked through the gardens of the Vatican alone. It had been almost a week since the near destruction of the Church and the world and while there were many questions she still wanted answering, she was still questioning her own beliefs.

She was a woman of science, she always knew that and was always proud to say it; but seeing what she had seen, was well beyond her own scientific explanations.

She looked around her at the manicured gardens and thought about her life and if she should really be following the path she had taken so long to find. She needed questions to be answered and she continued to walk.

Around her, groundskeepers were busy working, a few priests were quietly chatting to each other and in the shadow of the Basilica Dome, fully repaired to its previous magnificence, she saw Cardinal Conquezla.

"Your Eminence." She said.

"Miss Kennedy," Conquezla said smiling and kissing her hand, "I was looking for you. I believe you have some questions."

Laura smiled and as the Cardinal led her into the gardens, she prepared herself to ask the questions. "I have so many to ask," she said, "but I think the first one is -"

"What happened when you started the Pope's heart?" Conquezla asked, interrupting her. Laura felt embarrassed at the question that she had mulled over and debated within herself for the past week.

Conquezla motioned for her to sit down and he turned to her. "As Cardinals and devout Catholics, we believe that when we elect a new Pope, our decision is guided by the Holy Spirit. We believe that that force, within each of us, the force that emanates and originated from God is what helps make our decision.

"Being the Pope isn't about being a politician, it's about being God's voice here on Earth. God is essentially choosing who he wants to represent him here. When that decision is made, the connection between the Pope and God remains intact until the mortal Pope dies and when that happens there is no connection between heaven and earth."

"So when we re-started his heart?" Laura asked, half knowing the answer.

"Yes, when we made the connection once more, the energy you saw was the power of God reaching down to his representative on Earth. We assume God always knew we were in trouble and things were getting out of control, but by the time we reached the critical point, Pope Pius was under the control of Lucifer and with nobody here to be connected to, he couldn't make his presence known and help us."

"What about Houseman? He was elected pope."

Conquezla sat silently for a moment. "He wasn't chosen or guided by the Holy Spirit. It was a lack of choice and options, not spiritual intervention."

"Did you know that would happen? The power of God thing?"

Conquezla shook his head. "No, I honestly thought that all we were doing was saving one man's life. I thought if we could revive him, he might be able to broker a deal with those things."

There was a few minutes silence as they both sat and looked at the manicured gardens. Conquezla knew she had more questions, and after what they had been through, and the help she had given, he allowed her to find her own questions in her own time. He continued to watch a gardener as he tidied a flower bed.

Laura was trying to comprehend the explanation given by the Cardinal. There was part of her that understood it, but another part of her that couldn't believe it. She looked up at the Dome, "I've seen the news and there are no reports of anything happening. There're no reports of the deaths, the wraiths, the Devil. The Dome there was destroyed, yet here it is now repaired as if nothing had happened. But we remember it all. How is that possible?"

Conquezla nodded to a young priest who passed them, and he answered Laura with the same gentle calming tones he used during confessions. "We were at the epicentre of the whole event and we were also in the Vatican. If it was a combination of both that allowed us to remember those terrible days, I don't know. But as the energy wave swept across the globe, it wasn't just removing the demons, wraiths, Hashalanths and Lucifer from the Earth it was also repairing it all, wiping people's memories, putting things back the way they were before these terrible events unfolded." He paused for a moment as he gathered his thoughts.

"However some people couldn't be saved." Conquezla said, "Fr. Julio Yegros is one of them. Why he wasn't brought back, I don't know. But there are others who are missing too, some of my Knights are still unaccounted for. Perhaps they were an intricate part of the events and their return could jeopardise the new order of cohesion and equilibrium that has been created."

"What about Masterson and Sunrise?" she asked. His central role in trying to bring the destruction of the church had been on her mind since she had heard his television comments. She used to respect him and his company, but now she despised everything about him and was prepared to write her resignation letter as soon as she was back on American soil.

Conquezla nodded slowly, "Yes," he said, almost trying to choose his words carefully about the man who was pivotal in bringing the Devil to his doorstep, "we have had contact from Mr. Masterson. It appears that he was rather panicked and emotional. I believe that while things have been returned to their previous state, Mr. Masterson has been left with the memory of what had happened, and his involvement. Perhaps allowing him to keep the memories of the past few weeks was deemed as an appropriate punishment. One might say." He added with a sly smile.

"Why shouldn't everybody remember the events to show there really is a God looking over them?"

"We prefer to believe what Jesus said to Doubting Thomas as quoted in the Bible when he finally saw him and acknowledged his presence after his resurrection."

"And what was that?" Laura asked.

"'Because you have seen me, you have believed; blessed are those who have not seen and yet have believed.'

"As for the future, this has never happened before, and we have no idea how, over the coming months and years things will develop. Will people begin to remember some of the events? Will there be inconsistencies that the sharp eyed people will pick up on? I don't know." Conquezla paused for a second and thought. It was a question he hadn't really considered. "Maybe there will be and if there are I imagine there will be stories and conspiracy theories for many years to come. The media will once more bang on the door of the Church shouting ridiculous questions, and the internet will be awash with proof."

"What will you do?" Laura asked looking up at the magnificent dome of the Basilica above them.

"We will do what the Church always does," Conquezla replied, "what we always have done. We'll continue with dignified silence. The rumours will die out, Miss Kennedy, but the Church will continue."

They both sat in silence for another minute, listening to the birds singing in the trees, interspersed with the car horns of the Italian drivers across the city.

It was incredible, Laura thought, that so much had

changed, yet everything seemed to be the same.

"What about Peter?" she asked suddenly, breaking the silence.

Conquezla looked at her, staring into her eyes. "I'm afraid we lost Peter Morgan, he didn't make it."

Laura looked away from Conquezla and bowed her head. Her mind turned to Fr. Peter Morgan and despite only knowing him for a few days, he had been such a major factor in her life. He had selflessly acted to protect her from the Hashalanths, the Wraiths, and Kronos. Despite her attachment with the corporation that allowed the Devil to come perilously close to dominating the world, Peter Morgan had still found it in his heart to help her, and protect her.

"He was a good man." Conquezla said, almost reading her thoughts. "He was a good priest, and he will be missed by us all."

Laura looked back at the Cardinal and took a breath to steady her nerves and calm herself. "He was an incredible man. The world needs more people like him."

EPILOGUE

The ball hit the back of the net and the boy ran around the pitch waving his arms around, pleased that he had scored the goal. His family watched proudly and cheered his success. In the crowd, the off duty nurses and doctors of Makenza Hospital watched as their patients played like children should.

The goal scorer's teammates ran over to him and hugged him too, running their hands across his head, each giving their own congratulations to him.

Near the side of the pitch, a pickup truck door slammed shut and Fr. Peter Morgan watched the children cheer and restart the game. He had expected to see Carlos either at the airport or there at the hospital, but there was no sign of him. Before he left Rome, he had been briefed by Cardinal Conquezla and had sat down in a private meeting with Pope Pius XV, and they had discussed the new world they were now living in.

"Some people were resurrected," Conquelza had said, "others were not brought back."

Silently, Morgan sat and listened and his heart sank as he knew that Conquezla was referring to his friend Fr. Julio Yegros. Morgan was coming to terms with never seeing him again, and as he watched the children play on the field, he knew he had lost Carlos too. Why he wasn't brought back, Morgan would never know, but he hoped that wherever he was now, he was safe.

Pope Pius personally thanked Morgan for his actions in

saving the Church and the World, and as a sign of gratitude he offered Morgan any post, any position within the Church, anywhere in the world. Morgan didn't have to think for a second and he said "With all due respect, I would like to return to Venezuela. I still have a job to do there, and the kids need me."

Pope Pius gave a small smile and shook his hand, thanking him again for his actions and blessing him for a safe journey.

Morgan walked back with Cardinal Conquezla to the offices in the lower levels of the Vatican. "What shall I tell Miss Kennedy?" Conquezla asked.

Morgan stopped and looked out of one of the tall windows overlooking the Papal gardens. "I've been thinking about that for a few days now." He turned and faced his Cardinal. "Our Order is one of secrecy and we work best when we're working in the shadows. I don't think I could continue my duties if I knew she thought I was alive."

Conquezla nodded and patted him on the arm. "I'll tell her." He said.

Morgan hated making the decision. He wanted to say goodbye to her, to thank her, and to reassure her. He knew that the events of the last week would be emotionally and mentally tiring and scaring. He wanted to personally help her through the coming weeks and months as she tried to understand what had happened.

Morgan knew that he himself would take many months to fully accept what had happened, and he had been trained and totally immersed in religious doctrine; so he knew it would be difficult for Laura to comprehend the events.

He saw her in the gardens below, her hair gently fluttering in the light breeze as she looked up at the Basilica Dome. He wanted to say goodbye to her, he wanted to speak to her, but he knew that his vows came first and for him to fulfil them he needed to walk away.

Finally after a long flight and two hour drive, he was back where he loved to work, with the families and children staying at the hospital.

A young girl saw him first and she shouted across and walked as fast as she could towards him. The other children saw him too and they too ran across. Within seconds Morgan was inundated with children hugging his legs and waist and he fell to the floor as they scrambled all over him.

After what he had been through, to be back with children he had vowed to help, and the staff who dedicated their lives to continuing the momentous uphill battle against cancer, to be back to normality, was the only thing he ever wanted.

THE END

ABOUT THE AUTHOR

David Whelan is a new British writer based in
Worcestershire. Writing since his teens, he has written
screenplays, short stories, and poems
Currently working as a Forensic Scene Investigator for West
Midlands Police, he has an extensive knowledge of forensic
practices and techniques.
He lives in Bromsgrove, Worcestershire with his wife Alison,
and son, Joshua.

http://birmingham-writer.blogspot.co.uk/
On Facebook: David Whelan – The Writer

3867175R00139

Printed in Great Britain
by Amazon.co.uk, Ltd.,
Marston Gate.